RECKLESS

It was fully dark now. Maggie Rose thought if she could pinch herself she would to see if this was a dream. Surely she wasn't actually lying in Chris's arms in the lounger on his porch looking up at the same stars she looked at from her own window when she was yearning for Chris instead of sleeping.

At first she'd been startled but there was really nothing to fear, not with Chris, her hero since the ninth grade. He would always protect her even when he was upset with her.

"This is nice," she murmured.

"It certainly is," Chris responded. "And this is nicer." He turned her face to his and brushed her lips with a whisper of a kiss, back and forth, tantalizing and slow, waiting until she let him know she wanted more.

RECKLESS

Adrienne Ellis Reeves

BET Publications, LLC
http://www.bet.com
http://www.arabesquebooks.com

ARABESQUE BOOKS are published by

BET Publications, LLC
c/o BET BOOKS
One BET Plaza
1900 W Place NE
Washington, DC 20018-1211

All Kensington Titles, Imprints, and Distributed Lines are available at special quantity discounts for bulk purchases for sales promotions, premiums, fund-raising, and educational or institutional use. Special book excerpts or customized printings can also be created to fit specific needs. For details, write or phone the office of the Kensington special sales manager: Kensington Publishing Corp., 850 Third Avenue, New York, NY 10022, attn: Special Sales Department, Phone: 1-800-221-2647.

First Printing: April 2003
10 9 8 7 6 5 4 3 2

Printed in the United States of America

This book is dedicated to the men in my family. May they live long and well: Caswell, Nathaniel, and Firuz; and Lafayette, Roscoe, Lateef, William, Allen, Jason, Jonathan, Robert, Michael, Mosi, and Elliot.

ACKNOWLEDGMENTS

With appreciation and gratitude to my critique partners, Nina Bruhns and Priscilla Kissinger; to Karen DeLonge and her Carousel Riding School; and particularly to Denise Mitchell for her computer skills and her constant encouragement.

Chapter One

"Can you come up with your five thousand by July fifteenth?"

"How much?" Maggie Rose Sanders blinked. She pulled back from the telephone as if it had bitten her.

"I've gone over the figures several times since our last conversation. We're going to have to come up with ten thousand dollars to get the business ready for us to take over." Ginnie Steed's voice was practical and reassuring. "Five from you and five from me."

"Why five? Can't we get by for three or even three thousand five if necessary?"

Maggie Rose frowned at the five and three zeros she'd jotted on the telephone pad. Drawing a heavy line through them, she wrote three thousand. That looked much better. It looked doable even though this was already March.

"My aunt's lawyer said we have to put at least five thousand down in order to take possession of the business." Ginnie sighed.

Ginnie had told Maggie Rose a year ago that her aunt Henny was retiring from the Mailroom, which had begun as a small service attached to her grocery store. Although the grocery had suffered when a large chain market moved in two blocks away, the mail service continued to prosper.

"Aunt Henny wants me to buy her out," Ginnie had confided. "But I can't do it alone. I need a partner and you're the only person I'd trust. Come back home and let's do this together."

Maggie Rose had been in and out of the store all her life. She'd always dreamed of owning her own business, and the idea of saving it for people in the community who found it hard or inconvenient to get to the post office appealed to her. In the ensuing months she and Ginnie had examined the proposition in detail and agreed to a partnership.

"I can get the down payment together because I've been working overtime in my consultant job and saving ever since Aunt Henny first mentioned it," Ginnie said. "It's the best chance I'll ever have to own a business."

A trickle of cold air hit Maggie Rose. Telephone in hand she walked over to the window and pushed it down firmly. A blast of frigid air from Canada had invaded Connecticut that morning and now outside her bedroom window in Hartford, the snow fell in heavy wet flakes.

"What's the weather like at home, Ginnie?" Maggie Rose watched the wind pick up the snow and swirl it around.

"It was sunny and sixty-five this afternoon. Of course it's cooled down this evening." Surprise at the change of subject was clear in Ginnie's voice. "Why? What's happening in Hartford?"

"Cold, snow, and wind. I hope it's not freezing by morning." She'd probably leave her car in the garage and take the bus to work.

"Just the thought of that weather chills me!" Ginnie was sympathetic. "Jamison, South Carolina, will look very good to you when you get here."

"It certainly will." Back in her chair, Maggie Rose looked at the figures again. "My half is for the licensing, redecoration, purchasing stock, and other incidentals. Is that right?"

"Yes, can you manage it?"

Maggie Rose responded to the anxiety in Ginnie's voice. "Don't worry about it, Ginnie. That's five months from now. I'll have five thousand when we need it."

Getting the money had seemed a straightforward matter to Maggie Rose. She snatched off her ivory silk jacket, flung it on the bed, and kicked off her ivory pumps on the way to the bathroom. She splashed cold water on her face, then examined it critically for a clue to what had gone wrong today.

The smooth brown face, framed by well-groomed shoulder-length brown hair, had long-lashed wide brown eyes, high cheekbones, a small nose, a generous mouth and a tiny mole at the end of the right eyebrow. A determined chin, but that hadn't helped matters thus far.

Just a face, she concluded. Nothing remarkable. However, it did show more maturity than when she'd left Jamison twelve years ago and that should have been a plus today.

With a frustrated look, she dried her face, dabbed it with cream, and stomped to the kitchen.

A few moments later she plopped down in the blue wing chair opposite the windows and let a long sip of iced lemonade slide down her throat. Heavenly. The only thing right on this first day of June that had been filled with such promise.

Resting her tired feet on a hassock, she gave thanks once again that her Southwind apartment here in Jamision provided a view of parklike expanse of lush grass bordered by flourishing trees.

If only the job hunting she'd been on for the past two weeks had proven so fortuitous. With the first swallows of lemonade cooling her, she was content to slowly sip the refreshing beverage as she pondered her dilemma.

It was supposed to have been so easy. After all, the city of Charleston was just forty minutes away and surely she'd find plenty of jobs with her employment background. It was only two weeks ago that she'd resigned her position as administrative assistant to a vice president in the legal department of the Travelers insurance company in Hartford.

She'd decided to interrupt her promising career to come home before it was too late. Too late to make her dream of being in business for herself come true. Too late to do something about her younger sisters, Alicia and Jerlene, and Jerlene's ten-year-old son, Covey. Too late to be a support to Mama and Daddy, now in their sixties and with the beginning of health problems.

The final drop of lemonade trickled down her throat. She began crushing the ice cubes with her teeth. They made a satisfying sound and Maggie Rose decided she'd released enough tension to look at her problem objectively.

From her bag she pulled out the interview sheet she'd prepared for herself. She'd selected eight positions from the want ads and faxed the requested résumés. Four had responded and interviews had been set up for today.

The shrill of the telephone on the small table beside her startled Maggie Rose. She glanced at her watch. It was four-thirty. Mama, anxious to hear how today had gone, was the likely caller.

"Hi, Mama."

"Magnolia Rose. How'd you know this was me? Suppose it had been someone else, dear? It could have been embarrassing."

She called me Magnolia Rose, so she's a little upset.

"You're absolutely right, Mama, but I had a feeling you'd be wanting to know about the interviews today. I think I have a solid prospect."

"That's wonderful, Maggie Rose." The relief in her voice was clear.

"The first three places gave me the same excuse I've heard before—that they couldn't pay me what my experience calls for. But the last one was the Elliott Law Firm on Greenleaf Street down by the bay."

"Your dad was showing me those new offices last month. They look so smart."

"They are good looking, Mama. I figured a business that could afford such an office ought to be able to pay me a good salary. The inside was as nice as the outside. The receptionist even served me coffee while I waited to speak with Mr. Elliott."

Maggie Rose heard her mother chuckle. "That

was different from the way the other people treated you. What's Mr. Elliot like?''

''Prosperous looking, in his fifties, pleasant manner. Talked with me about the office administrator position and asked in detail about my work at Travelers.''

''Did he make you an offer?''

''Not yet. He said he'd speak with me in a day or two.''

''What's your feeling about it, honey? I don't see how anyone could be better qualified for the job than you.''

Mama was so loyal. Maggie Rose wished she could be as certain that qualifications alone would secure the position. She knew now that was not enough. Even now some relative of Mr. Elliott might already have it. But she put on a brave face for Mama. ''He seemed impressed and I'm hopeful.''

''Things are so different than when I looked for work. It was easy to get a job,'' Mama said. ''These days salaries are higher but jobs are more scarce.''

''This is the first time I've had to go job hunting since I was in high school. It's not a pleasant experience. When you keep getting turned down you begin to wonder about your abilities.''

She hadn't meant to say that. She hadn't meant to acknowledge the sense of humiliation she was beginning to feel after applying at fourteen places and still no job! She hadn't meant to display that weakness, especially not to Mama, who'd tell Daddy and they'd both worry. Maybe she could clean it up a bit.

''If this one doesn't come through, I'm applying for a job at the technical college,'' she said brightly.

"I think I'd like working there." The college was her ace in the hole.

"That's a good place to work. Jerlene worked there for a while as a temp in the admissions office. She liked it."

The wistful note in her mother's voice made Maggie Rose grit her teeth. Her twenty-eight-year-old sister, Jerlene, never kept a job. She talked too much and in an overpowering manner that soon rubbed people the wrong way. Although she was neither malicious nor mean, there were times when she could be spiteful. But tact was a concept she couldn't seem to understand.

The only time that Jerlene demonstrated that she could be silent when it suited her was when, at eighteen, she'd had Covey. She had never revealed the name of his father to her family or to anyone, as far as Maggie Rose knew.

"How does Jerlene like her new job at Kiddie's Korner?" Maggie Rose asked.

"She likes it. The people are friendly and she hopes to stay there," her mother said. "But Covey had a little mishap this afternoon."

Maggie Rose shot up in her chair. "What happened?"

"He came home with a black eye about an hour ago. He got in a fight with a boy who tried to take his bike away from him. Tommy was with him and saw the whole thing."

"Did Tommy get hurt?"

"You know Tommy. He just watched. He says he doesn't like fighting. I wish Covey felt that way."

"Where's Covey now, Mama?"

"In his room with an ice pack on his eye."

After the conversation, Maggie Rose pondered

what she could do for her nephew. Summer was just beginning, with unlimited time for trouble. He'd been fiercely uncooperative about camps or library summer activities. "I like to choose my own books," he'd said with finality. Maggie Rose couldn't help but agree with him.

It wasn't her job to worry about the boy or about Jerlene. But Jerlene was a sometime parent and when her own life became her consuming interest, she'd always had Mama and Daddy to pick up the slack.

Maggie Rose recalled the past Christmas. Jerlene had been in the throes of one of her ardent love affairs with a new boyfriend. The careless way she'd treated Covey when the boyfriend was available had been the cause of a bitter argument between the sisters. Jerlene had been defensive.

"I love Covey, he's my son," she'd snapped at Maggie Rose, her hands on her hips and her cheeks red with anger.

"You don't act like it," Maggie Rose had said unforgivably.

"What would you know about raising a son?" Jerlene had taunted.

Maggie Rose cringed inside. She wished with all her heart that she had a son or daughter, but marriage hadn't come her way. Now, at thirty, she wondered if it ever would.

Doing well in her studies and on the job had always been her priority because she had confidence in those areas. Confidence evaporated when it came to dating. She could manage in group situations, but not on her own.

"You act like you're scared of boys," Ginnie had

said when they were seniors in high school and their double dating had been a failure.

"I'm not scared, I just don't know what to say," Maggie Rose said defensively.

"Find out what the boy likes," Ginnie explained. "Basketball, football, cars, and ask him about it."

That had worked until the date with that lout who was only interested in rubbing Maggie Rose's leg and trying to feel her breast. When she didn't cooperate he called her an unflattering name and walked out, leaving her angry and embarrassed.

Eventually she learned how to handle men like that, and while she was working in Hartford, she'd become part of a group that enjoyed a lively social life.

However, a deeply unhappy love affair with Lem Norris when she was twenty-five confirmed her suspicion that she lacked the talent for a one-on-one relationship.

That argument with Jerlene last Christmas had helped fuel her determination to return to Jamison. Maggie Rose had no faith in Jerlene changing her ways and giving Covey the kind of loving support and guidance he needed, especially in the total absence of a father. The whole situation was taking its toll on her parents and would be even worse as the boy grew older.

I have to find something for Covey to do this summer, she thought as she gazed at two squirrels playing up and down a large tree. She wondered if Covey liked animals. He'd loved Buster, the family dog, and had cried when Buster had to be put to sleep. Maybe he could find something to do with animals and see if it piqued his interest.

It was hard to tell what he really liked. He was

as quiet and reserved as his mother was talkative and open.

Maybe he was like his father. For the thousandth time Maggie Rose pondered the reason her sister would not reveal his identity. She thought it must have been an older married man attracted to Jerlene's buxom figure, high energy level, and flashing smile.

Jerlene loved to flirt and it had been rumored that she was running with an older crowd that included Chris Shealy and his buddy Bill Denton. Perhaps someone else in that crowd might be guilty, but Maggie Rose shied away from the notion that Chris could be Covey's father—although heaven knows he'd been attractive enough and wild enough to sweep a naive girl off her feet.

Chris had been her secret hero since grade school. Surely he hadn't been so irresponsible. Especially with *her* younger sister!

With a sigh, Maggie Rose dismissed Jerlene and Covey from her mind. Time to go back to the job situation, which translated into her financial situation. The funds she'd brought from Travelers included her severance pay and her savings. Setting up the apartment had used some of this money. She'd anticipated that plus living costs for one month.

But now two months had passed and the money allocated toward the five thousand was being eaten into. She had no job and no prospect of one. For a panicky moment she wondered if she'd made the wrong decision in leaving Travelers.

No, she knew she had to come home. It would work out even if she had to put two small jobs together. Maybe she'd end up like Lucy Fairfax, her old schoolmate.

"Lucy's back in town with her two children," Mama had said. "She's divorced and at first she worked in an office but she couldn't live on the salary. She began cleaning houses. She built up a good clientele and is making the best money she's ever had."

The very thought of it made Maggie Rose grimace. But if she had to do it, she would. She was becoming desperate for a job.

A growl from her stomach reminded her that she hadn't eaten since breakfast. She stretched her tall, slim form as she got up. In the bedroom she'd changed into worn jeans and a rose top that had seen better days. Catching a glimpse of herself in the oval mirror on the opposite wall, she thought she'd never have Jerlene's curves, but she'd lived long enough with her body to accept it.

She put on a Grover Washington Jr. CD and opened the refrigerator. Nothing she saw interested her; in fact she didn't feel the least bit like cooking tonight. She closed the refrigerator door, went to the telephone, and ordered pizza.

"What toppings would you like?" the lady asked.

"Pepperoni, Italian sausage, and mushrooms," Maggie Rose said, feeling greedy.

She moved to Grover's jazz as she took her place setting to the heavy dark table she'd bought at a yard sale because it was much like the one she'd grown up with in her parents' house. It had a few nicks and scratches but she'd polished it lovingly and now it shone almost like new. Matching chairs and a sideboard bought at the same yard sale completed the dining area. As soon as she got a job, she'd have her family over to dinner. Menu items were already popping around in her head.

The doorbell rang and a male voice called, "Pizza." Maggie Rose took a twenty-dollar bill from her bag, and hurried to open the door.

Everything inside her stopped. She looked blankly at the tall man at the door, his dark eyes watching her, a small smile curving his lips.

"Where's the pizza man?" Maggie Rose heard herself say.

"Right here." He extended a large pizza box. "Christopher James Shealy at your service, ma'am."

Chapter Two

Nothing had changed, Chris thought. He'd first met her when he was eleven and she'd been a skinny girl with fat pigtails flying, being chased by two older boys in the schoolyard. That hadn't been uncommon. But as they had come around the swings toward him, he saw the girl was crying. Without thinking, Chris had reached out and put her behind him.

"Why don't you pick on someone your own size?" He glared at the boys, his fists clenched.

"We were just teasing." The boys backed away.

Even then it had been known that Chris Shealy never avoided a fight and usually won, even if it meant being suspended from school.

The girl wiped the tears from her face with the back of her hand, when Chris turned to her. "What's your name?"

She looked up at him, her brown eyes still moist. "Magnolia Rose Sanders."

"How old are you?"

"Nine."

Her eyes, with their long, wet lashes, held a shy appeal that had made Chris feel funny inside. He'd wanted to protect her from teasing boys and anything else that might harm her.

Now, standing at her door, the pizza box forgotten, he was mesmerized as he gazed at Maggie Rose.

How could her eyes hold that same appeal after so many years? Each time he saw her on her trips home during the time she'd been in Hartford, he'd expected her to change, especially in the past few years after growing into a mature woman, successful and confident in her work and social life.

Did she look at other men like that, as if she knew she could count on you no matter what happened? How many guys in Hartford had responded to that appeal?

Chris gave himself a mental shrug. Maggie Rose was home now, he'd known her almost all of his life, and although he recognized that look of hers, *he* was immune to it.

"Aren't you going to invite me in?" He raised a questioning brow. "I have a pizza to deliver."

She stepped aside so he could come in, then looked down the hall.

"What happened to the pizza man?"

"We happened to meet at your door and I took the pizza." He set the box on the dining table.

"But I didn't pay him," she protested.

"It's paid for."

He hadn't seen her since Christmas. He knew

she'd been back for Easter but he'd been in Atlanta. What was she thinking as she stared at him as if he'd appeared via crystal ball?

Did she still think of him as that "wild Shealy boy"? He was trying to put that past behind him. It was plain bad luck that a cop and a photographer had shown up a few weeks ago when he'd been separating two guys and had received a punch in the eye for his trouble.

He knew his reputation had made her wary of him, but did she ever remember their school encounters, especially that study session in the library? She'd helped him with his English assignment, and afterward the two of them had walked outside and talked about school, movies, and what they wanted to do after graduation.

She was an honor student, protected by strict parents, with college as her future. He was an orphan living on a farm with his uncle and not particularly interested in school. They seemed so dissimilar and yet he'd never forgotten that conversation, because neither one had wanted it to end. There'd been an openness between them, and something else he couldn't name at the time. Later he'd identified it as an innocent intimacy. Its essence lingered with him still.

The light floral fragrance he always associated with her filled his senses as he stepped closer and gave her a careful hug. Despite himself, he was swept back to prom night, when even though he wasn't her escort, he'd put his arms around her for the first time and kissed her. Twice.

He clamped down on that memory and gave her a light kiss on both cheeks, reminding himself to do nothing that would endanger his mission.

"Welcome home, Maggie Rose."

"Chris Shealy," she breathed.

He'd bet she was remembering that prom night, too, from the look in her eyes and the flush rising in her face—unless he was fooling himself and she was just startled.

She seemed embarrassed by her reaction and suddenly held out the twenty-dollar bill to him, but he shook his head.

"Since you delivered the pizza, this belongs to you," she insisted.

He gently folded her fingers over the bill. "It's paid for," he repeated. "However, I wouldn't mind sharing some of it since I haven't had dinner yet," he said to silence her protest.

Her face brightened. "That's the least I can do," she agreed and began setting a place for him.

He watched her slim figure as she reached to take dishes from the cupboard, unconscious grace in every movement. This was his lucky day, catching the pizza man at the door, because sharing a meal with her gave him time to easily achieve his objective.

While she was at the refrigerator getting drinks, he asked, "When did you get home?" He was making idle conversation to put her at ease, because he already knew exactly when she'd arrived.

"Two months ago yesterday." Maggie Rose set the pitcher of lemonade on the table, along with two ice-filled glasses and some napkins.

Chris stepped behind her to hold her chair. The clean scent of her hair drew him to brush it with his lips. As he bent closer the sound of her indrawn breath saved him from that folly. He'd better watch it, he thought, as he seated himself opposite her and reached for a slice of pizza.

As Maggie Rose chose one for herself and took a small bite, Chris said, "So you got tired of big-city life and decided to come home to Jamision?" His dark eyes smiled at her.

"That was partly it."

Most of the time when they'd seen each other on her trips home, their encounters had been characterized by the friendly teasing that had carried on from high school days. Although he made her nervous because he made her blush, she'd always been enlivened by these meetings. Running into him had lent a secret spice to her visits.

For a scary but exciting moment at the door, she thought he was going to kiss her on her lips as he had at the prom. It was just as well he hadn't. They weren't kids anymore.

She was thirty and he was thirty-two and everyone knew Chris lived a wild life. In fact, his latest escapade had made the newspaper, with his black eye showing up dramatically. She wouldn't know what to do with such a man. Particularly if that man was Chris Shealy!

Chris took another bite. "This is good. I'm glad I invited myself to have some. I always picture you as cooking for yourself."

She saw that teasing glint appear in his eyes.

"I pictured you making a delicious meal for some lucky guy in Hartford."

He'd thought of her in Hartford! That sweet idea was something to ponder on later. "I do like to cook, but nothing in the fridge appealed to me."

"I'm interested to know what made you come

home after all these years, if you don't mind telling me."

Maggie Rose welcomed the question. A mundane conversation would relieve the edginess she felt in Chris's presence.

"When I went right from the University of Connecticut into Travelers, I was glad to have a job with a future and relieved that I didn't have to look for work. Interning with them in the summers made a difference. But then it gradually came to me that no matter how good the job was, I couldn't see living in Hartford until retirement. It was too far away from home and my family."

"You didn't want to get a transfer to an office in Charleston or in a nearby city?"

"No, I didn't. Ten years was long enough to be in the insurance business."

"I know they tried to get you to stay," he said decisively. "They wouldn't want to lose a valuable employee like you. They probably even offered you a raise."

"Not only that, but a promotion as well."

Chris smiled at her hint of smugness about the promotion. It confirmed his long-held idea of her abilities and skills.

"You weren't tempted?"

"Not tempted, no." Maggie looked at Chris, surprised at how easily they were talking. "I'd anticipated the raise proposal but not the two-level promotion. I did wonder for a moment if I should stay, but it was only for that moment. I'd made my decision before putting in my resignation and had begun packing."

"I'm glad you didn't change your mind." His

eyes held hers as he picked up his glass, then set it down again.

"Didn't you mind leaving your friends? You must have had a pretty good life in a city like Hartford, especially with New York a couple of hours away."

"When I first started working, I made the usual party rounds. That included going to New York many weekends with a group and hitting the clubs."

"Must have been fun."

Her eyes sparkled at Chris. "It was great fun while it lasted, but after a while that running every weekend became boring. Same people, same places."

"So you became a stick-in-the-mud? That's hard to believe." He leaned across the table, smiling.

"Of course I didn't," Maggie Rose said indignantly. "I simply began doing the kinds of things I really wanted to do." She looked at him demurely. "I prefer a quieter lifestyle."

Chris shifted in his chair, then took another slice of pizza to keep himself from wanting to touch her.

"Describe this quiet lifestyle to me," he said.

She told Chris about going to the movies she wanted to see regardless of anyone else's taste, to concerts, plays, and museums, or to a lecture that interested her. Sometimes she went with friends, more often by herself. "And I read a lot," she concluded.

"You didn't leave a man who's likely to come after you and take you back to Connecticut?" he asked softly.

Maggie Rose looked at him sharply. "No, I didn't." A tiny frown appeared between her eyebrows.

Chris saw the frown. "So there's no one special, Maggie Rose?"

She shook her head no. "What about you?" she asked.

Chris shook his head and felt the air hum between them. Maggie Rose broke the spell by picking up the glasses and going to the refrigerator for more lemonade.

Chris accepted the icy lemonade with thanks. "I know your mom and dad are glad to have you home."

Maggie Rose cut the pizza with her fork. "They're one of the main reasons I came home. Being here only for holidays was all right when they were younger, but not now."

"I see Jerlene out and about and I run into Alicia occasionally. Young Covey nearly ran me down on his bike the other day. How's he doing?"

"Not as good as he could be. He couldn't be persuaded to go to camp this year and he's too young to get a job, so time hangs heavy on his hands."

Maggie Rose pushed her plate away. Despite herself she wondered if Chris was interested because Covey was his son. You couldn't tell by looking because Covey had the same eyes, shape of face, and coloring as Jerlene.

"I remember myself at that age," Chris mused.

Had he read her mind? Maggie Rose knew she wasn't good at hiding her emotions. Best to be truthful with him. Maybe he could suggest something helpful.

"Mama said he came home today with a black eye from a fight with someone who tried to take his bike."

"I had several of those fights myself." His mischievous grin suddenly made him look like the lanky boy she'd known in school, and she smiled in response.

"Maybe I can help." He moved his plate to the side and held his glass with both hands. "You may not know that after Uncle Henry died five years ago, Tallie Sims moved in with me. He'd always helped around the farm. After the funeral he seemed lost so I invited him to take one of the empty bedrooms and keep on with the odd jobs."

His deprecating shrug told Maggie Rose that it was more likely the basic kindness that Chris tried to hide that had provided Tallie with a home.

"I remember him. He and Daddy are acquainted. I haven't seen him in years." She recalled a medium-sized man who gave the impression of wiry strength. "What does he do on the farm?"

"He keeps an eye on the place while I'm at work, and he likes to cook most of the meals."

Chris had been taken in by his father's brother after Chris had lost both parents by the time he was five. Henry Shealy had raised his nephew single-handedly on his large farm a few miles outside of Jamison. Maggie Rose assumed the property now belonged to Chris, as no other Shealys had ever shown up as far as she knew. It sounded as if it was good for Chris to have Tallie there not only for work but for companionship.

Where would Covey fit into this picture? "Do you still plant crops?" Maybe Chris saw the boy helping out in the fields.

"The crop land is leased out," Chris said. "But I still have cows, hogs, chickens, and geese. How does Covey feel about animals?"

"The only thing I know is that he loved Buster, our dog."

"I know Tallie would love to have the boy around to keep him company, and he could help Tallie with the chores. I forgot to say that Tallie plants a large garden every year. It takes a lot of work. Of course I'd pay Covey a salary."

Maggie Rose's eyes were shining again. This sounded like the perfect solution for her nephew's summer.

"One of the chores where Tallie could really use help is with the horses. They need daily care to keep them in prime condition for the riding school I have."

Fear invaded Maggie Rose's body, causing a sheen of perspiration on her forehead. She clenched her hands so tightly it made her knuckles whiten.

"No! He can't go near any horses!" she blurted.

"What's the matter, Maggie Rose? Is Covey afraid of horses?"

She saw the surprise and concern in his eyes. "They're so big and dangerous. He's never been near one. He could be hurt or killed." She knew she was babbling but she couldn't help it.

"Children can begin to learn to ride when they're three or four years old." Chris's voice was quiet and soothing. "You needn't be afraid for him, Maggie Rose. The first thing Uncle Henry taught me when I came to him was how to handle horses. I'd never been near one, but I was riding three months later and I was only five."

His description of how patient and gentle Uncle Henry had been with him and how he would be the same with Covey began to penetrate her panic.

Chris took her hands in his and gently rubbed them. "You've known me all your life, Maggie Rose. Do you think Tallie or I would let Covey get hurt?" His eyes held hers steadily.

She felt his strength as he tightened his long fingers around hers.

"He'll be safe with us." His reassuring voice soothed her and the warmth of this hands comforted her.

"It's Jerlene who has to give consent," she murmured.

"I don't think that will be a problem. You didn't answer my question."

"Will you or Tallie always be able to keep an eye on him?"

"You have my word on it."

"It's not my decision."

"Don't you trust me?"

The hesitancy in his voice made her look at him searchingly. Why should she doubt him now when he'd given her no reason to do so? She'd first met him as a protector when she was nine, and though many years had passed, she couldn't believe he'd changed that much. Still, there were other issues that plagued her.

"It isn't a matter of trust, Chris," she said. "Anyway, you'll have to talk to Jerlene. Covey is her son."

Is he yours as well?

She saw the flare of disappointment in his eyes. He got to his feet as if he couldn't sit still any longer.

"How about some coffee?" she asked as she carried the plates into the kitchen.

"Coffee sounds wonderful."

Chris moved around the living room portion of the apartment as the fragrance of perking coffee filled the air. He noted how Maggie Rose had emphasized the demarcation of space between the dining and living room areas with a vivid rug of deep reds and blues enclosing a cream center. Two love seats and several chairs echoed the colors. A pair of table lamps were a soft green while two others had a golden scroll on a cream background.

While Chris found the effect visually inviting, his mind was still occupied with what had just happened. Maggie Rose's attitude about horses puzzled him. What was it about them that disturbed her? He tried to remember if he'd ever known of her riding when she was still in Jamison. He didn't think so. Maybe it was just her unfamiliarity with them. Horses, after all, were very large creatures who could move fast and their hooves could inflict serious damage. He was used to them but not everyone was. Looking at it objectively, he could make a case for her reaction. She was essentially a city woman, he thought, and horses were outside of her experience. He'd have to see what he could do about that.

Maggie Rose brought in a tray with the coffee, cobalt-blue mugs, cream, sugar, spoons, and napkins.

"Black for me," Chris said before she asked. He took the coffee with thanks and drank it as they both stood looking out the window.

Maggie Rose had always been so restful, he thought. Not a lot of useless chatter to fill up space. Silence didn't scare her.

"You have a nice place here, Maggie Rose." He set his mug on the tray.

"I was fortunate to get this apartment with the view. It had just become available when I applied. Let me show you this other room."

He followed her to the first door down the hall.

"This is the office, library, TV room, and guest bedroom all in one," she explained. She'd put a lot of thought into decorating her apartment and was proud of how it had turned out.

A cranberry couch sat against one wall opposite the television and the computer. Bookcases were stacked against a third wall and an upholstered chair sat on each side of the window on the outside wall.

"A woman after my own heart," Chris said admiringly. "You've created inviting rooms."

"It's nice of you to say so, Chris." Maggie Rose flushed with pleasure.

"Would you like a dish of chocolate ice cream with a second cup of coffee?"

"I certainly would."

Maggie Rose wasn't in a hurry to throw him out, and maybe they were both relaxed enough now for him to get to the core of his mission.

Maggie Rose was the key and he was more determined than ever to be successful before he said good night!

Chapter Three

"I like your red clock," Chris said. He stood in the kitchen doorway watching Maggie Rose dishing up the ice cream.

"It's the best I could do to get some color in here. There's so little wall space." She flicked a glance at him. The tall, thin boy she'd known had changed. Now he had broad shoulders, a long torso with a flat stomach, and narrow hips. He looked so attractively masculine standing there, making her small kitchen seem even smaller.

A third scoop of ice cream fell into the glass bowl. "Is this enough?"

"Yes, thanks." He took the bowl and spoon, his fingers brushing hers. She looked at him but met a bland, innocent gaze.

It just isn't fair, she thought, as they ate their ice cream. In his black linen slacks, white sports shirt, and polished half boots, he managed to look so casually elegant, while she looked her worst. He could at least have called to say he was coming by. Give a girl some warning so she wouldn't answer the door looking like something the cat dragged in. And that was another thing.

"How did you know where I live, Chris? I've only been here three weeks."

"I ran into Jerlene at the steak house. I asked how you were settling in and she told me about this apartment. Didn't you want people outside your family to know?"

She heard the surprise in his voice. She took her last bite of ice cream to hide her embarrassment. "It's all right. I just wondered how you knew so quickly. You're my first guest outside of family."

"I'm honored." Chris placed his empty dish on the table, then reached for her hand, raised it, and brushed his lips across her knuckles before releasing it.

She drew in her breath and busied herself pouring coffee from the thermos jug.

The breeze blowing in the open window had begun to cool. In another half hour it would be dusk, but now, in the softened light, the sound of children's voices drifted on the air. Meat was cooking on a grill and the occasional chords of a guitar could be heard.

"This is very pleasant," Chris said. "How do you like it here?"

"I was in my parents' house until I was almost nineteen; then I went to Hartford to Aunt Harriet's. This is the first time in my life I've been alone, the first time I've had an apartment. I'm surprised myself at how much I like it."

"You're lucky. Many apartments aren't like this. I work for a corporation that owns them."

Somehow Maggie Rose had never associated him with working any place but on the farm. She visualized him dressed in business clothes, running an office. His angular face with its dark brows, deep-set eyes, and firm chin that had shown stubbornness as a boy now had the maturity and strength to manage a business or anything else he decided to do. She could see that now, but the idea took a bit of an adjustment.

"What do you do for the corporation?"

"Everything." This conversation was perfect. It was leading to his goal without him forcing it. "I collect and bank the rents, hear complaints, oversee the upkeep of the units, and of course, arrange the advertisements."

"How many units are there?"

"Seventy-two at the moment."

"Don't you have any help?"

"Each building has its own manager who reports to me. I hire service people as they're needed."

"It's still a big job."

"Agreed. Once in a while a serious problem comes up." *Like now.* Every time he relived the scene he got angry again. "I came in one morning to find records pulled from the files and dumped all over the floor."

Maggie Rose was horrified. "Did the police find who did it?"

"Not yet. There'd been a break-in at another office a couple of months ago but the guy who did that is still in jail. I didn't find anything stolen, I don't keep any money overnight. The police said it must be an angry tenant."

"Who do you think did it?"

"I don't think it was a tenant, because they only know about the manager's office in their building. It probably was someone looking for money."

That made sense to her. "What happened to the records?"

"Right now they're sitting in a spare room at home all jumbled up."

"Don't you have a secretary or a receptionist who could work on them?"

Chris shook his head. "It's a one-man office. An answering service takes the calls and relays them to me. My time there is minimum because I'm out checking the units, supervising the maintenance, and taking care of serious complaints. The farm, of course, is still my primary concern."

She looked at him with new respect, thinking of the horror stories her friends in Hartford had told her of neglected apartments where complaints were ignored until the tenants refused to pay their rents. From what Chris said, she doubted that he had such problems.

Now is the time, Chris thought. "It's been a long time since you've seen the farm, Maggie Rose. All the buildings have been repaired and painted. We've built fences, planted shrubs and flowers. I'm anxious to show you what I've done since you were there for Uncle Henry's funeral."

The work had been hard, tedious, and expensive, but rehabilitating what Uncle Henry had entrusted to his care had driven Chris to extraordinary effort. It had given him deep satisfaction that helped assuage his grief at the death of the man who'd been a father to him since he was five.

He leaned forward in his chair, his hands clasped, holding her gaze with his.

"Will you come and see it with me after work tomorrow?"

When she didn't answer immediately, Chris began to feel anxious. There was speculation in her eyes and she was still silent. Quickly he said, "I'll be by at five to pick you up. Is that a good time for you?"

"Five is fine. I'll be ready," Maggie Rose said.

Maggie Rose was not prepared for what she saw when Chris turned into the long lane leading to the farm buildings. When he had proposed the idea yesterday, the visit appealed to her. She wanted to see how the once familiar farm looked now and to assess its fitness as a place for Covey to spend his summer.

The potholed narrow dirt lane had been widened and graveled. The cornfield on the left was now a pasture. On her right as they neared the house was a tidy building with a large sign reading HS STABLES OFFICE. The lane curved, then opened up to the house on the right and a group of buildings off to the left.

"Take a minute to look around; then I'll give you a tour," Chris said as they stepped out of his dark green Toyota SUV.

She'd taken care with her appearance and from his appreciative look it had paid off. She wore slacks, a soft yellow shirt with matching earrings, and sandals. Her shining hair swung against her smooth face as she turned her head to look first in one direction, then another.

She recognized the big old barn in the distance and several other buildings, but there were some new ones also. The house itself was the biggest surprise. The four steps up to a small porch had been replaced with wider steps and a wraparound porch with several loungers, large plants, and a wicker table enhancing its attractiveness.

But it was the totality of the appearance of the entire property that made the greatest impact. Every building and all of the fences gleamed with white paint. The plots of healthy green grass were neatly mowed. Trim, glossy shrubbery grew around the porch and office. Flowering plants in large pots were strategically placed for their greatest effect.

"It's beautiful!" Maggie Rose turned to face Chris. "It hardly looks like the same place. I know your uncle would be pleased with what you've done, Chris. It's truly impressive."

Chris breathed a sigh of relief. "I worked on it for three years after Uncle Henry died," he explained. "Some of it he and I had talked about before he got sick, and some of it came about because of the riding business."

"Did you build the porch yourself?"

"Tallie and I did it. Come inside and let me show you what else we did."

The last time she'd been in the house was after Mr. Shealy's funeral when everyone had gathered for the traditional repast. Remembering Mr. Shealy with his kind eyes and the gentle way he'd always treated her had kept her in tears, so she'd busied herself in the kitchen helping out with the food.

She recalled how the ladies from the church had tried to spruce up the living room. Mr. Shealy had followed the old habit of heavy drapes drawn against the light, and the room was dark and life-less.

What she saw now was a transformation. There were ivory walls, sheer curtains at sparkling windows, a new rug, and a couch with gay-colored cushions. On the outside wall where a dark sideboard used to stand was a full-size brick fireplace adorned with a maple mantel.

"I wouldn't have recognized this room," she said. "How did you happen to put in this fireplace?"

His hands in his pockets, Chris sheepishly explained what must have been a boyhood fantasy. "When I was small, I used to look at pictures of families gathered around a roaring fireplace. The mother would have some sewing or a baby on her lap, while the father read a story to the children sitting on the floor."

The wistful note in his voice reminded her how Chris had often lingered at her house after a school meeting had been over. Mama had liked Chris and made him feel welcome but Daddy had reservations about his hotheadedness.

Chris was smoothing the mantel as he spoke and Maggie Rose realized that another facet of his personality had come to light. Chris wanted to be part of a family.

Chris confirmed her idea as he continued, "I guess that family-around-the-fireplace image stayed in my subconscious, because when I decided to get the house in better shape, I found that fireplace was already in that particular spot."

On the mantel was a picture of Mr. Shealy as a young man and one of Chris in cap and gown.

"Have you used it yet?"

"I initiated it three years ago with a New Year's Eve party. I wanted you to be here but you had to hurry back to Hartford after Christmas."

She responded to the hint of accusation in Chris's voice. "I couldn't come when I wasn't invited."

They regarded each other across the mantelpiece. "You never needed a special invitation to come to my house," he said emphatically. "Jerlene came and Bill Denton and a lot of our old school friends. You'd have enjoyed it."

"I didn't know about your party, Chris," she repeated.

"I'm inviting you right now to the next one, this coming December thirty-first, so you'll have no excuse not to come."

"Suppose the weather is in the seventies?" she challenged.

"We'll still light a fire and have a party. Is it a date?" He quirked his brow and a smile curved his lips, but his voice was uncompromising.

"It's a date," she agreed.

The tour continued as Chris pointed out other changes, like the hardwood floor in the dining room, modern touches in the upstairs bath, and the eighteenth-century rice bed in his bedroom.

"I indulged myself a little here," he acknowledged.

A second bedroom was sparsely furnished with twin beds and a dresser. In the third bedroom was a desk and a daybed, and was filled with boxes.

"These are the twenty years of records?" she asked. She felt him watching her as she stood in his sunny room, flipping through the five-by-five cards. "Why isn't this stored on computer disks?"

"The corporation began very small. Since I've been at the office there's been no one to do the job. But I'm working on it."

Her attention had wandered. She suddenly had the notion that this was meant to be a nursery, because it was so different. The walls were a daffodil yellow with a border of spring flowers around them. Pale yellow sheers were at the window, through which the sunlight poured. The rug was a deep-piled ivory.

"A lovely room," she murmured. "Where does Tallie sleep?" Maggie Rose left the nursery, avoiding Chris's eyes.

"He wanted to be off the kitchen. Said he didn't need to be climbing the stairs several times a day. I put in a shower for him next to his room."

He guided her down to the kitchen and through the door onto the screened porch furnished with a small table, chairs, and a gas grill.

"We eat out here a lot. Tallie likes cooking outside."

"Where is Tallie? I thought I'd see him."

"He had to go into town."

Four young trees separated the backyard from another fenced lot. As they went down the steps, Chris explained that he used the lot to help new students become comfortable with their horses.

Maggie Rose controlled a shudder at the thought of getting close enough to such a creature to become comfortable with it.

They saw the empty stables, its nine stalls, the tack room, the grain-storage section, and the big barn where hay was kept and the cows stayed. While she wasn't interested to know details of caring for horses, it was important to see where Covey might be working.

She listened carefully to Chris's comments about the building work. That he could take on an enterprise this large was a revelation; it refuted his earlier reputation of reckless irresponsibility. She saw clearly the time, planning, sheer hard work, determination, and expense that had gone into taking the farm from a collection of dull brown buildings, some in poor repair, to this attractive, prosperous-looking property.

At the office building where, he explained, riding customers came to enroll and to buy riding clothes, she laid her hand on his arm.

"I can see all you've accomplished here and the effort it took to make the place look like this. It's a fine advertisement for your business, Chris."

He covered her hand and squeezed it. "I'm glad you like what I've done."

It felt so good to walk back to the kitchen arm in arm, their steps evenly matched. He smiled at her and her heart skipped a beat.

"I have to go soon," she reminded him before she got carried away with her inappropriate reaction.

"Let me give you some iced tea first."

As soon as he'd served the tea, Chris said, "I've a business proposition for you, Maggie Rose. Could you transfer those records onto computer disks for me?"

Some things about Chris hadn't changed, she thought. He was still unpredictable.

"I can't. I'm interviewing for a job tomorrow. You don't really need me, anyhow. There are a lot of people and agencies who know how to do

computer work. You can easily find someone else."
She recalled their earlier discussion. "When we
were looking at the records, you said you were
working on getting them done."

He gave her a wry smile. "That's exactly what
I'm doing now. Offering you the job at a very good
salary. I can't let just anyone handle those records,
since most of the people are local and the information is confidential. Also, you know as well as I do
that people who advertise their skills aren't always
reliable. Their work is full of errors. The corporation can't afford that. I need *you* to take it on."

She acknowledged there was some truth to his
reasons, but when would she have the time once
she started working? Mr. Elliot had not called her
but she had planned to interview at the college.

"I don't see how I could do it, Chris."

"You could do it in the evenings. I have no deadline," he said persuasively.

There was a flicker in his eyes and Maggie Rose
sensed that he wanted something else from her.
The files were just one part of it. Maybe her intuition was learning to anticipate his unexpected
moves.

"Listen to me, Maggie Rose. The South Carolina
Riding Association will be evaluating this area in
a few weeks. I intend for HS Stables to win the
highest award in my category this year, but that
requires a top-grade office manager. I need *you* for
that position."

The statement was made with such certainty that
Maggie Rose was bewildered. She knew nothing
about riding stables except that they involved
horses, which made the whole proposition immediately untenable. She couldn't even consider it, but

curiosity made her ask, "Don't you have an office manager?"

"I had one," he said grimly. "She walked out two weeks ago to move to Tennessee."

"Surely you advertised for another?"

"I got six high school graduates and four from college. Not one of them could do what has to be done. I need a competent, experienced manager. It's you I need," he repeated for the second time.

His voice carried an authority she'd never heard. This must be the Chris Shealy of the real estate corporation. All business. Determined. She knew the type from her previous position. Good to work with as long as you did *your* job well. But with Chris there would be a very personal element. She'd better decline politely and leave.

"I'm sure if you look hard enough," she began soothingly, "you'll find—"

"You don't understand the situation." Chris rose from his chair in one quick movement as if his suppressed energy demanded an outlet. His hands clenched the counter, his eyes were intent.

"I began planning HS Stables several years ago because Uncle Henry's dream had been to ride horses for a living. He never wanted to do anything else but he got stuck with the land his father wanted him to farm. It had been in the family since slavery ended. Then he got stuck with me after my parents died. He took on that responsibility whether he wanted to or not. I don't know what might have happened to me if he hadn't taken me in."

Chris moved from the counter to the window in two quick steps and stood with his back to Maggie Rose. "I think I was a burden and a disappointment to him in many ways because it took me a long time to settle down," he said quietly.

Maggie Rose was stunned at these revelations. Who would have thought Mr. Shealy, that quiet man with kind eyes, had carried in him the passion to be a jockey or a cowboy? It seemed that same passion now burned in Chris to create HS Stables as a memorial for his uncle, whose dreams had been denied.

"I made myself a promise to straighten up and to create HS Stables in his honor. Last year we came in second place." Chris turned around to face Maggie Rose. "I made myself another promise that this year: his stables would come in first.

"Neither Tallie nor I can do the office work. I have my job and I give the riding lessons after work and on weekends. We both take care of the horses."

He dropped down into the chair again, his eyes never leaving hers. "Your work would be with the student enrollment, the parents, keeping the records, ordering the supplies, ordering and selling the equestrian clothes for the shop. But the most urgent matter is that the official opening of the summer season is in two weeks and there's still a lot to be done."

He leaned forward, took her hand in his. "Will you do it, Maggie Rose? Please?"

She felt Chris willing her to understand and acquiesce to his imperative need for her services. It was clear he must have someone capable immediately, but how could she be that someone? No, it was impossible.

She sighed, then took a deep breath. "Chris, even if I took the job it could only be for six weeks, and you need someone long term."

He looked at her blankly. "I don't understand."

"One of the main reasons I'm home is to go into business with Ginnie Steed. We're buying her aunt Henny's place, the Mailroom."

"I heard she was retiring. *You're* one of the new owners?" His words came out disbelievingly.

"We take possession July fifteenth."

The shock on his face made Maggie Rose feel sorry for Chris. He'd been so certain about her as his office manager that even she had begun to wish she could take the position, while knowing it would never happen. She could never work around horses.

"What were you planning to do between now and July fifteenth?" he asked.

"Find a job," she admitted.

His face cleared. "I'm offering you a job and you needn't worry about the length of time. These next weeks are crucial ones so when the evaluators visit, everything will be in the best possible condition."

His eyes were shining now and Maggie Rose could see he was marshaling all the forces he could think of to obtain her agreement. She had to deflect him.

"Chris, I need to have five thousand dollars by July fifteenth. I'm sure your office manager didn't earn that."

He didn't even blink. In fact, he looked relieved, she thought.

"If that's the only problem, then we've nothing to worry about. I'll be happy to pay you that if you'll just take the job."

How could he afford to pay her that much for six weeks of work? He must earn a lot on that job of his, or maybe it was a sign of how far he was willing to go to get what he wanted.

Could she do the job? It would be great to know the five thousand was hers by July fifteenth. She didn't see how she could pass that up, as desperately as she needed it. Perhaps with skillful juggling she could manage to avoid the horses altogether, she thought, as her mind replayed the list of functions Chris mentioned.

Those seemed easy enough and might even turn out to be interesting, especially getting ready for the season opening. She enjoyed that kind of challenge.

She'd be able to keep an eye on Covey. She tried to ignore the thought that she'd have the opportunity to observe what relationship, if any, there might be between the boy and Chris.

Maggie Rose suppressed the spark of excitement that the idea of working with Chris awakened in her and considered her options soberly.

She had to have the five thousand. The only obstacle was something Chris knew nothing about, and perhaps if she was clever and watchful, he'd never need to know in the six weeks she'd be working for him.

Chris squeezed her hand lightly. "Will you take the job, Maggie Rose?"

His eyes were hopeful, beckoning her to say yes.

She had everything to gain as long as she was careful. Even so, risks had to be taken sometimes.

"Yes," she said, and a moment later was lifted to her feet and smothered in Chris's exultant hug.

Recklessness had its immediate rewards sometimes, she thought with a secret smile.

Chapter Four

Covey Sanders rolled out of bed. Usually he jumped out and was dressed within minutes but this morning was different. He was going with Aunt Maggie Rose to begin working. He'd never had a paying job before and he wasn't sure what to expect. Would working with the Mr. Sims at the farm be hard or easy? Was he mean or nice? Covey was just supposed to follow along and do whatever Mr. Sims wanted him to do in the garden or around the barn. He would learn how to take care of horses and that would be good. He'd always been interested in horses, though he'd never had a chance to be around one.

Covey had washed his face and brushed his teeth. In the mirror he saw a narrow face with thin lips and brown eyes. He didn't like to look at himself too much because if he did he would begin to wonder about his daddy. Who was he and what did he look like? Why had he gone away and never come back? Had it been because he hadn't wanted his son?

Once when Covey asked his mom about his dad, all she said was that he liked horses. While Covey pulled on his jeans and a shirt, he thought that maybe the Mr. Shealy who owned the place might be his dad. It made him both excited and nervous about working there this summer. He wasn't supposed to know that Mr. Shealy might be his dad. He'd heard about it by accident from three boys talking together in the rest room at school.

"My dad said I could have some riding lessons," one boy had bragged.

"No one around here gives lessons," a second boy taunted.

Covey, in one of the two stalls, couldn't help but hear the conversation.

"Sure they do. A Mr. Shealy has stables where he gives lessons on weekends."

A third boy said, "I know something about Mr. Shealy I bet you don't know."

Covey knew the voice. It belonged to Eddie Stockton, who was a year older than Covey. Eddie always knew stuff about people that other kids didn't know.

"What about him? Aren't his horses any good?" asked the first boy anxiously.

"I guess they're all right," Eddie said. "I heard my parents say that he might be Covey Sanders's dad."

There was utter silence for a moment. In the stall, Covey froze in shock. Then the bell rang.

"Let's go," Eddie said, and Covey heard the door

open. A moment later other boys surged in and Covey felt safe to leave.

For the remainder of the afternoon, Covey's mind couldn't focus on anything except the possibility that the Mr. Shealy he had known as a friend of his mom and his aunt might be his dad. He didn't know much about Mr. Shealy, but the few times they'd met, Mr. Shealy had always been friendly and had talked to him directly as a person. Covey hated it when adults talked with him as if he were only someone to be noticed for a second.

Was Mr. Shealy married? Did he have other children? Covey wished he could ask his mother about it but he knew from experience that she would only tighten her lips and change the subject. Once he'd asked Grandma who his dad was. She'd looked at him sadly. "I don't know, Covey. Try not to worry about it because we all love you so much." She'd hugged him tight for a minute, then let him go.

At breakfast Covey said, "Thanks for letting me go out to Mr. Shealy's with Aunt Maggie Rose, Mom. This'll be my first real job."

"You be very careful and listen to what you're told."

"I will," Covey promised. He didn't have to try to find out from his mom if what Eddie had said was true. He'd figured out a way to find out for himself that would let him know for sure one way or the other.

"Finish up, your aunt will be here to get you soon," Jerlene said.

She, too, was glad about this job for Covey. He was only ten so she didn't know how much of a real job it would be but it would keep him off the street for now. *I wonder what made Chris come up with the idea,* she mused, as she got ready to go to work. What did he have in mind? Maybe she needed to keep an eye on him. After all, she had the best excuse for a casual visit now and then. Chris had her son.

When he'd called to talk about Covey, he'd only said Tallie could use help this summer as they'd be very busy with the riding school and since Maggie Rose would be driving out every day, Covey could come with her. Would that be all right? he asked, after naming the kinds of things Tallie would want Covey to do, and the salary Chris would pay.

Of course she had no objections. Now she wouldn't have to worry that Covey had been in a fight or something worse. She didn't exactly have objections to Maggie Rose working with Chris, either. She knew it wasn't wise, but how could she stop it? Even if she could, it would put Covey out of luck for something safe and productive to keep him occupied.

"But how did this happen?" she asked Maggie Rose on the phone after Chris had hung up. "Thought you were getting a job with a law firm downtown. That's what Mama told me."

"I thought so, too, but they hadn't called so I took Chris's offer. I'm not wild about it but it is a job I know how to do and I'll get a check every week."

"I didn't know he was looking for an office manager. He didn't mention anything like that the last time I saw him. Several weeks ago, I was having dinner at the steak house with some other people when he came over to say hello. Shanta, one of the girls I was with, hadn't met him before and she thought Chris was too fine! I told her not to get her hopes up about him because he's been fine a long time but he's still single and apparently intends to stay that way. Then this other girl, Delora—you remember her, don't you?—she said she's been trying to get his attention for years and he's friendly but that's all. Anyway, how did he come to ask you to be his office manager?"

"He said the one he had went to Tennessee and didn't come back. He's getting ready for the opening of the riding school for the season and he needed help fast. When he found out I'd come home to stay, he asked me because of my experience at Travelers."

As she gave Jerlene this information, Maggie Rose wondered if there had been a message in Jerlene's prattle. Was there a warning for her about Chris Shealy? Not to get her hopes up? Hopes for what? Nothing she'd ever said or done was a basis for Jerlene to think Maggie Rose entertained any kind of "hopes" when it came to Chris Shealy. How could she possibly have hopes for a relationship with a man who might be the father of her nephew? Maybe Jerlene was speaking of her own experience.

Maggie Rose had planned to have a sound night's sleep before starting the new job, but sleep had been elusive. When she finally stopped trying to find a comfortable spot and drifted off anyhow, her dreams were disturbed by visions filled with flashing hooves and screams. The screams had her shooting upright in bed, her heart beating fast, and the bedclothes tangled about her. With a trembling hand she turned on the lamp.

It was only four o'clock. She hadn't had the nightmare in a very long time. It always left her shaky, terrified, and feeling cold inside. This was the last thing she needed just now.

Maggie Rose washed her face in the bathroom, drank some water, then straightened the bed. It was useless to think she could go back to sleep no matter how tired she was. She returned to bed, picked up her book, and settled down to try to clear her mind by reading the newest mystery by a favorite writer.

In trying to figure out which one of the six characters being introduced would be murdered and which would be the murderer, the terrifying images of her dream faded away. When her alarm went off at six she found she had been able to fall asleep.

A long shower helped clear away the cobwebs. She wanted to look professional, competent, and smart on this first day of her new job. Deciding on an oatmeal ankle-length A-line skirt with front and back darts that emphasized her waist, she added a grass-green silk blouse and matching earrings. Her chocolate leather loafers had contrasting stitched trim that matched her skirt.

She looked at herself critically and decided the outfit would do. For a fleeting moment she anticipated the look on Chris's face when he saw her. The makeup she applied was soft and subtle. She brushed her hair until it swung glossy and free at her shoulders.

By the time she went to the kitchen, she thought she was composed and ready for breakfast, but the very smell of coffee and toast was nauseating. This was a delayed reaction from the nightmare, she knew, but one she didn't want to have to deal with today of all days.

After rinsing out her mouth with cold water, she slowly took twenty deep breaths. The tension in her stomach muscles relaxed, giving her hope that the worst was over and she could face the day with equilibrium.

When she stopped the car in front of Jerlene's apartment, Covey opened the door and came running out.

"Hi, Aunt Maggie Rose. Do I look okay?" He indicated his jeans and the black T-shirt. "I wanted to wear shorts because it's so warm but Mom said to wear jeans."

"You look fine, Covey. Tomorrow you can bring some shorts and I'll keep them in the office for you to change into when you get too hot." Covey was all arms and legs, causing Jerlene to complain about how fast he outgrew his jeans. "Your mom's already gone to work?"

"She had to go a little early today because someone was going to be absent, she said. She told me to tell you she'll talk to you tonight."

The going-to-work traffic was heavy as Maggie Rose guided the car through Jamison to come out on the south side toward highway 90. She could tell Covey was nervous by his unusual flow of conversation. Unlike his mother, the boy was quiet most of the time. But now he was commenting on the cars they passed, houses where someone he knew lived, and in between the impersonal, injecting seemingly casual questions that told Maggie Rose about his anxieties.

"Will there be other kids at the farm?" he asked.

"I don't think so, Covey. Mr. Shealy isn't mar-

ried. The only other person who lives there is Mr.
Tallie Sims, the man you'll be helping.''

"Is he a relative?"

"No. He used to help Mr. Shealy's uncle and
after he died, Chris Shealy asked him to live on
the farm and keep helping.''

Driving down highway 90 was almost like being
under a canopy, Maggie Rose thought. All her life
she'd been up and down this two-lane road but
never tired of its restful beauty. Occasionally devel-
opers had petitioned to have the road widened
and had put forth various strategies to make some
of the parcels of land open to development. All
such efforts had failed and highway 90 remained
an untouched piece of rural South Carolina.

"How much farther, Aunt Maggie Rose?"

Maggie Rose saw that Covey was looking straight
ahead instead of looking right and left as he had
been doing. Nervous tension flowed from him.
Already vulnerable, Maggie Rose felt his tension
infect her. The nightmare and its aftermath, an
empty stomach, the knowledge that in a few more
minutes she would be near horses, and the need
to hide from Chris and Covey the terror the beasts
invoked coiled her nerves tighter and tighter.

"We're almost there," she said. "Look down the
road on your right and you can see the white fence.
That's the beginning of it.''

She began practicing deep breathing as unobtru-
sively as possible and shortly afterward turned off
the highway into Chris's place. She saw him immediately, standing by the pasture fence with Tallie.
She flicked a hurried glance behind him. There
were no horses in sight. Her tension drained away,

followed by euphoria. She parked the car and stepped out with Covey beside her.

"Hi, Chris. Good morning, Mr. Tallie. I haven't seen you in a long time. I've brought you your helper. This is my nephew, Covey Sanders."

"Glad to meet you, Covey," Tallie said.

Chris was dazzled by the radiance of her smile. The thread of anxiety he'd had as to whether she'd show up vanished. She looked wonderful and she smelled wonderful. If she kept smiling at him like that, how was he going to keep this the purely business proposition he'd promised himself to do?

"Morning, Maggie Rose," he managed. He turned to Covey and extended his hand. "Good to have you here, Covey. Tallie's going to show you around while I show Maggie Rose her office."

"You're looking very well this morning," he said as they walked across to the office. "You must have had a good night's sleep."

"Actually, I didn't, but I feel great now." Another dazzling smile made Chris glad they'd arrived at the office. "Welcome to your new home away from home." He pushed the door open for her.

They stepped into a large, attractively painted room. "As you can see, this front part of the building is for the clothes shop," Chris explained.

There was a large assortment of pants, jodhpurs, tops, jackets, belts, hats, and helmets. There were also boots and other accessories.

Another room held a desk, computer, file cabinets, and several chairs and a worktable. The building also had a bathroom and a storage room.

"It's larger than it looks from the outside," she remarked as she glanced at the pictures of students and awards that decorated the walls.

Chris ushered her into the contoured desk chair. "It's your office now." He took the chair on the other side and beamed at her. "Are you comfortable?"

"Yes, I am. Tell me about your office procedures and your students."

Chris said there were currently eighteen students coming for instruction on Friday afternoons and all day Saturday. Two or three came on Thursday afternoons.

She looked at the list of students' names. "How long are the lessons?"

"Beginners come for half an hour; then they move into the one-hour group class. A few come for an hour's private lesson."

"How do you keep the schedule straight?"

"I keep it in my head but now that I have my new office manager I'd like to have a large chart because changes do occur." His hands deftly indicated the size of the chart and the wall space beside the desk where it should hang.

"I know the kind you mean, erasable and color coded," she said, making notes in the tablet she'd brought with her.

"After the opening I hope to have many more students." He straightened the certificate on the wall that named him as a registered riding instructor.

Maggie Rose stopped writing to look at Chris. "Can you teach them all, Chris? There're only so many hours in the day."

"In the summer there're more hours in the day because of daylight savings time, you know. Last summer I had an advanced class that began at seven-thirty P.M."

"Have you thought of hiring someone to help you?" she asked with concern.

"I will if I get enough new students."

Maggie Rose nodded, satisfied. "As I see, it the most urgent business is the opening. Can you give me a picture of what happens?" Her pen flew across the page as Chris described the event.

"Basically, I invite a lot of people to come to the stables, have refreshments, visit the shop, ask about lessons, and watch the students ride. The idea is to impress on them that this is a good place for riding instruction. That's why I worked so hard to change its appearance, so people will see this as a prosperous and secure business." His voice was filled with determination.

"The first thing, then, is the invitations. Have they gone out yet?"

"No, they're still at the printer's. I'm picking them up as soon as I leave here."

"Where is the mailing list?"

Chris dug it out of the file cabinet. As least he had that in order.

"Is it completed and updated?"

"Yes, I've been working on that myself and it's ready."

He laid it in front of her. She quickly glanced through the two hundred names to be sure each had an address.

He watched her, thankful to see her in possession of his office, managing this part of the business and leaving him to concentrate on the rest.

"By the way," he said, "we use Perfect Words for our printing. We have an account there and one at Staples for office supplies. The petty cash is here." He showed her a metal box in a locked desk drawer. "I'll get you a set of keys while I'm out."

"What about publicity?" Maggie Rose asked.

Chris rubbed his hand over his face "That's one of the things that fell through the cracks when Venetia moved back to Tennessee."

Maggie Rose made more notes in her tablet. "Don't worry about it, it'll be taken care of," she promised.

Alone in her new office, Maggie Rose took a deep breath. This job was going to be exciting if she could just avoid the horses. Chris's office procedures were easy to understand, no problem there. She already saw a number of things she could do for the opening to make it a truly gala affair. From what Chris related, last year's opening had been small, but she would make this one successful beyond his wildest dreams.

Instead of snacks served on the porch, she'd have a marquee with tables, chairs, and a serving bar. People could sit after touring the stables and watching the riders. In such comfort they were more likely to decide on riding lessons for themselves and their children.

She'd make the shop more attractive, order new stock, and put some on sale. Order a sign and cards. People liked to take something home. How about a pen or key ring with HS Stables on it? The stables needed a distinctive logo. Maybe Chris already had one. It should be printed on all of their paper products and signs.

The door opened and Chris breezed in. She looked up at him with a smiling welcome.

"It's great to have you here, Maggie Rose," he said, placing the boxes of invitations on her desk.

To her surprise he held out his hand, his eyes meeting hers. Hesitantly she put her hand in his. She felt his warm breath on her palm, then a soft brush of his lips. He'd kissed her hand before. Was this a romantic gesture he gave any woman to whom he was being attentive for the moment? She'd pay it no attention, even though it did create a warmth, which gradually spread as he continued to hold her gaze and her hand.

She saw the look in his eyes change. Then instead of his releasing her hand, his mouth moved down to the sensitive spot on her inner wrist. She held her breath as his lips lingered there, his eyes closed. Tendrils of heat fanned out inside her. She felt an errant desire to caress his head as he bent it over her wrist.

The room was still as he opened his eyes and released her hand. She wanted to see if her wrist had a red spot where his lips had been but she couldn't look away from their locked gaze.

"Thank you for coming to help me," he said softly.

"You're welcome," she whispered.

The invitations. That was what she was supposed to be doing. She took a card from the box. The standard "You are invited" form was adequate but had no flair. Next year would be different. She'd— Maggie Rose stopped. Chris's kiss on her wrist really had confused her if she was thinking of being here next year.

"I was thinking that out of the two hundred people, maybe seventy-five will come. Sundays in June are pretty busy," Chris said. Chris was standing away from the desk, turning in his hands a wooden horse sculpture.

"You're thinking right," she agreed. "That's why my idea is to go all out and make this a gala occasion to attract more people, if that's all right with you."

"The sky's the limit as far as I'm concerned."

"What kind of budget do you have for this?" Maggie Rose asked. "Can you give me a dollar figure?" Her hand hovered over her pad waiting for his answer.

Chris avoiding looking at her. She'd shown him she could be as businesslike as he despite random kisses on the palm and wrist.

"Tomorrow you give me as thorough a list as you can of what you need and then we'll be able to work from there. I have to go to work for a few hours now." He looked at her briefly. "When are you and Covey leaving?"

"I thought we'd come at eight-thirty as we did today and leave at four-thirty."

"That's fine. As long as the work gets done you can set your own hours." His mischievous smile was back. "I'm no slave driver."

He wouldn't drive her as he drove himself, but he didn't need to. He'd seen her work ethic was as strong as his.

"You'll get your full eight hours, boss." She was surprised to see a hint of embarrassment in his expression.

"Be sure to get some lunch. I know Tallie made some." He closed the door quietly behind him.

Chris scarcely noted the heavy traffic at the major intersections as he drove back to the farm that afternoon. Thank God he was his own boss and could leave the job when he wanted to. All afternoon he'd thought of Maggie Rose.

He felt a deep sense of satisfaction knowing she was at her desk working for him. He hadn't been sure he could pull it off, but he had. Running the stables and working for the corporation were two full-time jobs and he couldn't do it without Tallie and a competent office manager. He'd been frantic when Venetia had left.

The idea of securing Maggie Rose to fill that spot had been an inspiration and now she was here. He knew her to be skilled and a hard worker. He could count on her and that was what he needed if he was to turn HS Stables into the kind of riding business that would win him the coveted award as well as demonstrate his stature as a sound businessman, not an irresponsible person unable to leave his wildness behind him.

He could not afford to become involved emotionally with Maggie Rose. He hadn't meant to touch her in any way, but when he'd brought the invitations in and she smiled at him with such warmth he'd reacted unthinkingly with the kiss on her palm. But he discovered that wasn't enough. The pulse at her wrist beckoned him and with closed eyes, he savored the tender, silky skin. He heard her indrawn breath and felt the tiny tremor in her arm as he tasted her. When the image of continuing the tasting all the way up her arm took hold of him, he was on dangerous ground.

He had to create a distance between them and so he had stepped away. From now on he had to stop the eye contact that he had always sought with Maggie Rose. Keep strictly to business. He never had mixed business with pleasure and this was no time to start. For the next six weeks there wasn't going to be any pleasure in the social sense; he had his hands full with the corporation in the day and working flat-out to achieve his goal with the HS Stables business.

With this intention firmly in mind he had no problem greeting Maggie Rose and thanking her when she showed him the boxes of invitations ready to be mailed. She was on her feet, putting the last of the envelopes in a box. "If you'll get Covey for me, I can get them to the post office and metered in time to go out in tomorrow's mail," she said.

He stepped to the door. "Covey," he yelled and followed that with a whistle. He grinned at the startled expression. "Just want to be sure he hears me," he said. He pulled four twenty-dollar bills from his pocket. "This will cover the mailing."

Covey came running from the barn to the car as Chris put the boxes of invitations in the truck.

"Hey, Covey," he said, "how'd it go today?"

Covey had a few pieces of straw in his hair, dust on his jeans, and a smudge on his face. "Mr. Tallie said I did a good job." He grinned at Chris, trying not to look proud as he climbed into the car.

"Thanks for everything, Maggie Rose," Chris said at her window.

He stepped aside and she started the car. "Come back tomorrow," he heard himself say.

"I will," she promised.

"Me, too," Covey said. "Mr. Tallie showed me how to do so many things, but I didn't get to do anything with the horses today. He said they have to get used to me. But in a little while I'll be able to help with them. I can't wait to tell Mama."

Covey's thin face, so often somber and quiet, was animated with happy anticipation.

Dealing with horses was Covey's idea of heaven; the same idea was the opposite for her. Yet whatever it took for her to deal with them, she had to do it for his sake, and for the sake of her business goal with Ginnie.

Part of that was concealing from Chris the terror that horses caused in her. Every day she would have to be wary of avoiding them without arousing Chris's suspicion. It was like walking a tightwire, especially with the pull between them generated by Chris this morning. Whatever had led him to kiss her palm and then her wrist in such a tender way, which even now made her tingle, had to be ignored. Maybe he was reacting to getting her to take the job.

Whatever it was, she would be very careful to keep her hands and wrists to herself from now on. The job would be all business.

Across town, the telephone was ringing as the man opened the door. He caught it on the last ring.

"I was going to call you later. Any luck yet?"

"Yeah, I've made a solid contact."

"Good. Don't do anything to mess this up. You know how important this is."

"I know. Don't worry."

"I'll call you next week."

Chapter Five

"Maggie Rose?"

"Hi, Jerlene." Maggie Rose eased into the slow lane, where guiding the car with one hand and talking into the cell phone was less dangerous. "We're five minutes away from your house. I had to stop at the post office." She knew she was running a little late.

"That's why I'm calling you. I won't be home until later, so drop Covey off at Mom's. Okay? See you later."

Jerlene disconnected before Maggie Rose could reply. *I'll bet it's not the job that's making her late,* she thought with exasperation. *That's why she hung up so fast. Doesn't she care how much Covey wants to tell her about what happened today?* She took time putting the phone back in its cradle and watching the traffic before she turned to Covey.

"We're going to Grandma's. Your mom said

she'll be late. Probably has to wait for some parents to pick up their children."

The resignation and disappointment in Covey's thin face as he turned away to look out the window made Maggie Rose furious at her sister.

"Grandma's already cooking dinner," she said, "but whatever it is, we can have ice cream for dessert. Do you want to go to Dairy Queen or Baskin Robbins?"

She was counting on getting Covey's attention, as he seemed never to get tired of certain flavors of ice cream.

"Tommy said he had a new flavor called watermelon at Dairy Queen." Covey looked at her hopefully.

"Are you sure it's ice cream? Sounds more like sherbet to me."

"He said ice cream but it does sound weird. Can we try it?"

"Sure, but why don't you call Grandma and see what kind she and Granddad want?"

By the time of the purchase of a pint of watermelon ice cream as an experiment and a half gallon of tried-and-true chocolate chip was accomplished, Covey had regained some of his earlier enthusiasm.

"Mr. Tallie said he's known my grandfather a long time and for me to tell him hello for Mr. Tallie."

"Grandad'll be glad to hear that."

Laurel Street, where her parents lived, had retained the air of comfort and livability with which Maggie Rose had grown up. The one- and two-story houses, each with its own yard, were kept up through the encouragement of a committee of the Laurel Street residents. Covey had spent a good part of his young life here, she thought as she parked the car in her parents' driveway. Maybe that stability, represented by his grandparents, had become a part of the boy's character and would sustain him through the times when Jerlene failed him.

Frank Sanders opened the door as they came up the steps, Covey in front carrying the ice cream. A big man with heavy features topped with iron-gray hair, he nodded a greeting.

"I was watching for you. That ice cream must be melting in this weather. Ada, they're here." His resonant voice filled the room.

Ada Sanders was a quiet-moving, genteel woman whose family was the mainstay of her existence. She greeted her daughter and grandson lovingly.

"Hello, you two." She opened the freezer side of the refrigerator. "Here, Covey, I made room for your ice cream on this shelf. Dinner's ready soon as you wash your hands."

Covey began talking as soon as grace was said. "Mr. Tallie told me to tell you hello, Granddad. He said he's known you a long time." He passed his plate around and had it come back with a thick hamburger patty, an ear of corn, a mound of beans, and some tomato slices.

"He's right, we go back a long way. We worked together building houses before I started with the phone company. I remember once—" He interrupted himself. "What's the matter with your food?" Covey wasn't eating.

"Can I have my hamburger in a bun with mustard and pickles and mayonnaise?" Covey asked.

"You certainly may when you're eating at a fast food place," his grandmother answered, "but here at the dinner table you eat it with a fork with the rest of your food.''

"She told me the same thing, and then Alicia and then your mom,'' Maggie Rose confided. "It's not bad that way.''

Covey picked up his fork reluctantly. "Go on with your story, Granddad.''

"I'll tell you later. I want to hear all about what you did out at Henry's place.''

Covey frowned. "Who's Henry?''

Maggie Rose and her mother glanced at each other. Frank Sanders still disapproved of Chris for giving his uncle problems. He refused to acknowledge that Henry Shealy's property now belonged to Chris even though Henry had been gone five years.

"Henry Shealy owned the farm,'' Ada explained. "He was Chris's uncle but he's dead now and the place belongs to Chris.''

The frown disappeared and in between the stops for chewing and swallowing Covey related how Mr. Tallie showed him how to feed the cows, hogs, chickens, and geese. "I can't spread the clean straw in the barn and the stall for the horses yet but Mr. Tallie said I'd learn.''

"What did you like best?'' Ada asked as she gave him another ear of corn.

"The horses. They're so beautiful,'' he said simply, his voice full of wonder.

"Did you ever ride horses, Granddad?''

"Sometimes, when I was growing up like you. How many horses does Shealy have?''

As the conversation continued in detail, Maggie Rose breathed deeply, took small sips of water, and tried to shut it out by thinking of the Mailroom figures she and Ginnie were going to discuss later.

"Maggie Rose, you ready for ice cream?" Her mother was looking at her oddly and Covey was on his way to the refrigerator.

"Bring on the watermelon flavor," she said as she helped clear the table.

"I'll pick you up at eight in the morning," she told Covey later. "Be sure to bring some shorts with you."

At the door her father said, "You tell that Chris he better not let anything happen to Covey over there."

Maggie Rose reassured him and went to her car. Before she could find her keys, an unfamiliar red car turned into the driveway and stopped beside her.

"Maggie Rose, I'm glad I caught you," Jerlene called, scrambling out of the car. "I want you to meet Dan Montgomery."

Dan was tall and rangy with light brown skin and brown eyes. He responded to Jerlene's introduction with a brief smile and handshake.

"How'd the job go?" Jerlene asked but in the next breath explained to Dan that her son and Maggie Rose had begun working at the Shealy stables that day.

Everything about Jerlene seemed to be filled with movement—her short, dark curls, her flashing eyes, and her hands that made descriptive gestures. She turned from Dan to Maggie Rose. "Did Covey like it?"

"Very much. He's anxious to tell you all about it. I'll pick him up at eight tomorrow."

She'd been right as usual, she mused as she drove

home. When it came to Jerlene, too often male companionship came before Covey, and this latest male, Dan Montgomery, was like the others. Physically attractive but seemingly all surface. Still, she'd reserve judgment on him; he might turn out to be better than the others.

Chris often thought the early morning routine with his horses was the best part of his day. These handsome, intelligent creatures had distinctive personalities and behaviors. He enjoyed their company and he knew they enjoyed his as he checked them each morning to see that they were in good health and talked to them.

His favorite was a Morgan he'd named HS for Henry Shealy even though she was a mare. "I'm showing you off today," he said, rubbing her muzzle. "I want you to be good and don't scare Maggie Rose when I bring her to see you." HS dropped her head and nickered as if she understood, then nudged Chris's hand for the carrot he'd brought her.

The black horse with a white patch on her rump was next. "Chica, no tricks from you today," Chris admonished the flighty paint, who had a mind of her own.

"Maggie Rose is going to love you," he told Starlight, a silvery gray quarter horse.

"Maybe she'll like you best, Windsong. You're an elegant beauty." He patted the horse that was a favorite of the female students.

The last horse was Nicky, a reddish brown pony. "I know she'll like you because you're so gentle," he said, checking Nicky's eyes.

By the time he had groomed, watered, and fed
the horses and mucked their stalls, another hour
had passed.

There was an understanding between Chris and
his horses. He could remember times when they
had seemed to be his only true friends. They
accepted him as he was. Often he'd been able to
ride out his frustrations on their backs and find a
resolution to his problems.

He was going to show off his beauties to Maggie
Rose today. She needed to know them by name,
breed, and appearance so she could answer questions from prospective clients. He realized she
might be a little unsure around them at first but
that was all right. She'd get past that.

He took a final look at the stalls. Five glossy heads
with glistening alert eyes and pricked ears looked
back at him. With a whistle and a light step Chris
left the stable and went in to breakfast.

At eight-thirty he saw Maggie Rose's car come
down the lane and was ready to open her door
when she stopped.

"Good morning." He smiled.

"The same to you. You're looking very chipper
today," she replied.

"Hi, Mr. Chris." Covey came around the car.

"Covey. Glad you came back. Tallie'll be glad,
too. He's in the kitchen."

Chris thought Maggie Rose looked smart in her
cool linen outfit of tailored pants with a matching
short-sleeve top, white earrings, and sandals.

"It's going to be a hot day but you look cool.
Cool, calm, and collected?" He lifted an eyebrow.

"But of course." Maggie Rose smiled as she
started toward the office. "I made the lists you

asked for and I need to go over them with you so I can begin lining up what we'll need for the opening."

"That can wait a little while," Chris said. "There's something I want you to see first. I have five beauties in their stalls waiting to meet the newest addition to our business."

"Can't that wait a little?" Maggie Rose said, her heart beating fast. "I need to have time to discuss this list with you before you go to work."

"We'll have time," Chris began but was interrupted by a call from Tallie that Chris had an urgent message from one of his apartment managers.

"I'll be back," Chris said as he hurried to the house.

Maggie Rose reached her office and dropped into her chair. She put her head down between her knees until the dizziness passed. She devoutly hoped Chris would be called away at least for a while. She sat up slowly, rubbed her cheeks to restore color, and breathed deeply.

"I'm sorry but I have to leave. There's been a severe domestic fight in one of the buildings. See you later." Chris was in and out of the office before she could say anything.

She went limp with relief.

The morning sped by as Maggie Rose found and priced the marquee, plus tables and chairs for one hundred guests. She hoped she wasn't being over-optimistic. She didn't know what Chris had used last year but this year there'd be one or two portable toilets. She called Catering by Leah, run by a friend whose food and service were first class. They discussed appropriate food for such a gathering and how it would be served. She gathered several quotes from sign makers and from companies who provided party favors.

At noon she joined Tallie and Covey for lunch at the kitchen table.

"Mr. Tallie let me watch when he turned the horses out from their stalls into the pasture," Covey announced.

"You've got a smart nephew here," Tallie said. "He already knows which horse is which."

Keep yourself steady now, breathe slowly and deeply, she told herself. Then she was ready. "Can you name them, Covey?"

"Sure I can. Their names are HS for Mr. Chris's uncle Henry, and then there's Nicky, Starlight, Chica, and Windsong. You want me to take you to see them?" he asked eagerly.

"I think Mr. Chris wants to do that when he gets back and I have to get back to work in a minute."

The first thing she did when she got back to the office was to look at the files of the horses. Chris had called them beauties, and they were indeed handsome creatures. But they were also huge and fearsome and she didn't know how she was going to get near them when just looking closely at their pictures made her begin to feel dizzy and nauseated. She prayed that Chris wouldn't get home before she left.

Three-thirty came and went. Maggie Rose allowed herself to be hopeful. She was taking inventory in the storage room as her last task of the day when she heard the outer door open.

"Maggie Rose?" It was Chris's voice but dull and slow.

She hurried back into the office. Chris was

slumped in a chair, his long legs out, his head back with his eyes closed.

"It must have been a bad day," she said sympathetically.

"Bad," he echoed. "This morning a guy tried to use his wife as a punching bag. He damaged the place, then took on several family members who tried to restrain him. It took most of the morning to deal with it."

"Does that kind of thing occur often in your buildings?" It occurred to her that she didn't know where the apartments he took care of were located. Not that it mattered, since abuse happened everywhere.

"Not often, but it does happen. Then this afternoon a woman came home and found she'd been robbed." Chris sat straight and rubbed his eyes. "They took her television and stereo but what she couldn't stop crying about was that they took the silverware her grandmother had given her."

His weariness made Maggie Rose wonder how often he'd brought such depressing problems from work. Did he talk with Tallie about them or keep it all inside?

"It hadn't occurred to me," she said, thinking aloud, "that your job meant running into such problems. That must be very hard for you, Chris," she added gently.

The sympathy she felt seemed to register with Chris. His eyes lost their dullness and took on some warmth as he and Magie Rose looked at each other.

"Your listening helps, Maggie Rose," he said quietly.

He glanced at the wall clock and she saw him remember. He came to his feet, his energy restored. "There's just time to finish what we started this morning."

Before she could pull herself together he had her outside and walking toward the stables. Maggie Rose tried her breathing ritual but her heart pumped rapidly and she could manage only short, shallow breaths. Chris said something about how they had added new stalls but she couldn't respond.

Her whole focus was on staying upright but the dizziness came. She missed her footing and twisted her left ankle, crying out with pain as she lurched against Chris.

"What's the matter, Maggie Rose? What happened?" He put his arm strongly around her, holding her so her weight rested on him.

"My ankle. I twisted it."

"Can you put your weight on it?"

She shook her head no, biting her lip to hold back the tears.

The next thing she knew Chris picked her up and began walking toward the house.

She felt awkward and self-conscious until Chris smiled at her. She could see the fine hair on his face and a few fine lines around his mouth.

"You may as well enjoy the ride," he said, shifting her a little so that her head fell naturally on his shoulder.

"That's better," he said softly.

Maggie Rose marveled at his strength. His breathing was even, his carriage straight. The protectiveness she sensed made her nestle against him and she felt his arms tighten around her.

In silence they covered the distance to the house, up the steps, and into the sunlit living room where

Chris transferred her from his arms onto the couch as if she were a porcelain doll that might break.

"How are you?" he asked anxiously.

"All right. I enjoyed the ride." She felt shy and couldn't quite meet his eyes.

"So did I," Chris said quietly. He seated himself on the couch. "Now let's have a look at that ankle."

Her ankle was swollen and painful but even so, Maggie Rose was conscious of how gentle Chris was as his long fingers carefully probed the injury. She winced as he touched a particularly painful spot.

"Sorry," he said. "I'm trying not to make you feel any worse."

"Do you think it's sprained?"

"No, only twisted, and I know just the right thing for it. I'll be right back." He reappeared with a flat plastic bag of ice, a towel, and a glass of water.

"That's what my aunt used when I first tried ice skating in Hartford and twisted this same ankle," she recalled.

"Then you know ice helps the swelling go down." He produced a small bottle of aspirin from his pocket and shook two out for her. "I want you to take these and relax on the couch for a little while." He waited until she took a sip of water and the pills. He elevated her ankle, which he wrapped with the towel holding the ice in place.

"Are you comfortable?" he asked, bending over her.

Maggie Rose felt a complex of emotions. The near fall with the consequent twisted ankle had shaken her. Then Chris had carried her here to the house and treated her with a solicitude that brought her to a dangerously vulnerable condition.

Tears were near the surface but so was the urge to touch Chris. His face was so close and she couldn't stop looking at the way his mouth was shaped. His lips looked as if they would be firm, supple, and warm.

"Maggie Rose?" Her named floated on the hushed air.

She saw a question in his eyes and realized that in another moment he was going to kiss her. She raised her hand and caressed his cheek.

"Thank you for taking care of me."

Chris caught her hand. He pressed a fervent kiss on her palm while his eyes told her it was her lips he wanted to touch.

Reluctantly, she gently pulled her hand away. "I'll rest awhile; then Covey and I have to go home."

She saw his disappointment; then he straightened up. "Don't worry about that now. Let the swelling go down." He checked to see that the makeshift ice bag was secure on her ankle, then quietly left the room.

Maggie Rose turned her head on the cushion to find a comfortable spot, then with the palm that bore the imprint of his kiss against her lips drifted off to sleep.

"Aunt Maggie Rose?"

She opened her eyes to see a worried Covey standing next to her. "Are you all right? Mr. Chris said you hurt your ankle."

"I did, but it feels better now and we need to get home."

Chris appeared from another room as she sat

up, and he saw that much of the swelling had disappeared. "Let me help you," he said.

Maggie Rose stood and, leaning on Chris, put her weight on her left foot. Although the pain was no longer acute, it was still there.

"Covey, give your aunt that cane against the wall," Chris said. "It was Uncle Henry's and I thought it might help," he told Maggie Rose and added, "I'm driving you home."

"That isn't necessary," she objected. "I can drive."

"I'll also come and get you in the morning," Chris said as if she hadn't spoken.

Maggie Rose felt her temper begin to rise. "No, you won't. You've done enough, and I'm perfectly capable of driving."

Covey said, "There's a man coming up the porch, Mr. Chris." A moment later the bell rang.

"Mr. Shealy? I heard you have a good stable out here and I've come to find out about riding lessons. I'm Ross Peters."

Maggie Rose couldn't see the speaker but he sounded like a young man.

"Covey," Chris said, "why don't you take Mr. Peters to the office for me? I'll be there in just a minute."

Covey beamed. "Sure, Mr. Chris." He darted out the door and Maggie Rose saw him going down the steps beside a young man in jeans and a T-shirt.

"I guess I'm going to have to let you take yourself home even though I don't want to." Chris was disgruntled.

"I'll be careful," she promised as they made their slow way to her car.

When he'd seated her she said, "My purse is in the bottom desk drawer. Please have Covey bring it when he comes."

"Don't come tomorrow if you're not up to it."

"Of course I'm coming; we have to decide on the plans for the opening."

"That can wait another day."

"No, it can't." She turned the ignition on. "You've a student waiting."

"You're one stubborn lady," he said with a smile.

"Just trying to keep up with one stubborn man." She smiled in return.

Chris stretched out on the porch lounger. The night sky, brilliant with stars, and the caress of the warm breeze across his body clad only in his shorts, gave him the peace that had eluded him all day.

His anger and frustration at the assault and robbery were fading. Tighter security arrangements for the apartments were already in hand. He'd long ago concluded that he couldn't control the behavior of his tenants. Reasonable safeguards had been established and that was as much as he could do. Still, serious departure from those safeguards depressed him, especially when people suffered needlessly.

What a blessing it had been to come home to Maggie Rose and to have her warm understanding calm his spirit. He was still disappointed that he hadn't been able to show her his horses.

On the other hand, the last thing he'd expected was to be able to hold her in his arms!

He made a wry face at how his body had reacted long before his mind when she went down. He'd

picked her up immediately and she fit perfectly in
his arms. Her fragrant softness and the way she
nestled against him filled him with sensations that
rendered him speechless. She, too, was quiet, but
he knew some other kind of communication was
taking place between them.

That he might be able to ignore. What he
couldn't ignore was that the loneliness he had felt
since completing the rebuilding had abated with
the daily presence of Maggie Rose. But it returned
stronger than ever in the long hours of the night
after she left. Like now.

With a sigh of relief Maggie Rose slid into bed
and turned off the lamp. What a day it had been!

Another facet of Chris Shealy's character had
come to light. Never before had she seen him
unhappy or depressed. He'd never seemed to take
life seriously. But now it was apparent there was
more to him than he let people see. His guard had
been down when he sat in the office, disconsolate
about the hurting people in his apartments. Had
she followed her instincts she would have gone to
him and held him to let him know she understood
and he was not alone. But she couldn't allow herself
to do that. Who knew where that might lead?

Then the ordeal she'd dreaded that morning
and thought she'd avoided was suddenly thrust
upon her when Chris said he was taking her to the
stables. Her pleasure at seeing him come out of
his despondency was immediately overshadowed
by the specter of panic and the corresponding need
to conceal it from him.

When the dizziness made her stumble and crumple against Chris, he had her up and into his arms before she could think.

Maggie Rose burrowed deeper into her bed as she recalled the hardness of Chris's strong body. She'd never before been held in a man's arms like that. But as she snuggled close to him, she suspected it was only Chris Shealy whose arms could produce such sensations. Thrills coursed through her when he tightened his grasp and she reveled in the sweet shelter he represented.

Although she couldn't be certain of his feelings, she was aware that an exchange of emotions had occurred that needed no words as he carried her to the house. That emotion had almost propelled her into a kiss. A kiss she wanted and was ready to give.

They'd missed it by a margin so narrow it scared her. She was the one who had pulled back. Even now she wasn't sure why.

Maggie Rose turned on her other side, resolved to stop reliving those moments of unexpected conflicting emotions and go to sleep.

She resolved also that she must not and would not get that close to temptation again.

Chapter Six

Chris came out of the house as Maggie Rose parked her car the next morning. Covey said, "Hi, Mr. Chris," and went to find Tallie.

"How's the ankle this morning?" he asked.

"Much better, as you can see." The smile she gave him belied the signs of strain he saw around her eyes and mouth.

"You should have stayed home today."

"Not at all." Maggie Rose glanced at him. "I've a lot of work to do if we're to be ready for the opening." He liked the way she said *we*, implying that she felt, as he did, that this was more of a partnership than just a job. Her whole posture said she didn't want his assistance as she walked carefully to the office, so Chris refrained from offering his arm. He had to admire her fortitude as he moved ahead to hold the door open.

At her desk she looked very businesslike in a plain

shirt and summer-weight black-and-white-checked pants. Her nail polish matched her rose lipstick and he was glad to see she didn't sport the long scarlet nails some women wore. They just wouldn't have been appropriate on Maggie Rose, he thought, as he watched her take her tablet from a drawer and get ready to work on the list.

"Did your ankle keep you awake?" he asked.

"No, it didn't. I gave it first a cold, then a hot treatment, kept it elevated, took two aspirin, and went to bed."

"Good. Yesterday I went to look at where we were when your ankle gave way, because I don't want anyone else getting hurt. Did you feel your foot get stuck in a hole or did it hit something?"

Chris's questions caught Maggie Rose totally unprepared. How could she explain what had happened with him looking at her so intently?

"I'm not sure," she said vaguely, looking down.

"Because the path was smooth, no breaks in it that I could see." He was puzzled. "I don't see how it could have happened. I don't want Covey or any of the people coming for the opening to have any kind of injury."

Maggie Rose looked as puzzled as he felt. She was fiddling with her pen as she said, "I think my knee buckled, which made me turn the ankle." She frowned as if trying to recall the sequence of events.

"Were you feeling well? You looked very pale."

"I remember feeling a little dizzy," she said after a moment. She added nothing to that but busied herself going into her purse for a handkerchief.

Why were you feeling dizzy? Chris wanted to know but he'd already asked too many questions. Maggie

Rose must feel as if she were on the witness stand. She only twisted her ankle, yet somehow Chris felt there was more to it than that.

"The young man who came to the door yesterday, is he going to be a new student?"

Chris accepted the change of subject. "Yes, he is. You'll see where I put the details in the student roster. He looked at this watch. "Let's go over your list before I have to leave."

Her subdued expression changed immediately. Her eyes sparkled as she turned the tablet's pages to her list, then for the first time looked at him with the endearing openness that characterized Maggie Rose for him.

She is hiding something from me. He knew it with a certainty that made hurt and disappointment slice through him. A few minutes ago he thought they shared a partnership here and last night he thought how soothing it was to have her here when he came home from work.

Now he wanted to lean across the desk and demand to know what it was that she felt she couldn't tell him. He couldn't do that, but he could get up and walk away from her. Go to the job where all he had to deal with were breakdowns in apartments or issues like yesterday among tenants. Not this kind of breakdown with Maggie Rose! With an effort he tuned in to what she was saying.

". . . so my idea, if you think it's okay, is to create a gala atmosphere. That's why I've looked into putting up a marquee on the lawn where the guests can sit after they've seen the stables and can have refreshments. Catering by Leah can provide us with small sandwiches, cakes, and soft drinks. I think we need to rent a portable toilet because we don't want people using the ones in the house. The more comfortable they are the longer they'll stay to watch the riding and to buy from the shop."

Maggie Rose stopped for breath, her face alive with enthusiasm. "What do you think so far?"

"I can see you've put a lot of thought into it. Anything else?"

Maggie Rose talked about ordering clothes for the shop, new signs, perhaps a trinket as a giveaway, and publicity.

His comments were brief but it was the best he could do. No way could he match her vivacity or pretend to the kind of interest she'd just knocked out of him.

The light gradually dimmed in her face and from time to time she shot him an anxious glance.

"What about parking if we get the crowd you're anticipating?"

"I thought I'd leave that to you and Tallie." He nodded and she rushed on. "I also considered a distinctive logo that can be put on everything to do with the stables so people will instantly identify your business every time they see the logo. It can go on all the paper the business produces as well as everything from the shop. It can be introduced on the giveaway trinket."

She stopped short and seemed to be holding her breath, uncertain of his response.

That was a brilliant idea and Chris told her so. The other plans she could implement according to her best judgment. He answered her questions about charge accounts and told her to make out any necessary checks for him to sign. His cool business manner got him through these arrangements; then he left.

Maggie Rose looked at the door that Chris had quietly closed behind him. He might as well as have slammed it. Hard. She had no idea what had caused him to change from his friendly and pleasant self to the formal, unresponsive person who listened to her plans as if they were total strangers.

She thought that under his coolness he was seething with some emotion. But why? Halfway through her presentation she had the wild impulse to lean across the desk and ask him what the matter was. At first she thought she'd gone too far or in the wrong direction about the opening. Perhaps he wanted it just as he had had it last year. This was going to be much more costly but she'd balanced the expense against the new customer base that would result; plus much would be deductible under advertisement and business expenses. She was prepared to justify it on those grounds but all he said was, "What else?"

At the end he gave her carte blanche, so it wasn't the expense or the new ideas. They hadn't talked about anything else except a few sentences about her ankle. So what had upset him so? By the time he left for work the atmosphere had chilled to about thirty degrees.

The question lay in her consciousness all morning while she was on the telephone ordering some of the merchandise on her list. Her activity came to a halt when she tried to find a company to create the logo. They'd be happy to do it, they said, it would only take three or four weeks. She closed the yellow pages in exasperation.

There must be someone she knew who could help her. It was eleven forty-five and she probably wouldn't catch her sister Alicia, who was teaching summer school, but she could leave a message.

Covey came in and held the door for Tallie, who carried a tray laden with dishes.

"We brought the lunch over here so you wouldn't have to move," Covey said.

"Wasn't that nice of you." She cleared her desk and accepted a chicken sandwich, iced tea, and a dish of melon chunks. Covey and Mr. Tallie sat at a nearby worktable.

"This is delicious, Mr. Tallie, but you know you don't have to feed us every day. It's extra work for you."

"I like to do it." Tallie Sims had a long face, light eyes, gray hair, and a wiry strength of mind and body under an unassuming manner. Maggie Rose thought that probably the only reason her father hadn't raised more of a fuss about Covey's presence on the Shealy farm was his respect for Tallie Sims.

"It gives me something different to do. I cooked for a living a long time ago. I miss cooking for Henry, and Chris often isn't home, so you two are doing me a favor."

Covey listened with close attention because he didn't want to have to bring lunch every day, Maggie Rose thought. Now he said, "I'm sure glad you feel like that, Mr. Tallie, 'cause I like your food."

"We'll have to see if we can put some pounds on you this summer. Maybe one or two on you, too, Maggie Rose. You look a little peaked." Tallie's eyes swept over her slim figure assessingly.

"I'm okay, Mr. Tallie. My stomach gets upset a little in this heat. I guess I have to get used to the humidity again."

"I'm through." Covey bounced up from his chair. "Mr. Tallie said I could sweep the porch, then hose it down," he told Maggie Rose, his eyes gleaming at the thought of playing with the water in the hot sun.

"It's a good thing you brought your shorts today," she said. Covey was turning out to be industrious. Goofing off didn't seem to be in his working vocabulary, at least not yet, she thought as he picked up his paper plate and cup. Maybe after the newness wore off he'd slack off like most ten-year-old kids. "Watch out for splinters," she reminded him.

"Anything I can do for you before I go?" Tallie asked.

"Will you please bring down the box of cards that are in the yellow bedroom? I want to get started on them."

Maggie Rose found that transcribing the tenants' records onto the computer was a welcome occupation to keep her from dwelling on Chris's change in behavior. The office was so quiet that she jumped when the phone rang.

"Maggie Rose? I only have two minutes. What can I do for you?" Her sister Alicia's clear soprano voice was pleasant but hurried.

"Don't you have a friend who does all sorts of graphics? I need a logo for this business."

"Janice Nesbit." Alicia gave Maggie Rose the phone number. "You'll like her work. She's good and she's fast."

Fifteen minutes later Maggie Rose and Janice had discussed the origin of the stables, its present circumstances, how the logo was to be used, and that it was already late so urgency as well as attractiveness was essential.

Satisfied, Maggie Rose went back to the cards and was considering getting up for a drink of water when she heard a car pull up. From the window she saw Chris's best friend and her old schoolmate, Bill Denton, with camera attached as always, coming toward the office. She pushed away from the computer and stood to welcome him.

"Magnolia! I heard Chris had snared you into working for him. You're looking good as always."

They hugged and smiled at each other wholeheartedly. "I can see life's been treating you well, Bill. At least you've been eating good." She glanced pointedly at his waistline.

In high school Chris and Bill had both been skinny but Bill's figure had expanded as he developed an interest in gourmet cooking second only to his passion for photography. Bill was the only person who called her Magnolia. It had begun in her senior year when he photographed her standing under a flowering magnolia tree, holding a perfect bloom in her hand.

"The name suits you," he had declared. The picture had won an award in a local contest and helped Bill decide on taking pictures as a career.

"It's true I don't miss too many meals," he acknowledged with a rueful grin. "But tell me about yourself. What made you decide to come home?"

They sat down, Maggie Rose at her desk and Bill in the chair opposite, relaxed and attentive. He was a good listener and she regarded him with affection as their conversation touched on her life in Connecticut as contrasted to the future she

desired in Jamison being in business with Ginnie
Steed.

It would be easy to have a romance with Bill,
maybe even marriage, she mused. She'd always
liked him immensely. But there was no electricity
between them. Bill didn't make her heart beat
faster like Chris did, nor did she have to stifle the
desire to touch him or wonder how his kisses would
feel. *Don't go there,* she told herself as she realized
how long they'd been talking and laughing. She
began to feel guilty about spending so much time
visiting when she should be working.

"Bill, I'm glad you came by," she said, "because
I want to ask you about being here for the official
opening of the summer season. We're planning a
gala affair on the third Sunday this month. Can
you cover it for us?"

Bill consulted his pocket diary. "Beginning what
time?"

"The invitation says two until five."

"I've a christening celebration that morning but
it should be over by twelve-thirty. I can come
straight from there to get some preliminary shots
before people start arriving." He made a note in
his diary. "Tell me everything that's going on."

"First, I want pictures to go with the stories I'm
sending to the papers. I'll want to get the story in
the Charleston paper before the event with Chris
mounted and the other horses close by. Most of
the students live in or close by Jamison, so we need
them covered for the Jamison paper after the
event."

"You'll be wanting candid shots as well on
Sunday?"

"Yes, and I'm thinking we can sell them if you

can use a polaroid, especially of the students who'll be riding that day."

"No problem. How are you handling the refreshments this year?"

"I'm getting a marquee and having it catered. Let me show you a sketch of where things will be set up. I'll also want shots of the equestrian shop."

Bill came to the desk, putting a casual hand on her shoulder as he looked at the penciled sketch. "What's this up here in the corner?"

"A portalet. If you're hoping to have a crowd you need one, don't you think?"

"Sure do. That's an improvement over last year, when people had to go into the house," he said dryly.

"I'm thinking of placing the marquee here." She pointed to a large area on the front side of the house.

"The marquee's a great idea. It instantly raises the status of the affair, and people react to it positively. I've often noticed it when I'm covering outdoor functions."

"I'm so glad you like the idea, I feel the same way," she said, smiling at Bill. He was giving her the kind of interest and response she'd expected from Chris, and she was grateful.

Chris had begun the day with a feeling of well-being. He had wakened with the memory of Maggie Rose in his arms. The early morning sky was clear and bright. He went to the stables while Tallie cared for the other animals. Chris loved the morning routine with his horses. It was second nature to him after so many years.

As he cared for and talked to his horses, one part of his attention was on what had happened with Maggie Rose yesterday and its lingering sweetness. He had almost kissed her. He was certain she was aware of his desire and wanted on some level to respond. Had it been any of the other ladies he'd known, the kiss would have been given but Maggie Rose was different. She was like a rare and delicate flower whose petals opened slowly but whose full bloom was unique in its pristine beauty. Such a blossoming should not be forced and it was infinitely worth waiting for.

Tallie prepared buckwheat cakes and sausage for breakfast. He put a four-stack and two fat sausages on a plate for Chris.

"How's Covey coming along?" Chris had an appetite this morning and he thought how lucky he was to have Tallie.

"He learns fast and he works fast. I have to slow him down sometimes."

"So he really is a help to you."

"Yep. He's crazy about the horses and working around them but he does most of the rest of the work willingly enough, all except the hog pen." He chuckled. "You like barbecue and bacon, don't you, I told him, so you better take good care of these hogs."

"Did it make a difference?" Chris figured it hadn't made that job any easier because that was the way he'd reacted as a boy.

"He doesn't complain anymore, just gets it over with."

"You plan on making lunch for him and Maggie Rose every day?"

Tallie looked at Chris in surprise. "You don't mind, do you?"

"Course not, do as you please. I'm sure they enjoy it." He nursed his mug between his hands and thought it was too bad he couldn't join this lunch crowd.

"That Covey can eat! He loves everything I make."

When Covey and Maggie Rose had arrived at eight-thirty she'd declared her ankle was much better. He had asked, out of curiosity, how she came to stumble, since he couldn't find anything on the path. Now he wished he hadn't raised the subject. Her indeterminate answers surprised him, but it was her general air of uneasiness that set off his alarm. When she deliberately changed the subject and regained her usual brightness he was certain something was wrong. The sense that she was being less than candid gave him a cold chill, which stayed with him all day. He intended to stay at work until she left. Maybe he'd feel better tomorrow.

But he found himself leaving work in time to be home before four-thirty. Preoccupied with what he could say and how she would respond, he drove more slowly than usual as he turned into his lane and coasted quietly to the office. A strange car was parked nearby. It was probably one of the numerous salesmen who came by in the hope of adding HS Stables as a client. He went in through the equestrian shop door but no one was there.

Then he heard Maggie Rose's laugh followed by a male voice. He stepped through the doorway to see Maggie Rose, vivacious and gay at the desk, laughing with Bill Denton, who was close to her, his hand on her shoulder.

Where had that gaiety and smile been for him this morning, and what was Bill doing standing so close and putting his hand on her?

"What's so funny?" he asked before he could stop himself. He saw the gaiety vanish from Maggie Rose's face and he felt a twist in his stomach.

"Hey, Chris." Bill came to the front of the desk. "Magnolia was showing me where the portalet is to be this year. I was telling her what happened last year with the little boy who couldn't wait."

"I thought there must be a salesman in here. I didn't recognize your car."

"Mine's in the shop and this is a loaner."

Maggie Rose was sitting at her desk moving papers around. "How'd it go today?" he asked, wondering if she'd look at him.

"I found someone who will do the logo and Bill will do pictures for all the publicity before and after." Now she looked up from her list, glancing at Bill, then at Chris. "We talked about him taking polaroid pictures to sell on the spot."

"Will people buy them?" Chris asked Bill.

The ensuing conversation covered the possible revenues from the pictures as well as other aspects of the gala. The three of them had talked together many times but never in an atmosphere like this. The usual give and take, the jokes, and the laughter were absent. He caught Bill stealing a glance at Maggie Rose's sober face, then looking at him.

He could read the question in Bill's eyes. *What is happening here between Chris and Magnolia?*

Chris sighed. If only he knew the answer.

Chapter Seven

"Girl horses are called mares and boy horses are stallions. Did you know that, Aunt Maggie Rose?"

Covey imparted this newly acquired knowledge as soon as he got into the car to go home.

"Mr. Chris only has mares but he plans to buy a stallion."

"How do you know that?" Maggie Rose looked both ways, then waited for three cars and a lumber truck to pass before moving out onto the highway from Chris's lane.

"Mr. Tallie told me when he was teaching me about grooming the horses."

It occurred to Maggie Rose that getting a description from Covey of each horse so she could speak of them knowledgeably might keep Chris from a second attempt at taking her to the stables. "Can you tell me how the horses look?"

"Course I can. They're different like people are."

Maggie Rose was amused at how Covey turned in his seat so he was facing her, his thin face in a serious lecture mode as he held up one finger.

"First is HS. She's the oldest and biggest. She's light brown with a white patch low on her face. The oldest students ride her."

"HS, biggest, light brown, white face patch," Maggie Rose repeated.

"Next is Starlight. She's silvery gray but her mane and tail are darker gray. She likes people and she always nudges Mr. Tallie. I think she'd like to talk if she could."

Covey glanced at her as if she might not believe his fanciful thought.

"Maybe she's talking in her own way with her nudging. Starlight is easy to remember with her color. Which horse is next?"

"Windsong. She's the prettiest one. She's a thoroughbred and she's brown, too, but you can tell her from HS because she's dark brown like a shining chestnut."

"Why do you think she's the prettiest?" Maggie Rose was curious.

"You ought to come see her. I don't know exactly how to describe her but she's graceful kinda like she wants to dance. Mr. Tallie said she's elegant."

"I like the name, it sounds like it fits her. Windsong, chestnut brown and elegant. Who are the others?"

"Chica is next and you always know her because she's a paint." He looked at Maggie Rose expectantly.

"What is a paint?"

"A horse that has a coat with patches of white or another color. Mr. Tallie said Chica is a piebald because she's mostly black with white on her rump."

"Covey, you're really learning a lot, aren't you?" She was impressed by his confident use of terminology.

Covey's face lit up with the unfettered grin of a mischievous, happy, energetic boy. "Mr. Tallie says I ask more questions than he can answer."

This is the way he should be at home, she thought, *and we have Chris to thank because the job on the farm was his idea.* She needed to remember that, because no matter how matters progressed with her and Chris, as long as she stayed on this job, Covey was the clear beneficiary.

"Nicky is the pony that the little kids ride. She's small, reddish brown, and very gentle."

"End of lesson just in time. See you in the morning." Maggie Rose paused in Jerlene's driveway and watched Covey until he was safely in the house.

"Good Morning."

Ramrod straight, Maggie Rose stood at the file cabinet looking through folders when Chris came in on his way to work. She wore a small-figured blue shirtwaist blouse with a straight white skirt. White earrings were her only jewelry.

She gave him her best employee smile, brief, civil, impersonal, touching only her lips.

"Morning." This morning Chris was dressed in light gray slacks, white shirt, blue tie, and navy jacket. Gleaming black half boots completed the attire of the successful businessman.

"I've work to do in town this morning but I'll be back early this afternoon to get ready for the Thursday students," he said.

His formal intonation was belied by something in his eyes that Maggie Rose couldn't identify. The heat and feeling there made her wonder if he could still be angry or upset, and if so, why?

Yesterday when he came home he acted almost as if he were jealous of Bill Denton being there and laughing with her, but that idea was too absurd to consider seriously. So until he decided to tell her what was making him act as if he'd just met and hired her, she was determined to act the same way.

"I'm getting the folders out now. I have one for Rachel Taylor and one for Jerry Watson. Isn't there a third one for today?"

Suddenly Chris was behind her as she sorted through the files. His long fingers brushed hers and for an instant both hands stilled.

"The one you're looking for is Dottie Adams." His slightly husky voice vibrated along her nerve ends. "She's new and maybe there's no folder for her yet."

He quickly flicked through the As as Maggie Rose, hands by her side, waited for him to move away. She was enveloped by his nearness, his warm breath on the nape of her neck, the faint scent of the soap he used in the shower. Why did he have to stand behind her like this?

All he had to do was stay on his side of the desk and give her the name of the third student. Was he deliberately teasing her? She dismissed that idea because he could have no inkling of the effect he had on her.

"Here she is." Chris pulled a single sheet of paper from the file, closed it, and laid the paper on her desk. "Venetia neglected to make a folder for her. These are just my notes." He stood at the side of the desk looking down at her.

Maggie Rose slipped into the security of her chair, opened a drawer, and pulled out a folder. "I'll fill out her registration form." Why didn't he go away?

"I noticed you began on the cards yesterday. You didn't bring them down, did you?" he said frowning.

"Tallie got them for me."

"Any problems with them?"

"None at all. I'll keep working on them in my spare moments."

"I appreciate it. You have my cell number?"

"Right here." She indicated the computer.

Chris grabbed a card from the box on the desk, turned it over, and wrote seven digits, then pushed it toward Maggie Rose. "Carry this one with you. I'll be back around one."

Maggie Rose picked up the notes Chris had written about Dottie Adams but she didn't see them. She saw Chris standing beside her at the desk making meaningless conversation as if he didn't want to leave, even though his manner was barely friendly. What was all that about? She tried to make sense of it but gave it up after a while. She found men hard to understand, and of them all, Chris Shealy was the greatest puzzle.

She finished the form, then called the supplier who had promised to deliver the erasable wall chart she needed to make the student schedule. The clerk said they could put it in today's mail.

"You promised to have it here by today," Maggie Rose said.

"I'm sorry, but we're a little behind."

Maggie Rose had promised herself to have the chart on the wall for the first students to come after her hiring. "I'll be right there to pick it up," she said.

"I'm the new office manager for HS Stables," she said at the shop. "We've done a lot of business with you in the past and I'd like to continue to use your services, but they'll have to be on time," she said pleasantly but firmly as she picked up the package.

The manager apologized and said it wouldn't happen again and was there anything else she needed?

"Nothing more today."

Some time later Maggie Rose looked at the color-coded chart with the current students and their lesson times neatly printed on it. She tacked it on the wall next to the file cabinet and wondered what Chris would say when he saw it. Maybe he wouldn't say anything. After all, it was part of her job.

There was a tentative knock on the equestrian shop door; then she heard Alicia call her name.

"Come on in," she answered and went to the shop to greet Alicia and Janice Nesbit.

Alicia, three years younger than Maggie Rose, had a square face like her sister's, but there the resemblance ended. Alicia's eyes were lively and curious. She frequently changed the color and style of her hair. For the summer she was wearing it in a tight bunch of reddish curls. Her passion for music poured itself into many outlets, teaching it in school, playing with a small band when possible, singing in choirs, and teaching private students.

"I didn't know you sold riding clothes here," Alicia said, moving around the shop, fingering items on display. "Look, Janice, how d'ya think these would fit me?" She held a pair of tan jodhpurs against her slim waist and hips.

Janice's delicate features shared a grin with Maggie Rose. "You know you'll never find time to ride with all you do."

Maggie Rose knew her sister well. "Who mentioned riding? She just wants to look smart and fool people into thinking she's an equestrian. It'll be one more outfit in her closet along with the others she may or may not wear."

"You're absolutely right," Alicia agreed. "Seriously, Maggie Rose, women who don't ride use some of this stuff in their casual wardrobe. You could create a good little business if you increase your selection."

"Why don't you and Janice talk about the logo she brought and I'll go through the shop and write down some ideas?" Alicia was already eyeing each jacket critically. She took the tablet and pen Maggie Rose gave her and began making notes.

In the office Janice laid out three designs. One was a perfect circle, one a rectangle, and the third was shaped like a watermelon. Inside each one were the words *HS Stables* and the outline of a horse with a flowing mane and tail. In letters that were smaller but no less distinct the address *Jamison, SC*, appeared.

"I used only black and white but they can be any color," Janice explained.

"We want to use it on all our paper products so

black and white is the best. It's a striking design, Janice, and all three look good. Fortunately, I don't have to make the decision. Chris will be here this afternoon to look at them and choose.''

Maggie Rose had intended to ask a painter to make the sign for the shop, but Janice's work impressed her with its quality and speed. Upon discussing it Janice said she would work with someone she knew to produce the sign.

Chris had an eleven o'clock appointment at the Jamison First National Bank and Trust. He was ushered into the president's office at once.

Millard J. Ravenel III, a bulky man with thin blond hair, heavy eyebrows, a large nose, and thin lips, now curved in a suave smile, stood with hand outstretched.

''Good to see you Chris. How's everything?''

''Fine, Millard. How's life with you?''

The two men had been acquaintances, never friends, despite knowing each other since school days. Millard's life had been focused on eventually becoming president of the bank his grandfather had founded. Uncle Henry had called Millard's father Mr. Ravenel but the first time Chris went to the bank he called Millard by his first name, as he'd been doing for years. He saw no reason to change just because Millard's father had retired, which boosted the son to the top job.

Millard said, ''I hear you've rehabilitated the property you inherited. I passed by there a while ago and it looked good from what I could see.''

''Next time, stop in and I'll give you a tour. Tallie Sims and I did extensive work on the grounds.''

After an exchange of pleasantries and comment on local issues, Chris mentioned that he was considering investing in two thoroughbred stallions.

Millard began to rub the knuckle of his right thumb, just as he'd done in school when he was the least bit upset or unsure. Chris saw the gesture but he knew he was on solid ground for the loan he was here to obtain. He made a practice of using the bank's money for certain large purchases. The loans, always for a limited time, were promptly paid, keeping his credit an A-rating. Meanwhile, his major capital, larger than anyone suspected, remained untouched as it continued to grow under his broker's smart investments.

"You still have the riding school." Millard and Chris each knew this was an opening gambit, as Millard kept himself updated on Chris's farm.

Chris nodded. "The number of students will double in two weeks when the summer season opens."

"You've five horses, as I recall."

Chris crossed one lean, muscular leg over the other and brushed an imaginary fleck from his sharply creased trousers.

"Right." Chica and Windsong, the two thoroughbreds, had been purchased with the bank's money.

"Surely it would be dangerous to let your students ride stallions," Millard said portentously.

In other words, Chris mused, *Millard thinks I don't know what I'm doing; therefore he's going to instruct me.*

"One stallion is for my personal use and the other will be put out to stud."

Chris knew that the bank president personally resented Chris's desire to extend his holdings and his business. Yet it was in the bank's interest to accommodate this successful businessman, lest he take his patronage down the street to the South Carolina Merchants Bank.

When Chris emerged from the bank later it was with a light step. He'd achieved what he'd set out to do. In his pocket was a sizable check for the purchase of one stallion with excellent bloodlines. By indicating he wanted two stallions, he'd been able to get sufficient funds for one on the terms he'd calculated before talking to Millard.

A smug look of satisfaction crossed his face. Dealing with Millard was a challenge he enjoyed, especially since it forced Millard to acknowledge Chris's business acumen.

The rescheduled meeting to arrange for the painting of the apartments in one of the corporation's units was next; then Chris was on his way home.

He chuckled inwardly as he thought of his session at the bank. His invitation for Millard to come see the farm was genuine. It would amuse him to see Millard find something to criticize but Chris could count on him doing so. He recalled others who had seen the results of his labor and they all congratulated him.

When Maggie Rose saw it, he expected her to say something appreciative as well, but he was surprised at the depth of gratification her words of understanding and praise gave him. What had happened to that attitude?

They'd been getting along so well. He looked forward each day to her arrival because she brought warmth and genuine interest with her. Look at all those great ideas she had about the opening. She was ten times better than Venetia. He was convinced part of it was because of their long association, because even though she'd been away, the tie they'd formed during their school years held fast. He never forgot Maggie Rose no matter how many other women he'd been involved with, and somehow he had the conviction she never forgot him.

After her fall she had felt so right in his arms as he carried her. The desire to kiss her had been so strong but he hadn't forced the issue, so that couldn't be why she had changed. The next morning she became evasive, a tactic he'd never seen her use.

A sudden thought struck him. Perhaps she was ill and didn't want him to know. Still, that seemed unlikely because there'd been no earlier indication. She seemed to be blooming with health, and Jerlene, who told everything, hadn't said her sister was sick. However, just in case there was something, he'd see if Tallie knew about her health since he fed her every day.

A horn blast from the car behind him shook Chris out of his reverie. He had drifted to the right without noticing. Lifting a hand in acknowledgment he corrected his steering and went back to thinking of his office manager.

This morning Maggie Rose had tried hard to be cool and impersonal standing at the file cabinet looking prim in her proper office attire. The tight smile she gave him didn't touch her eyes. He thought only of seeking her innate warmth.

Before he knew it he was behind her at the file, standing close with the excuse of finding the information on the Adams girl. It was ridiculous but he couldn't move away. The scent that was uniquely hers beguiled him. He closed his eyes, savoring it, and his fingers brushed hers. Maggie Rose was motionless as a trapped bird, yet he felt in her the effort it took to repress the same flutter of excited awareness that invaded him. Even after the Adams paper was found, he hadn't been able to turn away from Maggie Rose. Finally he ran out of things to say and had to leave.

Pathetic! That was what he'd been.

He'd put an end to that. Neda had called the other night and suggested going out. He'd make it a firm date for Sunday and put Maggie Rose out of his mind.

She was his office manager and that was all.

Maggie Rose's first encounter with the riding school routine had gone smoothly. Mothers arrived with their children, signed in, paid for the lesson, and took the receipt she gave them.

"When I first opened the school," Chris told Maggie Rose when he showed her the account book, "I sent out bills but I found people tended to be late or careless in how they paid. Some didn't pay at all. So now each lesson is paid for up front. Cuts down on paperwork, too."

Mrs. Adams arrived at three, a friendly, short woman who seemed to be about the same age as Maggie Rose. "I'm Risha Adams and this is my daughter, Dottie," she said smilingly, extending her hand.

"Maggie Rose Sanders." She shook Risha's hand and returned her smile.

Dottie, almost as tall as her mother, said, "Hi."

"Chris said he was looking for a new office manager." Risha signed the register and slid her check across. "I'm glad he found you."

"So am I." She began filling out a receipt as Risha continued the conversation, saying they'd moved to Jamison only six months ago from Dalton, Georgia, when her husband was transferred on his job.

Dottie's face brightened as Chris appeared to escort her to her first lesson. As a beginner she would be having several lessons by herself until she learned how to handle and control a horse. Then she would come an hour later and join Rachel Taylor and Jerry Watson in the twelve-year-old class held on Thursdays from four to five. Maggie Rose's relief that Chris hadn't required her to take Dottie to the stables had made her day end with heartfelt thankfulness.

Friday was another story. Four hour-long classes involving eleven students began at one o'clock. Jack and Zack Denby, six-year-old identical twins, were to start today. Chris explained the situation to Maggie Rose just before he left for work. "Beginners are usually taught by themselves but the Denbys asked if I would teach the twins together, at least at the start. I said I'd see how it goes. I'm squeezing them in today and I won't be able to leave the stables, so when they arrive, bring them down as quickly as you can."

After Chris left, apprehension became a suffocating cloud that grew stronger every hour. The only glimmer of light that penetrated it was being able to tell Janice when she called how much Chris liked the logo.

"It's the watermelon shape he likes, says he can almost feel the horse running on that one."

"That's my favorite one." Janice's delight came clearly over the wire.

"And mine," Maggie Rose added. "We'll need it camera ready by Monday."

The rest of the morning she worked on the cards, a dull, automatic task that kept her fingers moving while her mind dealt more and more frantically with what she could do to save her job when Chris saw what being near horses did to her. Why had she been so foolish and reckless to take the job and try to get away with it?

Tallie brought in a sandwich, homemade cookies, and iced tea for her lunch. He put the tray on her desk and swept her with his casual glance that missed very little.

"You don't look so well today. Can I get you something?"

"It's just a bad headache but I think it'll go away pretty soon. Thanks for lunch, I may eat some later." It was already five minutes till twelve and classes began at one. *I can't put this off any longer,* she thought.

As soon as Tallie left she took a dark red pillbox from her purse. Inside were two whole pills and two halves. She hesitated, then picked out a half pill, took a small bite of sandwich, then swallowed it, the pill, and some iced tea. She had hoped not to use the potent tranquilizer but her symptoms said she had to.

I only have to deliver the twins, she reasoned, *and Chris will be too busy to try to show me the horses.* The tranquilizer began to take effect. Her stomach muscles relaxed and the perspiration ceased. Chris

returned, the first students arrived, and Maggie
Rose felt calm and relaxed.

Her head was light and airy when the second
group signed in at two. The twins weren't with that
group; maybe they were coming a little later.

A third group of mostly ten-year-olds clattered
in at three and left an hour later. Still no twins.

Maggie could feel the diminishing effect of the
medication and the faint stirring of panic.

At four-twenty, Jack and Zack Denby raced in
with their mother apologizing for being caught in
heavy traffic.

"Mr. Shealy is waiting for the boys. Have a seat,
I'll be right back." Maggie Rose took each by the
hand as she headed toward the stables.

She went halfway down the path when the panic
began to bloom. She gritted her teeth, took deep,
deliberate breaths. *I can do this, this is my job.* She
repeated the phrase like a mantra.

"You're squeezing my hand too tight," Zack
complained.

"Mine, too," Jack said.

"I'm sorry." She relaxed her grip as she concen-
trated on putting one foot in front of the other.

Just as she wondered if she could make one more
step without collapsing, Chris came hurrying up
the path from the stables.

He greeted the twins, then looked at Maggie
Rose. "What took you so long?"

"The Denbys just got here, she said they were
stuck in traffic." She averted her face, hoping Chris
wouldn't look at her too closely.

"Let's go, boys," Chris said as he started back
to the stables.

Maggie Rose began to retrace her steps but nausea overtook her. She bent over clutching her stomach until it ceased.

She didn't see Chris glance her way as he arrived at the stable door, stop, watch her bend over, then, as if relieved, straighten and walk away.

Chapter Eight

Covey was unusually quiet on the way home. Every other day he had been a chatterbox regaling Maggie Rose with bits and pieces of what he'd done. He should be bubbling because Friday was payday. According to instructions, she had prepared checks for Chris's signature and passed them out to Tallie, Covey, and herself. Covey's face had lit up as he carefully folded the precious piece of paper into his wallet.

"Anything wrong, Covey?" she asked when they were halfway home.

Covey shook his head. Another few minutes of silence he said, "Mr. Chris probably isn't ever going to teach me to ride."

Maggie Rose heard the acceptance in his voice that most things you really want aren't likely to happen. Yet he couldn't repress the longing underlying the statement.

"Why do you say that, Covey? Did Mr. Chris say he wouldn't?" If he did, she'd have something to say about that. At first the thought of Covey on or near horses had petrified her but that was before they came to the farm and she saw his enchantment with and knowledge of the creatures increase. There was no reason for him not to have his chance to learn to ride and she'd see to it that he had it.

"No, he didn't," Covey replied.

"Have you asked him?"

"No."

"Why not? You see him every day."

"It's Mr. Tallie I'm with all day. I don't really know Mr. Chris." Covey explained this so patiently that Maggie Rose felt as if she were the ten-year-old and Covey the adult. This was not uncommon. Jerlene's casual and disorganized way of raising her son had made him wary of adults. Tallie Sims had broken through that mistrust by his natural kindness and his consistent treatment of Covey as a bright and responsible person that Tallie was glad to have working with him.

Covey said he didn't know Chris. Maggie Rose wondered if that implied a lack of the instinctive pull Covey would feel toward Chris as his father, or simply that he hadn't had the opportunity to get to know him.

Her thoughts were interrupted by another statement from Covey. "Mama has a new friend, Mr. Dan."

"Yes, I met him the other day."

"He said he rode horses all the time when he lived in Texas. He knows a lot about them."

"Is that what he does now?"

"He sells cars. Mom said she met him when she took the car in for a checkup."

A car salesman. That fit Maggie Rose's impression of him, but at least he talked with Covey about a mutual interest, and that was more than Jerlene's other friends, who largely ignored him. She'd have to give him a second look.

Chris was restless. After the final student had gone, he did the evening stable chores. When all was done he made his way to the kitchen.

"Thought you forgot about supper." Tallie handed him a plate of pork chops, baked potato, and green beans. "How'd the twins do?"

"Jack follows whatever Zack does."

"Not so good."

"Right. They'll have to be separated after a while so Jack can become confident on his own."

Tallie nodded, swallowing his food. "How about Covey?" he asked, looking at Chris.

"How about Covey what?" The piece of meat on Chris's fork stayed halfway to his mouth as he stared at Tallie.

"The boy's about to die if you don't put him up on a horse pretty soon. He didn't want to do anything this afternoon but watch you and the kids. I know you saw him hanging on the fence."

"I saw him." How could he avoid it? The boy's thin body had been filled with eager longing while he had watched the class. He reminded Chris of himself at that age. He knew Covey yearned as he had to be up on a horse. He could have started with him the first day but he realized now that

Maggie Rose's anxiety about Covey and horses had subconsciously held him back.

It wouldn't keep him back any longer. It wasn't fair to the boy.

"I'll start him when I get home Monday."

Chris finished his food and took the piece of apple pie Tallie handed him.

"Thought I might have to make another pie for you and me." Tallie chuckled. "Covey ate two pieces and thought about another one but I told him that was enough."

"Does Maggie Rose like your cooking too?" Chris asked casually.

"She hardly eats, Chris. Like today when I took the lunch in. She didn't look too good but said it was a bad headache and she might eat something later. I think I've seen her eat lunch once a week." Tallie looked at Chris with concern. "You reckon she's sick or something?"

"Maybe it's just the heat," Chris said, "or she's not in the habit of eating lunch."

Tallie wasn't convinced. "The other day she mentioned an upset stomach and now today she looks bad. She ought to see a doctor is what I think."

Chris changed the subject to the proposed purchase of a stallion. After supper he went to his bedroom to resume reading the South Carolina periodicals that advertised horse sales. It would take a while to find the stallion he wanted but he enjoyed the research.

His attention began to wander and his restlessness increased. Maybe he should take a run into town, see what was going on. Instead he found himself going silently down the steps and out the front door to one of the loungers.

The image of Maggie Rose bent over and holding her stomach came up, implacably distinct, in his mind. He'd avoided it for hours but it had to be dealt with because it wouldn't go away.

When she came down the path with the twins he'd been shocked at her appearance. Her eyes had a glazed look, her mouth was pinched tight, and her face was drawn. He had wanted desperately both to confront her and to comfort her but he had the twins to consider. It was clear she hoped he wouldn't notice because she kept her face turned away.

Anger began to burn in him. She must think he was a fool and a dolt not to notice her condition. Something told him to look back at her and he saw her bending over as if she had to throw up. Tallie said she scarcely ate anything and had complained of an upset stomach.

She had become dizzy Tuesday while on the way to the stables with him and as a result twisted her ankle. She'd evaded discussing it the next morning. Her manner had changed, and for the first time since he'd known her when she was a nine-year-old kid on the playground, she had not exactly lied but had certainly been less than honest with him.

His agitated thoughts tumbled about, causing him confusion and apprehension. He tried to dwell on other matters but his mind kept pulling him back to the one conclusion that fit all the signs. He could no longer suppress it.

Maggie Rose was pregnant!

Chris bounded from the lounger. Merciful God!

That couldn't be right. It wasn't possible. Not his Maggie Rose.

Before he realized what he was doing, he skimmed the steps and went pounding down the lane trying to outrun his thoughts, his hands clenching and unclenching, his heart thumping, and perspiration dripping down his face.

He came to his senses when he reached the point where his lane joined the highway and a car blinded him with its lights. He slowed to a walk and moved over to rest against his fence and catch his breath.

Gradually his heart slowed to its normal rate. His eyes adjusted to the night sky, the occasional car swooping past, and the scanty woods on the other side of the highway.

Deliberately keeping his mind blank he began counting cars. He'd go back home after the tenth car went past. Number seven was a high-riding SUV on his side of the road with its bright lights on, traveling at a slower speed than the ones preceding it. As he watched it, Chris saw the brights glinting on a vehicle parked about the length of half a block from his lane.

His adrenaline still high, Chris pulled out his key ring, found the powerful penlight attached to it, and turned it on. He'd just see who was in that vehicle, who had the nerve to park next to his fence, practically on his property. If it turned out to be a couple, the penlight should give them plenty of warning.

The vehicle turned out to be a black pickup truck with its windows closed. There was nothing in the seats or on the floor or in the bed of the truck. Chris felt cheated. It had a license-applied-for notice so that wasn't any help. He knew it hadn't been there when he came home. Maybe the gas tank was empty and the driver had hitched a ride, since the doors were locked.

He'd report it in the morning if it was still there. Chris turned off the penlight, walked quickly to his lane, and turned in.

The dark figure across the road remained motionless. That had been too close a call. He decided to wait a full hour before moving the truck away so the occupants of the farm would be asleep and not hear it.

Chapter Nine

Maggie Rose rolled over to look at the clock whose alarm she'd turned off earlier before drifting back to sleep. It was eight o'clock and she was due to meet Ginnie for a workday at eight-thirty. She scrambled out of bed, took a quick shower, pulled on work clothes, found her keys, and drove up to the Mailroom with a minute to spare.

"I brought cheese danishes to go with the coffee I hope you're making," she told Ginnie, who unlocked the door, let her in, locked the door, and closed the blinds.

Ginnie Steed, with a generously endowed figure, wore her brown hair in strategic swirls that pointed up her dark eyes, broad nose, and sculptured lips. She smiled as she led the way to the small utilitarian kitchen behind the office.

"Not only coffee but some melon, cheese, and a few other things. This is a workday, girlfriend, and we've got to have sustenance. I'm dying to hear about your new job," she said as they began breakfast. "Is Chris Shealy still gorgeous even when you see him day after day?"

Maggie Rose answered Ginnie's mischievous grin with one of her own. "I don't know about that but he's okay to work with. He works a lot harder than one would suspect from the reputation he's always had. You should see how he and Mr. Tallie have transformed that place."

Responding to Ginnie's questions, Maggie Rose described her first week on the job and also Covey's progress, omitting anything about horses. That was her secret.

"I'm looking forward to your opening next week," Ginnie said, as they cleared away the breakfast. "Seriously, Maggie Rose, how are things with you and Chris?" Ginnie's eyes had the penetrating focus Maggie Rose recognized that meant she intended to get a straight answer and you may as well give it to her immediately.

"At first they were friendly, warm, and fun," she answered. "Then he backed away as if I'd done something wrong but I can't figure out why. Now he's very businesslike. So am I."

Ginnie gave her friend a thoughtful look. "Chris always liked you. I guess you know that."

"Chris Shealy likes a lot of girls," Maggie Rose said dismissively.

"I know he's popular with the ladies. That's not what I'm saying. I'm saying I think you're special to him and always have been."

Maggie Rose stared at Ginnie, the dish towel in her hand. "You're serious."

"Of course I am. One of the reasons I think so

is that when you were coming for a visit, he'd manage to talk to me and bring up your name to find out what I knew about your schedule. At first I didn't put it together; then I just waited to see where he'd catch me.''

"Catch you?"

"He'd call me at home, or drop in to see me at the office, or come up to me at a social occasion. But he never missed.''

"I can't imagine why.'' Maggie Rose was puzzled. "He never asked me for a date.''

"But I bet you saw him, didn't you?''

"Ye-es. He was always around somewhere, teasing me and making me nervous.''

"Why did he make you nervous?''

"I was never sure when he was being serious and when he was being funny, so I was edgy around him. You know my one-on-one relationship record has never been that successful.''

"True, but it's improved since we were in high school, I hope. Do you remember the time we went to the junior prom together?''

"My first prom and I was so nervous I spilled punch on Kenny's white shirt.'' Maggie Rose grinned. "Served him right for stepping all over my brand-new sandals.''

"Then there was the time at the skating rink,'' Ginnie began. By the time she finished the story Maggie Rose had joined her in helpless giggles.

"Storage room next,'' Ginnie said when the kitchen was orderly. "Aunt Henny said she doesn't know all that's in here, so clean it out according to our judgment. Same with the files.'' She passed Maggie Rose some plastic gloves.

After several hours of strenuous work, Ginnie

called a halt, produced two cans of cool soft drinks, and followed Maggie Rose into the large central room where customer service took place.

"I've always wondered how Miss Henny got into this business," Maggie Rose said.

"She's my great aunt but she's only five years older than my dad, and he says that even as a child she scrounged around for little jobs but never spent the money. She got herself hired on as a helper in Owens Grocery when she was thirteen and went to full-time after leaving high school. Dad said she was a whiz at thinking of small ways to make the store better and bring in more customers."

"Just like she's done here," Maggie Rose recalled. "Remember when she had this room painted several times so it always looked good and each time she'd add a new candy machine or something?"

"We can learn a lot of lessons from her," Ginnie agreed.

"So she bought the store from Mr. Owens?"

"He was going to sell it to Aunt Henny and her fiancé, Ezell Addison, but Ezell disappeared after he robbed the bank in the next town. Turned out he'd done this before but no one here knew about it."

"How'd Miss Henny take it?"

"Dad said Aunt Henny was determined to have that store. She worked it out with the Owenses and two years later it was hers."

"Where was it? I don't remember an Owens store."

"It was right here but most of the original structure has disappeared in the years Aunt Henny has remodeled it."

"I've been thinking," Maggie Rose, said surveying the large space, "of how we might get the maximum use of this space without making it seem crowded."

"What do you have in mind?"

"This end of the room where Aunt Henny has the greeting cards and mailing supplies could support a counter. We can find someplace else for the card and mailers."

"What would we sell at the new counter?"

"Craft articles." She turned to Ginnie to make her pitch for an idea that had come to her several nights ago when she was thinking about Janice's work on the logo. "I used to go to a small shop in Hartford where craftspeople brought in their work but nothing was over twenty dollars. They did a great business. There are a lot of people here who turn out ceramics of all sorts, as well as jewelry and other items. I'm certain that if we can assemble a good variety for sale here, people will buy it. What do you think, Ginnie?"

"I don't want us to get in over our heads. We've already agreed that the business isn't going to be profitable to us personally for about two years. That's why we both have to keep on working. I don't see how we're going to add another segment to the mailing service so soon."

During the remainder of the day the idea became more distinct to Maggie Rose. Sunday morning she began to work it out on paper. When Ginnie called they discussed it again. "I'll work up a thorough proposal and we'll go over it. Okay?"

"Okay," Ginnie said. "Right now I've got my own proposal. We've done nothing but work. Dina called. She and Gwen want us to meet them at

Teddy's, see what's happening and have some ribs. All right with you?''

"Sounds good to me.'' She hadn't been out with the gang since returning home and it would be great to spend an evening with them. She'd been too tied up getting moved and trying to find a job but now she could relax and enjoy herself.

Working on the Mailroom project had pushed the HS Stables details to the back of her mind, but as she put the Mailroom folders away, she began thinking of what still had to be done this work week.

One of the jobs to do on Monday was to prepare publicity releases. As she began to give herself the manicure she needed, she thought of what should go into the piece—certainly a photo of its new appearance with the story mentioning its history, the types of instruction Chris gave, and a picture of Chris on HS, as well as details of the gala.

She'd call Bill first thing to see if he could come out that afternoon to get the picture of Chris as soon as Chris got home. That alone should attract the casual reader; he was so attractive, and for people who liked horses it would be a compelling sight if Bill did his usual magic.

She looked at her polished nails and wished there were some magic to fix her reaction to horses, or to fix whatever made Chris mad at her.

She ran a tub of water, put in her favorite bath fragrance, pinned up her hair, and slid in with a sigh of pure joy.

Ginnie had said yesterday that she thought Chris liked her in a special way, but she couldn't see it. If there was a tie between them, it was a fragile one linked to their school experiences when they were young. There had been one particular time that stayed in her memory when they had worked on an English assignment together, then walked around outside talking about nothing special but not wanting their time together to end. She was basically shy, but not so with Chris. His confident manner and the way he liked to tease her made her nervous, but on a deeper level they had an assured knowledge of each other.

With the water getting cool, she got out of the tub, dried herself with a fluffy bath towel, and began to sort through the closet for something to wear. She felt like wearing something other than pants and decided on an ankle-length apricot dress that showed off her flat stomach and slim hips. Steam from the bath had made her hair curly. She left it that way instead of brushing it into a smooth fall.

As she began to put on careful makeup she thought of how Chris had almost kissed her, but that still didn't necessarily mean that the tie between them was a romantic one. Proximity itself does crazy things to people, so she wouldn't put any emphasis on that moment.

She put dangling apricot stones in her ears and slipped into beige heels. The full-length mirror gave back a reflection of an attractive woman ready to have a good time. *That's just how I feel,* she thought. As she drove to Teddy's she discovered that one reason she felt so relaxed and happy was that in her subconscious mind she'd decided that whatever quirk Chris was dealing with, she liked him and nothing was going to stand in the way of their longtime friendship. When she saw him at work Monday she was going to be her own warm and understanding self no matter how he acted.

Teddy Reuben had forsaken the snow and ice of Chicago to settle in Jamison twenty years earlier, bringing with him years of experience of making superb barbecue. With patience and hard work he had established what was now an institution in Jamison. Teddy served the best barbecue in three counties in a tasteful restaurant that had three dining spaces, plus a bar and a postage-stamp dance floor. Monday was the only night it wasn't filled and on weekend nights there was a wait of an hour for a table.

When you hadn't been out for a while, the hour wait was part of the fun, Maggie Rose thought. You got to see people you knew coming in and going out. She wasn't surprised to see Jerlene and Dan leave just as her group was ushered in to a table for four where they had a good view of the bar and a smaller dining space through a large plate-glass wall.

"Who's the new man with Jerlene?" Gwen Aiken asked. An energetic, dedicated social worker, Gwen worked part-time with Ginnie.

"I wondered the same thing; this is the third time I've seen them," Dina Ramsey murmured. Dina was the owner of a salon and was her own best advertisement. She was sleek, svelte, and happily married, reserving her right to hang out with this group of girlfriends just as her husband hung out with his friends occasionally.

"He's a car salesman named Dan Montgomery," Maggie Rose said.

The waiter delivered their drink orders and took four orders of ribs with him.

Several couples stopped by to chat. Nearly every-one Maggie Rose had spoken with had compli-mented her on her appearance beginning with Dina, whose assessing glance had ended with, "You're looking great, honey."

Maggie Rose thought how good it was to be home. There were the Dukes, friends of her par-ents. She'd seen them in church last week and here came Raleigh and Ruth Short.

"Where have you been since you came home, girl?" Ruth wanted to know.

"Finding a place, moving in, looking for a job, the usual rat race," Maggie Rose said.

"You certainly don't look like you've been in a rat race," Raleigh said admiringly.

"He's right, you know," Ruth said. "Come see us soon." They moved on to a table.

"I sure never thought they'd last," Dina ob-served.

"How long's it been?" Ginnie asked.

"Ten years. I was in the wedding, remember?" Gwen said.

Their conversation paused while the waiter served them with plates heaped with baby back ribs, baked potato, coleslaw, corn on the cob, and rolls.

As the waiter finished unloading his large serving tray and moved aside, another waiter came into view leading a couple to their table.

"Look who just came in," Ginnie whispered to Maggie Rose after one swift glance.

Maggie Rose looked up to see Chris and a striking redhead passing by the next row over. The woman was nearly as tall as Chris, with a voluptuous figure that had the men they passed giving her a second look. The waiter seated her solicitously with her back to Maggie Rose, which meant that even with a table or two intervening, all Chris had to do was look around and he would see Maggie Rose.

"There's Chris Shealy," said Gwen, who saw everything and knew nearly everyone. "I don't know the girl's name but I've seen her before."

"Her name's Neda McCann," Dina offered.

"Is that hair color real or is it from your salon?" Ginnie asked.

"It's my best work if I do say it myself," Dina said. "She has lovely hair to work with."

"Where's she from, how long has she been here, and what does she do? Fill us in, Dina," Ginnie said.

"She's from St. Louis, been here about four months. She said she taught for a few years there. Now she writes training manuals for a large manufacturing plant."

Maggie Rose had been listening to the conversation while cutting the tender meat from the ribs.

"Didn't Ginnie tell me you were working with Chris now as his office manager?" Gwen asked. "It's a good thing for him. I knew Venetia. Nice girl but unreliable."

"He's always so easygoing," Dina said. "Is he that way at work?"

"He is so far," Maggie Rose said. "I've only been there a week so he might change."

"He and Neda are coming over," Ginnie said.

There was a small flurry of introductions. Maggie Rose sat straighter, her chin up, a friendly smile on her face.

"Hi, Neda," she said. "How are you liking Jamison?"

"It's very different from St. Louis, my hometown, except for this heat and humidity. We get the same thing this time of year."

In addition to her entrancing figure, Neda had huge brown eyes, long lashes, high cheekbones, and flawless skin. Looking at Neda, Maggie Rose wondered how she could have thought herself attractive in her bedroom mirror.

Although Neda carried herself with the confidence of a stunning woman, Maggie Rose thought she seemed genuinely friendly in the few minutes of conversation at their table.

Chris stood beside her talking and laughing but Maggie Rose could feel him willing her to look up. Gwen asked Neda a question, taking Neda's attention from Maggie Rose, who hadn't looked directly at Chris until that moment.

They might have been alone, so strong was his look of resentment and disappointment. The friendliness and warmth Maggie Rose had decided to extend him shriveled and disappeared as she flinched from that look.

She felt Ginnie glance at her curiously and she averted her eyes from Chris to join in the general laughter from something Gwen had said. Had her life depended upon it she could not have said what she was laughing about.

Chris took Neda back to their table. "Thanks for introducing me," Neda said. "When I meet more people I'll probably like Jamison better. I know Dina but tell me about the others."

While they made inroads on their rib dinners, Chris spoke about the three women and answered Neda's questions, mentioning at the end that Maggie Rose was his new office manager and that she'd recently returned home.

"Maybe I'll find myself returning home one day," Neda said wistfully.

Chris tried to keep his focus on his dinner companion but couldn't help looking across the tables at Maggie Rose occasionally. She'd taken his breath away when he first saw her in that marvelous apricot dress, her hair curling around her vibrant face. The sight of her happy and carefree brought back the hurt and distress he'd been carrying around all weekend. He had to get near her.

But when he'd been at her table with Neda, Maggie Rose had looked at everyone except him. When he'd compelled her to meet his eyes by the intensity of his gaze, her inability to sustain the contact strengthened in him the rightness of the conclusion he'd arrived at Friday night. He and Neda were still eating when Maggie Rose and the others left with a good-bye wave.

Maggie Rose was willow thin in her clinging dress. With an ache in his throat Chris wondered how long that would last.

Chapter Ten

Maggie Rose arrived at work Monday morning dreading to see Chris. Their meeting last evening at Teddy's had left a bitter taste in her mouth even though no words had been spoken.

She found she needn't have worried. The note on her desk was brief and curt: *Call on the cell phone if you need me. If I get back in time I'll give Covey his first lesson. Chris.*

He'd never left early before and she wondered if he was steering clear of her or if he had a genuine need to get to the job. Whatever it was, she found herself grateful. Not only could she work hard on the gala but the problem of Covey learning to ride was solved without her having to do anything about it.

She called Bill about photographs. He'd be out the next day. She wrote the story for the paper, received the excellent logo work from Janice, and took it to the printer with an order encompassing the several kinds of paper the business used. She was delighted with that particular accomplishment and remembered to prepare Janice's check for Chris's signature.

With other odds and ends the day went quickly. At four Chris rang to say he wouldn't be home in time for Covey's lesson but definitely would tomorrow. Maggie Rose told him to look on her desk at the items she'd left for him.

On the way home she told Covey Mr. Chris would give him a riding lesson the next day.

Covey's eyes grew big. "Are you sure?" he asked.

"He called to tell me to tell you. He wanted to do it today but found he wouldn't be here in time."

"I can tell Mom?" Covey asked.

"Of course."

On Tuesday morning the first thing Covey said when he got into the car was that his mom and Mr. Dan were coming to see him take his first lesson.

"Do you think that'll be all right, Aunt Maggie Rose?"

"I imagine so. Mr. Chris knows your mom."

I know her, too, and she's never been that anxious to see some of Covey's other activities. Is she coming to see father and son together?

"Will you come see me, Aunt Maggie Rose?"

"If I can get away, but if your mom and Mr. Dan come, that's enough of an audience for your first time."

Covey seemed content with that and was dreamily quiet the rest of the way.

This morning's note said: *Make any decisions you*

need to for the gala. I should be back for Covey's lesson before four. Chris.

Maggie Rose had a section in a loose-leaf notebook for the items concerning the opening. The next one to be taken care of today was catering. She was soon on the phone with Leah Johnson, owner of Catering by Leah and mother of ten-year-old Kayla, one of Chris's students.

"Leah, we talked about the food and agreed on small sandwiches, dips and chips, fresh fruit, and cold beverages."

"Right. Did you decide you wanted something else like buffalo wings?"

"Not that but maybe dishes of nuts."

"That's a good idea. Sometimes people only want something cold to drink and a handful of nuts."

"The main question is, do you need any electrical outlets? Because I'm not sure we have any for an outdoor affair like this."

"Since we're not serving any hot dishes we don't have to worry. We'll bring the ice we need. Also we now have a refrigerated unit in a light truck that is a blessing in carrying food like the sandwiches to keep them fresh."

Maggie Rose sighed in relief. "I'm so glad. What will we do if it rains?"

"It's June and if it rains, it'll still be warm. We'll just have everyone in the marquee at the same time but with the food, they'll be all right. Don't worry, Maggie Rose. I'll bring coffee also, in case."

"You sound so calm."

"I am because we've done this in all sorts of conditions and people still enjoy themselves." Leah laughed and concluded, "Kayla is so excited, it's her first time for something like this, and she and her dad predict that the weather will be absolutely fine!"

Maggie Rose noted the date of this final consultation with Leah and what they talked about. Hopefully the refreshments were taken care of.

Later in the day she called Alicia to see if they could go together tomorrow to select the items Alicia had suggested for the equestrian shop.

"I was going to call you tonight to ask about that. Sure, I'll go. I have a proposition for you and Chris. How about paying me to handle that shop for you on Sunday?"

"You sure you have the time? Can you get someone else to play the organ for church?"

"I have a substitute, don't have to use her often, but she's pretty good. I'll tell her now so she can practice for the service."

Maggie Rose marked that on her list. Alicia would sell more clothes than she would. She made a mental note to give her sister a bonus on Sunday.

A call to Janice Nesbit reassured her that the new sign for the equestrian shop would be ready for hanging on Thursday.

The portalet company called to see if it would be convenient to deliver it on Saturday afternoon rather than early Sunday, as they were going to be shorthanded Sunday.

"That will be fine as long as you're not charging overnight fees."

"The cost will be the one agreed on in the contract."

The voice on the other end of the line was going over the directions when there was the sound of a door opening and Maggie Rose looked up to see Jerlene, Dan, and Chris coming in together.

She hadn't realized it was so late or that seeing Chris after two days would make her heart beat faster. She sketched a hello to the three of them as she continued the conversation.

"Yes, that's right. No, you turn left at that corner." She deliberately spun out the conversation to give herself time to settle down before having to speak with Chris.

He and Dan were talking about horses and Dan was saying he'd ridden several years on Texas ranches and had also worked teaching people to ride. He asked Chris if he'd heard of the Lone Star Riding Academy in Dallas.

Chris said no, he'd done most of his training in South Carolina, but during the summers after he got out of college he'd traveled a bit, taking part in a number of events, and he had spent a couple of weeks in Austin during that time.

"That was a wild two weeks."

"I know what you mean," Dan said. "Texans are a breed unto themselves."

"They ride as if they were born in the saddle," Chris said.

"That's because someone holds the baby in front of them as they ride, even before the infant can walk," Dan explained.

Maggie Rose heard these remarks as the portalet man hung up the phone and she couldn't help wishing she'd been thus conditioned to a horse. She wouldn't have found herself in her present predicament. She joined the general conversation until Chris said he had to go get changed.

"Anything I need to do here or know?" He stood by her side looking at her.

"Janice is bringing the sign for the shop on Thursday, and tomorrow Alicia and I will buy additional clothes for the shop. Also, Alicia is going to manage the shop on Sunday if that's okay with you. That'll leave me free for the office and anything else that might come up."

His eyes searched hers as if there was more information he needed, but his expression told her nothing.

"Hey, guys, if Alicia is going to help on Sunday, maybe there's something I can do. And Dan, too," Jerlene said enthusiastically. "If you have a good crowd you'll need several pairs of hands."

"I know you haven't seen me ride but I'm available if you find you need help," Dan told Chris.

"I appreciate that. Jerlene, you know where the stables are. I'll meet you and Dan there in a couple of minutes."

Covey remembered Mr. Tallie describing Windsong one day as "jumpin' out of her skin." When Covey asked what he meant, he said Windsong was very excited and couldn't keep still. Covey felt that same way all day anticipating his first riding lesson.

He'd been working around the horses for a week now but somehow it seemed much longer, he felt so close to them. He couldn't wait each morning to get back to them. He loved to watch how they moved in the pasture, how they would have their heads down nibbling on the grass, then suddenly raise up, eyes alert, ears pricked, and stand absolutely still as if they were hearing sound Covey couldn't hear. He loved the way they stood still for the grooming Mr. Tallie had taught him to give them; they liked it a lot just like a person would.

He wasn't afraid of them even though they were bigger than he was. He knew they could hurt him if he was careless but he wasn't going to be careless. Mr. Tallie had talked to him very seriously about that. They were used to him now and their eyes seemed to recognize him when he talked to them.

Today he was finally going to ride one. He hoped. He hoped that Mr. Chris was going to skip the very beginning about grooming and how to bridle and saddle the horse because he already knew that. He had watched Mr. Tallie and had done it himself. Mom and Mr. Dan would be here and he wanted them to see him up on a horse.

"Is it about time yet?" he asked for the fourth time.

"Why don't you go outside and see if they're coming?" Mr. Tallie said.

Covey burst out the door and there they came down the path, his mom and Mr. Dan.

"Mom! Hi, Mr. Dan. Mom, did you see Mr. Chris? Is he here yet?"

"He's changing and said he'll meet us here in a minute."

Chris appeared and, taking Nicky from his stall, led him to the small paddock for beginners, all the while speaking softly to Covey, who walked beside him.

"You're pretty excited, aren't you?"

"I can't help it, Mr. Chris."

"I understand but I'd like you to try to calm down a little, Covey. You know why?"

"It might scare Nicky?"

"I don't think it would scare her but you know

horses are very sensitive. You've been around them long enough to know that, haven't you?''

"Yes, Mr. Chris."

"If Nicky feels your excitement, she might get excited, too, and right now we want her to be very calm.''

Talking the way he did, soft and slow in his explanation, made Covey feel less excited. He didn't want to do anything that would hurt his lesson.

Covey answered all of Mr. Chris's questions about how he had groomed Nicky, and Covey could see that Mr. Chris thought he'd done a good job. Then he put a bridle on Nicky, being careful to do it just as Mr. Tallie had taught him. Next came the saddle. Then he was allowed to lead Nicky around to limber his muscles. Finally the big moment came.

"What side do you mount from, Covey?"

"Left."

Covey stood on the mounting block while Mr. Chris showed him how to handle the reins and get his legs and weight smoothly over Nicky's back so that he was settled in the right place on the saddle. He sat straight and tall.

Covey couldn't help but smile. He was *on* a horse at last!

"Turn this way, Covey," his mom called. His mom, Mr. Tallie, and Mr. Dan were lined up on the fence smiling and his mom clicked her camera. Even Mr. Chris smiled. He wondered where Aunt Maggie Rose was but she went out of his mind as Mr. Chris started leading Nicky around the lot.

I'll never forget this, Covey thought.

* * *

In bed that night all Covey could think of in the moments before sleep came was the glorious moment on Nicky. He also thought he almost had the answer as to whether or not Mr. Chris was his dad. After another few lessons he would know for sure.

Chapter
Eleven

Maggie Rose walked into her office Wednesday morning and stopped dead still. Chris Shealy leaned against the table opposite her desk waiting for her. Feeling embarrassed that she had been so obviously surprised, she said, "Good morning," and went to her desk.

After all, Chris was her employer and had every right to be in the office, but since he had apparently made it his business *not* to be in the office the previous two days, she'd had no reason to expect him here today. Since he was here she would thank him for Covey's lesson.

"You certainly made Covey one happy boy, Chris. He can't talk about anything but his riding lesson and how much he loves horses. Thank you."

"No need to thank me. Since he's here every day I'll work in a lesson as often as possible. He's an eager student. Jerlene was very pleased for him.

I noticed you weren't there." The statement was flat, cool, his face unsmiling.

She'd known this was coming and had her answer ready, the same one she'd given Covey yesterday. Covey had been easily satisfied since his mom and Mr. Tallie had been there and his sheer joy had transcended a small thing like her absence. Chris was not Covey but she had only one answer and he'd have to take it or leave it.

"The phone began ringing right after Jerlene and Dan left. There were six calls from people who'd received their invitations and had questions. Their messages are here." She indicated a small pile of notes. "Then Janice and Alicia called."

"That took the whole forty minutes?"

"Once people began calling about the opening, I was afraid to leave in case I'd miss a call. Since Jerlene was there to see Covey I thought it was more important for me to stay here and take care of business." His eyes flickered and she knew she'd made a point he wasn't prepared for. But she didn't want to rub it in. Matters between them were difficult enough.

She handed him the message. "I imagine there'll be more calls asking for specific directions. Maybe next time there should be a small map in the invitation as well as the address."

He nodded as he flipped through the note. . . . "None of these people came last year. If new ones come plus most of the old ones, there might be a good crowd. I'm going to the office for a little while today but I'll be here the rest of the week so Tallie and I can get the stables and the grounds in perfect condition. I'll be around in case you need me for anything. Today you and Alicia are getting clothes for the shop?"

"Yes. I'm to meet her in an hour."

"Be sure to switch the phone to the stables when you leave."

"Chris, before you go I wanted to ask you about the inspector for the association that gives the awards. Will he or she be here Sunday?"

"I don't know. I sent an invitation to the association but they never tell you in advance when they'll visit your stables." He seemed to forget he was talking to a person he'd ignored the past few days, and began talking to Maggie Rose. "That's why if you're serious about winning an award every element of your stables has to be in top condition all of the time. The pressure really builds up."

"Would you recognize the person if you saw them?"

"Not necessarily. I've met a few of them but you never know who'll show up."

Maggie Rose thought about Chris's answers regarding awards as she drove to the sports store to meet Alicia. The award represented so much more to him than its intrinsic or publicity value. It would say to him that he had atoned for his failures with Uncle Henry, that he was a worthwhile person now, and that he could move forward with his life. Maggie Rose had always known Chris was a person of worth, that he was strong, generous, kind, and that he had a good brain. It was hard for her to imagine that Mr. Shealy had failed to see these characteristics of the boy he'd raised with a foundation of solid values. Undoubtedly Chris had been headstrong at times, but he'd not been mean or malicious.

She thought it was mostly in Chris's perception

that he'd failed his uncle, but if that was a reality to him, then getting the award was a need for him. She was going to work as hard as she could to help him reach that goal.

Alicia, in a white sleeveless sundress and sandals, was waiting at the door for Maggie Rose.

"How can you wear pants and blouse in this heat?" she asked.

"I'm working in an air-conditioned office but you look nice and cool," Maggie Rose said affectionately. Alicia was a pleasure to be around and as the hours went by on their search for the latest in equestrian wear, she was thankful Alicia had offered her services.

"You look droopy. Lunchtime." Alicia led Maggie Rose to a coffee shop a few doors down. "I don't think you're eating enough, Maggie Rose."

"This chicken salad looks good. Will you help me if I can't finish it all?"

Maggie Rose was amused at how Alicia loved to play the big-sister role although she was the younger of the two.

The waitress came back from the kitchen apologizing that the chicken was gone but they had a lovely tuna salad she could bring. Maggie Rose agreed.

As they ate they consulted the list of students and their ages to be sure that their basic client base was covered. "We've got riding hats, string gloves, a few jackets, breeches, and riding boots. For the adults whom we hope to entice there're leather-patched breeches, hacking jackets, stock-tie blouses, and a couple of other type jackets."

Maggie Rose frowned at Alicia. "Some of these items I agreed to only because you were certain you could sell them. I hope you're right. Otherwise Chris is going to think I'm crazy when he sees the bill.''

"You didn't pay retail for them and I am sure I can sell them. One or two things I intend to buy myself if no one else does. As soon as we finish here, I want to go back and look over the belts and jewelry. There were some nice horse-head cameos that I know will sell.''

By midafternoon Alicia was willing to call a halt and they headed back to the farm. Alicia went immediately into the shop while Maggie Rose went to her desk. "You know we're going to have to move some furniture in order to show the clothes off to their best advantage. Later we'll need to get posters of models wearing equestrian fashions,'' Alicia called back.

Maggie Rose switched the phone back to the office and read the messages on her desk. She took care of them, then went to the shop. Alicia's energy seemed endless, unlike hers. She didn't know if it was the heat or her lunch that kept her from feeling good but she hoped it would pass now that she was in the air-conditioned building.

"Maggie Rose, you know what's missing?" Alicia stood looking around, hands on hips.

"Customers to buy these expensive clothes?" Maggie Rose said dryly.

"You worry too much. They'll be here Sunday and they'll be interested. But they won't buy because they can't try them on! Why didn't I think of that before?''

"I see what you mean. That full-length mirror isn't enough. They have to be able to change their clothes.''

Maggie Rose remembered an idea she had had the first day Chris showed her this building. "There's a sizable storeroom next to the office and the first time I saw it I thought it would be more useful as a dressing room."

"This is just what we need," Alicia said when Maggie Rose opened the storage room door. "It's big enough that we can put some kind of partition in the middle and make it into two spaces. All we need are mirrors and hooks and a piece of carpeting on the floor."

"I don't think there'll be a problem with that. Chris said he'd be working here the rest of the week to get everything ready. He and Mr. Tallie can change this space, I'm sure."

"Wonderful!" With that taken care of Alicia was ready to return to the shop. "This is what needs to happen in here," she said, pointing out to Maggie Rose how the racks and the small furniture pieces that displayed clothes needed to be moved. She picked up one end of a rack. "Let's see how this one looks over there."

Maggie Rose picked up her end and when it was placed in its new position she could see immediately that Alicia was right. She worked steadily under Alicia's supervision and the shop began to look like a different place.

Despite the cooled air she began to feel overheated. Her stomach began to feel more uncomfortable.

The shop door opened and Chris came in wearing jeans, a T-shirt, and work boots. "I saw your cars were back," he said.

"How do you like the way your shop looks?" Alicia asked.

Maggie Rose, leaning against the chest they had begun to lift, suddenly felt her head whirl and her strength fail. She gripped the chest until her knuckles were white. She gritted her teeth and willed her legs not to give way. She was *not* going to fall again with Chris Shealy nearby.

In the distance, it seemed to her, Alicia cried her name in alarm. She tried to say she was all right but she couldn't open her mouth. She felt Chris's hand on hers loosening her grip while he made soothing sounds. She closed her eyes in an intense effort to keep down the nausea but it was no use. Chris had no sooner placed her in a chair than she lurched to her feet and made it to the bathroom, where all of the tuna salad came up. Alicia was beside her, steadying her while she retched, wiping her face with a cool, wet paper towel.

"It definitely was something I ate," Maggie Rose said with a touch of humor.

She hated to walk back out to where Chris was waiting, but after she'd washed her face twice, rinsed out her mouth, and finger-combed her hair, she had to go.

Chris was pacing and as soon as she appeared he took her hand and placed her in the chair again.

"What do you think you were doing, you and Alicia, moving that furniture?"

Alicia looked surprised. "It wasn't that heavy."

Chris continued as if she hadn't spoken, his attention focused on Maggie Rose.

"You're not supposed to be moving anything heavier than paper around here and I come in and find you moving furniture, and in this heat!"

Maggie Rose said quietly, "What made me throw

up was the tuna salad I had for lunch." From the corner of her eye she saw Alicia move soundlessly out of the office into the shop.

"If you need anything moved you tell Tallie or me. Is that clear, Maggie Rose?" he said through his teeth.

Maggie Rose could see that Chris was very upset. He was more than upset, he seemed to be angry. She was willing to give him some leeway but there was no need for him to speak to her as if she were a child. Her own temper began to rise.

"Why are you so angry?" She kept her voice low.

Chris paced again; then, as if he'd come to a decision, he came close and held her glance. "Are you all right, Maggie Rose?"

Now she was puzzled. "Of course I'm all right."

"Are you sure?"

"Why wouldn't I be sure?"

His eyes searched hers before he pulled back. "You may be sure but I'm not. This is the third time in the eight days you've worked here that I've seen you ill."

Maggie Rose was jolted by his response. She raised her chin and straightened her back. "I guess you'll just have to take my word for it."

They stared at each other; then Chris turned his back and left the office.

"What's the matter with Chris?" Alicia asked as soon as Maggie Rose returned to the shop.

"I don't know." Maggie Rose sighed. "Some bee in his bonnet about me confining myself to desk work. Don't pay it any attention."

"What did he say about the dressing room?"

"I'll tell him tomorrow."

Alicia giggled. "After the way he carried on about

the shop, he'll be pleased to do the dressing room for you."

Chris rode HS out of the yard. "I'll be back," he told Tallie.

It had been a while since he had taken the time to ride over his entire property. He felt the need to see it all this late afternoon when the sun illumined the fields and made dappled patterns in his woods. He rode easily, his thoughts moving randomly as he noted the crops planted by the two men who leased twenty of his fifty acres.

Uncle Henry had quoted his father, Hugh Christopher Shealy, who had expressed his love for the earth by frequently saying, "There's gold in that land." Gold was the highest compliment he could use for the riches the property produced for him through his careful husbandry. Old Hugh had left thirty acres to each of his three sons: Uncle Henry; Chris's father, Lee Christopher; and Hugh, Jr., the eldest son. Chris's father had gambled his away, then died. Hugh had lost his through poor judgment and debt, then disappeared. Old Hugh had left the best part of the land to Uncle Henry. It was the most fertile and had the brook running through it. Henry had bought twenty more acres and had made the investment pay. More than his brothers, he'd understood the value of land and that you were never poor as long as you had good land that was well taken care of.

Chris thought of this inheritance as he stopped HS by the brook, dismounted, and let the horse drink. He tied HS to a tree and sat back against it. What a joy it would be if Maggie Rose could be here with him. He'd never wanted a woman to ride over his land with him until now.

He would show her where he learned to fish in the brook, what it was like to hide away here on the hottest days lulled by the quiet, and how magical it was in the moonlight.

He would point out the various parts of his land, the leased crops, the old orchard that he wanted to restore soon, the fallow lands, the old trails he'd come across, and how he could expand the stables if he decided to.

There was so much he wished he could share with her, because she had been a part of his life from the ninth grade. She had seemed inaccessible to him for all of those early years, even when she lived in Hartford and came home on visits.

He'd wanted to ask her out on dates but hadn't had the nerve. He was sure she still saw him as wild and unreliable. He knew her father had a serious down on him, so although he made it his business to see her each time she was in town, he never proposed going out. He didn't want to embarrass her or hear her refusal.

He'd taken a great risk in asking her to work at the stables but it had paid off, to his astonishment and joy. Since she was home to stay and he had made a vow to do all he could to erase his earlier reputation and replace it with a good one, he thought the two of them could now take the opportunity to get to know each other as adults. To find out if there was substance in the spark there had always been when they were together.

It had started out well, but now, only eight days after she had begun working in the office, they were at serious odds.

He was hurt, disappointed, disillusioned, and hopelessly confused. What was it she was keeping from him? Why did she keep getting sick? But how could she be pregnant?

When he'd gone to see her at her apartment he'd asked her if there was someone in her life. She said no. He looked into her transparent eyes and believed.

Chris sat by the brook a long time but his thoughts didn't get any clearer. He mounted HS and made his way home.

Chapter Twelve

Maggie Rose watched the dawn break as she sat in her gown, feet curled up in the wing chair, and coffee mug in her hands. The faint pink in the east gradually strengthened, melded with orange streaks as the last veils of darkness disappeared and the sun broke through. Weary though she was, the glorious sight restored some energy to her and reminded her to give thanks for another day.

She had always valued calmness, serenity, and peace of mind. Her life had been relatively smooth compared to others she knew and that was the way she wanted it. Not for her a life on the fast track with numerous ups and downs. She wasn't the adventurous type.

The Lem Norris episode, brief and intense, had been her one departure from the norm and had been disastrous. After that she didn't mind if men thought of her as dull, too ordinary. In her last few years in Hartford no man had piqued her interest and she had returned to Jamison with a subconscious relief that that chapter of her life was over.

The Mailroom would open a new chapter, one that held a pleasant challenge in a field with which she was familiar. It did not disturb her peace of mind. Even agreeing to work for Chris, after the initial flutter his reappearance in her life caused, had not shattered her basic calmness.

The erosion of her peace of mind had begun the morning after she twisted her ankle and Chris probed at her reason for feeling dizzy. She couldn't tell him the real reason. Now as she sipped her coffee, she wondered if that had anything to do with his change in attitude. No, probably not, because how could he know her true reason? She had answered all of his questions well enough.

The atmosphere between them had been edgy in the office and had carried over to their chance meeting at Teddy's when he had made certain she saw his displeasure. On Monday and Tuesday he had even absented himself from their usual morning meeting.

She'd felt like a weathervane, trying to adjust her own attitude to however the wind blew his, but at the same time keeping her peace of mind—a contradictory state of affairs without a hope of success ending in restless nights and her watching the sunrise.

His attack yesterday afternoon about her being ill three times added to the confusion. What three times? Yesterday and after she twisted her ankle—that was twice.

Maggie Rose clutched the mug suddenly. The only other time had been after she took Jack and

Zack Denby to the stable. He must have turned around and looked at her while she was retching. Even if he had, what was so important about it that had set him off yesterday? It was a vexing puzzle.

The sun was well and truly up, heralding another hot day. She rose and stretched and wished she felt more tranquil about the remaining three days before the gala. The one blessing about being up so early was the ability to be leisurely so that by the time she arrived at her desk several hours later she was more relaxed and settled.

Chris came in ten minutes later in jeans and a T-shirt. Their "Good mornings" crossed as he sat down.

"The first thing I'd like to do is figure out the riding program for Sunday, and leave it for you to type. Okay?"

Their eyes met and Maggie Rose saw at once that the coldness Chris had displayed earlier was gone. His heated outburst yesterday must have shattered it, and although there was a little air of watchfulness about him, that was bearable. He could watch all he pleased. He would never see her sick again!

"Will everyone be riding?" she asked.

"All eighteen plus the twins make twenty. That's why families come and bring their friends—so they can show off their children."

"Do the children like it? I'd think some of them would be nervous and scared to ride in front of a crowd."

"A few are and the brand-new ones like the twins will just sit on a horse while Tallie or I walk it around a little. If they get too excited and frightened I have them just stand with someone else beside the horse so they can have their picture taken, but that doesn't happen often."

"Do you start with the youngest?"

"We want to show the skills they've learned and they're divided into those groups."

Chris pulled his chair to the desk and wrote the names of the students and the skills they would exhibit. With questions and comments from Maggie Rose the hour-long program emerged giving time for each group with a space between for changeovers.

They spoke together quietly and worked efficiently but there were no easy smiles and they were very careful not to touch.

"Can you have this ready to hand out to the parents today and tomorrow?"

"For them and for your Saturday students as well."

Chris looked at her in surprise. "You'll be here Saturday?"

"Of course. There's always last-minute things that come up and I want to be sure that what I'm responsible for gets done. I'm sure Covey will want to be here as well and he can help."

"Thanks, Maggie Rose."

That was the first time Chris had said her name in days. Maggie Rose tried to ignore the warmth that spread through her.

"I'll get these ready to hand out on Sunday, also," she said, "and if that's taken care of, I need to talk to you about the storage room before you go."

"What about it?" he asked.

"Let me show you," she said. The space in front of the storage room was narrow and Maggie Rose was again conscious of how she and Chris avoided physical contact as she outlined the idea of a dressing room. They stepped into the area and discussed what was needed. Chris said he and Tallie would get it done, as they had most of the material on hand. He'd get the mirrors the next time he was in town.

Without thinking they both started for the door at the same time. Chris stopped sharply and let her go through.

Was there anything else to be discussed before he went back outside? he wanted to know as he stood by the outside door. When she said no, he nodded and left.

Maggie Rose relaxed in her chair and rubbed her arms. Touching between her and Chris had always been natural, casual, and instinctive. It was strange, she thought, how their deliberate avoidance of it today produced an emotional tension that wouldn't have happened if they'd followed their usual habits.

When the phone rang an hour later Maggie Rose was sure it would be another person seeking direction to the Sunday affair but it was the party favor shop.

"Ms. Sanders? This is John at the Party Favors shop. The shipment we were expecting today has been held up and we can't guarantee that you'll have your key rings Sunday."

Maggie Rose had ordered two hundred key rings stamped with a horse's head for a giveaway. They weren't personalized for the stables but they were the best item she could find.

"If I can't have them for Sunday they'll be no use to me."

"I'm sorry, Ms. Sanders."

"So am I, but I'll have to cancel the order and request a refund on the deposit I gave you."

"I'll mail it to you."

Now what? She had already scoured the town and had been thankful to find the key ring. There had to be something, someplace, but time was short. She could go to Columbia but it was doubtful she'd find even one hundred of an appropriate trinket for what she had in mind.

Finally she picked up the phone and dialed Chris's cell number.

"This is Chris Shealy."

"Chris, this is Maggie Rose."

"What's the matter?"

"Nothing. I just wanted to tell you I have to go into Jamison to the print shop, but I'll be back as soon as possible."

"Be careful and thanks for letting me know. Switch the phone to the stable."

Maggie Rose wondered why he asked what was wrong; then it occurred to her it might be because she'd never used his cell number since he gave it to her.

At the printer's Maggie Rose was waited on by Gladys, the assistant manager with whom she had made her initial order.

"Did you come for your order, Ms. Sanders? It's to be delivered to you tomorrow."

"I want to add to it," Maggie Rose said.

She explained to Gladys her idea of a small notepad with the new logo on it to give to the guests on Sunday at their opening event. Was it too late or could she get them by Saturday?

"What size are you thinking of?"

"Purse size."

"How many?"

"Two hundred fifty."

"You might as well get five hundred. The difference in cost is minimal."

Maggie Rose left the shop thankful that that small problem had been solved. Gladys had assured her the notepads would be delivered with the rest of the order on Friday.

Shortly after twelve the office door opened and Chris came in with a card table under his arm. As Maggie Rose looked at him in surprise, the door opened again to Covey and Tallie, each carrying food.

"We're going to eat lunch in here with you," Covey announced gleefully.

"I could have come to the kitchen," she protested to Mr. Tallie.

"It seems cooler in here," he said, busily setting up green salad and a dish of glistening strawberries. Chris was silently assembling chairs and in another moment they were all seated at the table.

"This looks wonderful," Maggie Rose said.

"Everything except the rolls and the iced tea came from the garden," Mr. Tallie said proudly.

"I picked the lettuce and the green onions and pulled up two carrots, and then Mr. Tallie told me to find the ripest tomatoes on the vines. Do you like your salad, Mr. Chris?"

Chris had been figuring out that it was only thirteen days ago he had visited Maggie Rose in her apartment and sat across the table from her to eat pizza. Today he'd quietly suggested to Tallie that taking lunch to the office might be a good idea since Maggie Rose was so busy. He wanted to see that she ate and had been watching her while drinking two glasses of tea and slowly eating a roll. He'd purposely put Covey opposite her so his watching wouldn't be obvious. But that sharp-eyed Covey had noticed he hadn't touched his own salad.

"I'm sure I will, Covey. I was thirsty from the work we were doing so I had to drink some tea first." He picked up his fork and dug into the salad.

"I like it a lot, Covey." Maggie Rose was eating hers steadily, looking at Covey and Mr. Tallie. "Did you make the dressing?" she asked Tallie.

"It's just oil, vinegar, and some of my spices."

Tallie and Covey chatted away about their work. Maggie Rose listened and ate her salad. Chris, pleased, offered her the rolls.

"No, thanks. I'm saving room for the berries."

Chris filled a small bowl with the red fruit and handed it to her.

"They smell like they're really ripe." She watched him fill the bowl and put out her hand to take it from him.

Chris held on to the bowl. Maggie Rose raised her eyes to his.

He stroked her fingers under the bowl, then released it.

"Thank you." He saw the faint color come into her face.

"You're very welcome," he said softly.

Maggie Rose thanked her lunch companions for coming to the office but said she'd come to the kitchen the next two days because everyone would be so busy.

Covey, on his way out, turned back to ask Maggie Rose to come see him take his riding lesson later this afternoon.

"I'll come if I can," she said.

Chris, standing behind her, touched her on the arm. He felt the little start she tried to hide. *Good! I'm not the only one that's skittish,* he thought.

She turned to him, no longer trying to evade his glance.

"You had to go in to the printer's, is everything all right?"

Maggie Rose smiled, glad to give Chris good news. She told him how she'd thought of a notepad with logo when the original giveaway had fallen through and had rushed to the printer's rather than calling.

"I thought if I talked with Gladys and made her see the crisis I was in, I'd stand a better chance of getting her to do it by tomorrow."

"Is she going to do it?"

"Yes." Her uninhibited smile made his heart jump. "I think you'll like it, Chris."

"I'm sure I will. I'm also sure that you're a wizard at getting things done. Thanks, Maggie Rose." He couldn't look away from her. For the first time in days she was her old self with him. Despite all the unanswered questions between them, he wanted only to be close to the warmth and the sweetness that was his Maggie Rose.

"Mr. Chris? Mr. Tallie said he wants to show you something," Covey said, coming through the door.

Maggie Rose looked down and stepped back, disappointment in her every movement.

Chris swallowed an expletive. The precious moment was shattered and all he could do was to follow Covey out of the office.

Chapter Thirteen

Sunday dawned bright, clear, and hot. Maggie Rose turned on the weather channel immediately. She needed reassurance that the afternoon, at least, would continue to be clear. After that a snowstorm could come and it'd be all right with her. Just let the event be over first!

"No change for the next twenty-four hours," the announcer promised. Maggie Rose whooped for joy, then turned the channel off in case the announcer changed her mind. She laughed at herself as she decided she could stay in bed awhile longer since it wasn't six o'clock yet.

A storm would have been the last straw; enough had already happened. On Friday the marquee promised for Sunday had been damaged and no other was available from the company because they were all out for weddings. She'd been frantic until Janice, who had been supervising the hanging of the stylish new sign for the equestrian shop, told her about a new company call Celebrations. They had one and would install it at eight o'clock Sunday morning.

Alicia and Janice had priced the new inventory and added a few decorating touches including three distinctive chairs and a wastebasket from a flea market.

After the marquee near-disaster, Maggie Rose thought nothing more could happen. But later in the day Covey came running into her office, where she and Alicia were working.

"Aunt Maggie Rose, you've got to come with me, please." He held out his hand and she took it and went with him thinking something was amiss. Alicia followed them as Covey ran quickly to the lot where Chris had told her the beginning students learned how to handle a horse.

"See, Aunt Maggie Rose. This is Nicky, the pony I told you about, and I want you to stay and watch me ride because everyone's seen me except you, but if it wasn't for you I wouldn't be here and have this chance." The words tumbled out as Covey looked excitedly from Maggie Rose to Nicky, who stood on the other side of the fence watching him.

Before she could say anything Covey ran to enter the paddock from where Chris had apparently been waiting for him.

Her heart was pumping so loudly she could hear it in her ears. The perspiration began popping out on her face, and her stomach was tied in knots as the curious pony came closer to the fence. She could feel her eyes widen as she backed away.

She tried to take deep, slow breaths but all she could manage were short gasps. *I can't be sick again,* she told herself urgently as Chris and Covey came into the paddock and approached the pony. She turned her back to them and made a desperate attempt to control her reactions but the panic was too entrenched. The nausea that seized her made her bend over and hold her stomach.

With a half-smothered exclamation Chris came over the fence. He put his arm around her in support and made her lean against him.

Alicia's whole attention had been on Nicky as she crooned to him and held out her hand. Chris's quick move made her turn to see what was happening. She whirled around in alarm and hurried to her sister. "What's the matter, Maggie Rose?"

Humiliated beyond words, Maggie Rose kept her head down. Her pants had no pockets so she didn't have anything to clean her face with. Her legs were weak and she thought that if she fainted now she'd never be able to look Chris in the face again.

"Are you all right?" Alicia asked anxiously.

"No, she's not all right," Chris growled. He pushed his big handkerchief into Maggie Rose's hand and before she could protest, picked her up and for the second time carried her into the living room and laid her on the couch. Alicia and a white-faced Covey brought up the rear.

Chris brought a damp cloth from the kitchen and held it out to Maggie Rose silently.

She took it without looking at him and wiped her face.

"Alicia," she said, "please go to the office and answer the phone. I'll be there in a few minutes."

Alicia left, taking Covey with her. Maggie Rose lay with her eyes closed. How could she face Chris again? Something like this unanticipated encoun-

ter with a horse was bound to happen again. She'd
have a panic attack and would have to tell Chris
the whole story. He'd think she was a cheat and a
liar because she hadn't been totally open with him
when he offered her the job.

All the work she'd done for the opening on Sunday—how could she walk out now on Friday? Alicia
knew some of the arrangements because she'd
been working in the shop and a little in the office
but it wasn't the same. Chris had to win the award
and Maggie Rose was determined that he would.
This was only Friday and things could still go wrong,
even though she checked the items in her notebook constantly. Yet who could have foreseen the
failure just this morning of an essential such as the
marquee?

Even so, how could she possibly work with Chris
now? She couldn't even bring herself to look at
him. She could feel him standing by the couch
waiting for her to acknowledge him. The emotions
emanating from him were anything but positive.
How could she blame him?

She couldn't lie here forever so she might as well
get it over with. She opened her eyes and started
to speak, but nothing came out. She cleared her
throat and tried again.

"Do you want me to leave? I can probably get
Alicia to—"

He interrupted her. "What stupid foolishness
are you talking about?"

The strength of his angry voice shocked Maggie
Rose into looking up at him. His hands were
jammed in the pockets of his jeans as he paced
the length of the couch. He turned and seared
her with his gaze. He stopped beside her, his jaws

clenched tight. Then, "May the good Lord deliver me from crazy females."

Crazy? Who was he calling crazy? She might not have told him the whole truth about herself but she had worked hard since taking over his office, harder than most women would have done, because she was as involved in making Sunday a success as he was and she definitely was not crazy. Maggie Rose sat straight up and looked Chris in the eyes. "I am not crazy! You've got your nerve saying that."

"You may not be crazy, but there's something wrong with you that you're getting sick all of the time. What is the matter with you, Maggie Rose?"

Chris bit the words off because he had almost asked, "Are you pregnant?" He didn't want to go that far but he was worried about her. There had to be something seriously wrong and he had to get to the bottom of it. He couldn't keep on seeing her suffer so every few days.

Maggie Rose heard concern in his voice now and knew she had to give him some kind of answer. "I think it's just working hard and not getting enough sleep in this heat."

"You asked if I wanted you to leave. That's the last thing I want," Chris said. "But as your employer I am going to insist that you see a doctor as early next week as possible, Maggie Rose." The anger was gone but his authority was clear.

"I'll probably feel better after Sunday's over but I will see my doctor as soon as I can," she agreed.

Chris stared at her as if he wanted to say something else, then abruptly left the house.

That had been a very close call, Maggie Rose reflected as she looked at the trees from her bedroom window. She would keep her promise and see Dr. Moore. He would probably tell her to slow down and get more rest, and would give her a prescription for a nervous stomach. That would satisfy Chris until the next episode. Then what would she do?

She turned over restlessly and looked at the painting she'd purchased from an acquaintance in Hartford who was studying art. It was one of the series he called *Growing Up*, showing two round-headed little black boys jumping from a diving board into a pool while a little girl with braids, a doll dangling from her hand, stood looking at them. The look of wonder and yearning on the little girl's face had touched Maggie Rose. She saw herself reflected there. She had been like that little girl growing up, standing a little on the sideline, watching and admiring others who did things she couldn't do. Her only confidence had been in the schoolroom and in the home following her parents' instructions and watching over her sisters.

She thought she didn't have a reckless bone in her body, yet when Chris Shealy came to her with his offer she'd grabbed it with no apprehension. Now she had to acknowledge to herself that the underlying reason for that reckless act was the opportunity to be near Chris. She had never forgotten him. When she thought of men he was ever present in her subconscious but she hadn't realized it until she returned home.

Payment for that recklessness was now upon her and she didn't know what to do. All she knew was that with every day it seemed something else occurred to raise that payment higher, like on Saturday when she had gone to work again uncertain and concerned about what Chris's attitude toward her would be.

Two minutes after she arrived, Chris and Mr. Tallie walked in. "Did you see it?" Mr. Tallie asked.

"See what?" Maggie Rose was so aware of Chris standing a little behind Mr. Tallie with his eyes fixed on her that she had to make an effort to listen.

"Your new dressing room." Mr. Tallie gestured to Maggie Rose to come in as he opened the door to what had been the storage room.

The space was totally transformed. The walls had been painted ivory and decorated along the top with a border of ivory, blue, and green blossoms. An ivory divider five feet high made two separate dressing rooms. Hooks were on the walls for clothes hangers. A full-length mirror was on each wall facing the door while on a sidewall, a bench had been built. A soft blue carpet covered the floor.

Maggie Rose was speechless. How could they have done so much in such a short time? All she'd expected for the opening on Sunday was to have the storage removed, the place thoroughly cleaned, and the two mirrors put up. But this— this was a very attractive dressing room needing only customers trying on equestrian clothes. Gratitude and appreciation for what the two men had done welled up in her.

"How did you get all this done so fast?"

"Tallie wouldn't let us go to bed last night until it was finished," Chris said.

She turned to Mr. Tallie, who was looking at her with a half smile of pride. Maggie Rose threw her arms around him and kissed his cheek. "Thank you so much, Mr. Tallie. You've done a wonderful job and I'm sure we'll be able to sell a lot more clothes tomorrow because of this dressing room."

"Wasn't that hard," Mr. Tallie said. "Just part of the job."

Maggie Rose heard him walk out as she turned to face Chris standing in the opposite side of the small space watching her. She wasn't sure what to say or do but she knew she had to thank him also for this dressing room. She gathered no clue about this thoughts from his expression, but at least his eyes were neither cold nor angry, just watchful. Waiting to see if she had the nerve to thank him as she had Mr. Tallie. If that was what he wanted she'd prove she wasn't afraid.

She walked over to him. "Thank you, Chris, for this lovely room." She put her arms around him and stretched to kiss his cheek.

His arms closed tightly around her as he turned his face so that instead of her lips brushing his cheek they were captured by his.

It seemed to her they both ceased to breathe for a moment; when they breathed again it was as one entity. His kiss, warm and firm, yet tender and searching, made her legs weak. He tightened the embrace.

"Maggie Rose? Where are you?" Alicia's voice penetrated the sensual cloud surrounding Maggie Rose. She pulled away from Chris and stepped to the door.

"Come look at the dressing room," she called. A quick glance at Chris and she made a motion to wipe the lipstick from his mouth.

"Wow! I can't believe it!" Alicia said and spent the next few minutes going over everything that had been done. "You and Mr. Tallie are wonderful," she told Chris, who smiled through her exclamations while stealing glances at Maggie Rose whenever Alicia's attention was elsewhere.

"Tallie and I are going to lay out the parking before the students start coming. Anything you need before I go, Maggie Rose?" Chris asked when Alicia ran out of steam and they were back in the office.

Only to be back in your arms. "I can't think of anything now. We have a number of odds and ends to do for tomorrow."

Lying in her bed on Sunday morning, Maggie Rose thought that scene with Chris was like one of her favorite CDs, the ones she played over and over because they gave her such pleasure. All day Saturday she had relived that moment in his arms that had seemed an eternity. His kiss had shaken up her whole world and every time he'd been in the office their mutual awareness had been so strong she was sure Alicia had sensed it.

She still had four weeks of employment at the farm. How in heaven's name could she carry it out? In addition to the horse business, now this! Was it possible she and Chris could continue to work in close proximity on a professional basis with this, this, whatever it was, between them?

Maggie Rose rolled out of bed. She had to be at the farm before eight o'clock to be sure the marquee arrived and was properly installed. Chris would be there even if she didn't make it, but she felt it was her responsibility.

As she moved through her morning routine, it

wasn't the responsibility for the marquee that was foremost in her mind.

It was the escalating price she would pay for her recklessness.

Chapter
Fourteen

Chris felt a sense of calm for the first time in twenty-four hours as he rode elegant Windsong in the predawn hours of Sunday. He hadn't chosen HS this time when he went quietly into the stalls after a nearly sleepless night. Today he craved the gentleness and sensitivity of Windsong. He didn't want to race over his fields, he just wanted to ride slowly and let the soft breeze and quiet seep into his bones and give repose to his spirit.

The day lay ahead of him, busy, probably chaotic at times, full of noise and bustle. Now was his only opportunity to pull together the events of the past few days and try to bring some order to his heart and mind.

This seesaw business with Maggie Rose was driving him crazy. He'd accused her of being a crazy female, a definition she'd immediately rejected. She was right, or maybe they were both confused!

Every day it was something different. Wednesday
he had caught her moving furniture with Alicia
and then she threw up her lunch. He had every
right to be upset with her but she seemed surprised
at his agitation. He asked if she was ill and she said
no, and that he'd just have to take her word for
it. Couldn't she see that wasn't enough to reassure
him?

Thursday he'd had to sit near her while they
worked out the program. The tension between
them was thick enough to cut with a knife. He'd
decided to have lunch for the four of them in her
office so he could see if she was eating properly.
Watching her he felt his discomfort fade away and
his instinctive response to her sweet presence made
him touch her fingers as he handed her a dish of
strawberries.

She also had relaxed and later, after telling him
about her trip to the print shop, her wonderful
smile, which he hadn't seen in days, drew him like
a magnet. At that moment he didn't care what
might be wrong with her, he just wanted to hold
all of that warmth and sweetness in his arms. She
seemed to sense it too; then Covey had come in
with a message from Tallie.

Friday Covey had brought Maggie Rose and Alicia to the paddock to watch him ride but before
he'd mounted, Maggie Rose had been sick again.
He'd been so alarmed at the violence of the attack
he'd jumped the fence to hold her and then carried
her into the house. Thankfully, Alicia and Covey
went to the office because he was so angry and
upset he couldn't trust himself.

Maggie Rose was so pale and washed out she
couldn't even open her eyes. All he could do was

pace and wait until she said something. Then she had the audacity to ask if he wanted her to leave!

Leave? All he wanted was to know why she kept getting sick. Even if it meant, God help him, that she was pregnant; anything was better than not knowing. He made her promise to see a doctor and she agreed. That evening he had put all of his frustration into the transformation of the storage room into a ladies' dressing room. He worked so hard and so fast that Tallie had looked at him strangely but said nothing. He figured Tallie knew exactly what was going on anyway and it was okay.

He couldn't wait to see her face the next morning. He felt happy inside as she took in all they had done. She hadn't a clue how much more he would have done had she asked. Then she hugged and kissed Tallie and he was transfixed. Would she do the same with him?

He was careful to keep his face expressionless. She would have to come to him on her own.

He watched her eyes and saw her decide to take up the challenge. She came to him, put her arms around him, and aimed to kiss his cheek.

With enormous control he put his arms around her and moved his face slightly so their lips met. He lost his breath at that first contact, then gave himself over completely to the wonder of kissing his Maggie Rose. He'd just begun to take a second serving of the delectable feast when Alicia came calling Maggie Rose. But the sensation of holding her and feeling her response had stayed with him, illuminating the day and guaranteeing sleeplessness last night.

The sky was streaked with light, and dawn appeared like the muted strings of violins, but he knew that very shortly it would be the full orchestra telling him the business of the day was at hand.

He turned Windsong back to the farm. There was nothing, he decided, that he could do about Maggie Rose until she gave him her doctor's evaluation. Maybe it was the result of her overwork for today's opening and she'd be healthy again when this was over. He devoutly hoped that was the case. The restlessness he'd set out with was gone and a sense of composure settled within him. He would get through the next few days. He had to. He couldn't forget that it might be today that the people from the association would come for their evaluation.

He urged Windsong into a faster trot. He had a lot to do before people started arriving at two o'clock.

By one-thirty the troops had arrived ready for what they hoped would be the invasion of at least a hundred guests. Alicia, Janice, Ginnie, Jerlene, and Dan were in the office with Chris, Mr. Tallie, Maggie Rose, Covey, and Bill Denton.

"Ladies," Chris began, "you look wonderful. You're a great advertisement for the shop and I have no doubt all of you and Covey will make people want to buy from our shop. The important thing for all of us today is to see that everyone has a good time. There'll be a lot of children around and we don't want anything to happen to them so let's all of us keep an eye on them. Alicia and Janice will be here in the shop, Bill will be roaming around taking pictures. Jerlene and Dan, once the crowd gets thick and the program begins, I'd like you to

be with Tallie and me. Maggie Rose will supervise
everything at this end, Ginnie will fill in, and Covey
will be our gofer."

Covey, thrilled to have a particular job, said,
"What's a gofer, Mr. Chris?"

"The person who goes for this and goes for that
whenever anyone needs something. Is that okay
with you?"

"Sure." He threw back his shoulders and tried
to stand an inch taller in the new outfit Maggie
Rose had given him from the children's selection
in the shop.

"One more thing," Mr. Tallie said. "Last night
I made a peach cobbler and I've got some steaks
marinating. When this is all over everyone is invited
to stay for dinner."

His invitation was greeted with appreciative
cheers as the group broke up.

"Come outside with me for a minute," Chris
told Maggie Rose. She followed him out to stand
beside the office building, where they could look
at the whole layout.

"How do you think it looks?" he asked.

The buildings gleamed in the sun, the grounds
were meticulously clean and orderly. Pots of flowering plants and greenery stood here and there
decorating the scene. Signs for parking led to the
area beyond the paddock where two men had been
stationed to keep that in order. The deep green
marquee blended perfectly into the scene, as did
the attractive sign hanging above the door to the
shop. She hadn't been to the stables but she knew
from Covey how beautifully groomed the five
horses were and how that part of the farm had
been thoroughly cleaned and polished.

"If I drove in here for the first time I'd be very impressed. I'd think this place looked prosperous and well managed, that whoever owned it knew what he was doing. It's obvious that he cares for it," she said thoughtfully.

"I hope you're right."

She heard the thread of anxiety under his words and turned to him, her hand on his arm. "Chris, I'm being very objective here. No one, including the association person, could see it differently. So don't worry." Her radiant smile embraced him. "Just enjoy your day, Chris. You've worked so hard for it."

"So have you. Thank you, Maggie Rose," he said softly as he raised her hand and brushed a kiss on her palm. "See you at dinner."

Ten minutes later the first car turned into the lane, heralding a steady stream until the parking space was filled almost to capacity. Maggie Rose and the other women, wearing sleek-fitting riding breeches, tall flat-heeled boots, well-cut white blouses clinched in at the waist with horse-head leather belts, and hostess badges Janice had made with the logo in the corner, greeted the guests as they poured into the grounds, signed the guest register, and received their logo notepad.

Some went immediately to the marquee where Leah Johnson and Nancy Fisher served the cold beverages, sandwiches, dips with chips, platters of fresh fruit, and assorted nuts. Others wandered over to the fences to gaze at the five horses, who, brushed and groomed to perfection, seemed to know they were on stage and held themselves proudly as they gazed back at the people gazing at them. Bill Denton began taking his pictures.

Dina Ramsey and Gwen Aiken came through the crowd to speak to Maggie Rose. "Where's Chet? I thought I saw him with you," Maggie Rose said to Dina. Chris had mentioned that Dina's husband was interested in horses.

"He'll be as close to the horses as possible until we leave," Dina said, "but Gwen and I want to know where you got that great-looking outfit you're wearing."

"Let me introduce you to our equestrian shop," Maggie Rose said. "If you can't find exactly what you want we can order it for you."

The shop was crowded and vibrant with conversation from women and a few children urging their mothers to let them buy boots or breeches. Three women were in line to use the dressing rooms and Janice was busy at the cash register while Ginnie and Alicia consulted with other customers. How thankful she was that Alicia's part-time stint at the school made her presence here possible this past week.

Alicia was right about this venture, Maggie Rose mused. *In fact, if this keeps up we might sell out of our inventory.* She turned to greet a group of women and was surprised when the last one turned out to be Chris's friend, Neda McCann, wearing a knock-out dress of raspberry silk. A single strand of silver nestled on the smooth brown skin where the gown's neckline was cut just low enough to be attractively in good taste. Matching silver hung from her ears and raspberry sandals adorned her feet.

"Hi, Maggie Rose." Neda's face lit up with a warm smile. "I'm so glad to see someone I know." She glanced around and waved at Dina and Gwen.

"What a lovely shop you have here. When Chris told me last Sunday about this affair I thought I'd come because I've never been to a riding school."

"What do you think so far?" Maggie Rose was curious to know what a first-time visitor thought, and Neda seemed genuinely interested.

"Everything looks so well kept and efficiently run. I'm looking forward to watching the students perform, too. I'm thinking that taking riding lessons might be just what I need." In a lowered voice and with a touch of humor she asked, "Do you think I could find a pair of those gorgeous breeches you're wearing that'll fit these hips of mine?"

"I'm sure of it, but if we've run out of the size you want, we'll get them for you. Then if you want to sign up for classes you can see me in the office next door."

It was almost time for the program to begin, time, Maggie Rose thought, to embark on her experiment. Thirty minutes ago she had taken half a tranquilizer. Now she asked Ginnie to keep an eye on the office, saying that she had to take care of something outside. She went to the marquee, stacked two plates with goodies, filled two tall cups with a cool drink, and took them to the parking lot attendants. They thanked her profusely. She smiled at them and went to where she'd parked her car that morning. She got in and opened the windows to let the hot air out. Then she looked to the front pasture where the horses were. She stared at them for a long minute. No reaction. Chris and Tallie appeared and let the horses back into the stables. He had told her that would be the procedure as the students rode different ones. Maybe distance was all she needed. Distance, the protection of the car, and a tranquilizer. Could it be that simple? she wondered, putting her head back and closing her eyes.

When she opened them she thought she saw a movement on the other side of the car a little way down the aisle. She looked again and to her astonishment saw the reddish brown back of Nicky, the pony.

How could he be here when he should be ready to begin the program with the smallest riders?

Quietly she opened the opposite door, slid out of the car, and ran as fast as she could to the nearest attendant.

"Quick, run and tell Chris or Tallie that the pony is loose in the parking lot. Hurry!"

The man dropped his plate and ran. Maggie Rose stood in his place watching until she saw Chris, rope in hand, run from the stables and enter the parking lot.

Maggie Rose returned to her car. She heard the ringing of the bell that Tallie had hooked up to summon people outside to watch the riding program. Nicky was brought into the front pasture by Dan. Chris brought in Jack and Zack, introduced them, and had them take turns holding Nicky by the rope and leading him around in a circle. The mounting block was put in place and Zack mounted and clutched the reins as Chris led the pony ten steps forward and ten steps back. Then Jack was put up, following the same routine. The twins stood together and bowed to applause as Chris explained they'd only had two lessons and had done very well.

Maggie Rose stayed to watch Kayla, Leah's daughter, and then Covey, who displayed a confidence that made her proud.

In the shop only two women remained, saying it was too hot outside and they'd rather stay in here. Maggie Rose told Ginnie thanks and to go watch the show. At her desk she steadily drank water to help flush the rest of the tranquilizer out of her system. As the afternoon wore on, people began to drift into the office to inquire about riding classes. She handed out the brochure she'd put together and for those who were ready, took their applications and preferred days of the week for classes. She wondered if Neda would come in but she didn't, although three other adults signed up, followed by two men who inquired about the riding classes.

One was Mr. Neal, who worked in the bank. "Chris has a really great setup here," he told Maggie Rose after introducing Bob Kimbel, who was visiting him this weekend. "I haven't been out here for a long time but I see the improvements he's made."

"Are you thinking of taking classes yourself, Mr. Neal?" she asked.

"My wife keeps telling me I need outdoor exercise and I used to ride many years ago when I was limber and slimmer," he said wistfully.

"I'm trying to encourage him," Mr. Kimbel said. "I've been riding for years and it's a great pleasure. But maybe Mr. Shealy doesn't have room on his schedule," he said thoughtfully. "I saw by the program he already has twenty students and I'm sure you added more today."

"He's intending to expand his hours so he'll be able to accommodate more students. Would you like to take an application and brochure with you, Mr. Neal?''

"Yes, I would. Who knows, I might even get my wife to come with me. I know she'd love to have an excuse to wear the outfits you and your hostesses wore today.''

Maggie Rose looked at her watch after the men left. It was four-thirty and the office was quiet, the shop empty of customers as Janice and Alicia straightened up and sat down to make a final tally.

She stood carefully and went into the bathroom to examine her eyes. Satisfied that the effects of the tranquilizer were gone, she went to the marquee where Leah, her husband, Bill, and her staff were beginning to close up. "Do you think anyone else will come in?" Leah asked.

"No, the parking lot is empty of the guest cars. I checked," Maggie Rose said. "Is there any food left?" She forgot she'd eaten nothing that day and that Mr. Tallie's dinner was still a couple of hours away.

"Of course, I'll bring you a plate."

"Just a sandwich and some fruit, please."

It was a pleasure to sit and observe the competence with which Leah and staff worked as they put food in containers and set them aside. Next all of the tableware was packed in boxes. The tables and their covers were stored in the truck. Leah brought the food containers to Maggie Rose. "These are for you."

Maggie Rose was surprised. "Why?"

"They're included in the price we agreed on so they're yours. I don't think you'll have too much trouble using what's left because we estimate the amount pretty closely."

Bill and Nancy helped carry the containers to the office when Maggie Rose went to get the check for Leah.

"This is so nice," Nancy said, breezing through the shop.

"Most of the good stuff is gone," Alicia said, "but come again when we restock."

"You can count on it."

"Me, too," said Leah as she came in and looked around. "Although I can't see how we can wear these outfits to cater in, Nancy." She laughed.

"I think mother and daughter might look pretty snazzy in these clothes as they ride together," Bill said, his eyes fixed affectionately on the wife he'd married as a youth, lost, and then found again. He turned to Kayla as she followed them into the shop. "We might even become the family that rides together. Would you like that, sweetie?"

"I sure would, Daddy; then when little Billy gets old enough, I can teach him, too."

Maggie Rose knew Bill and Leah's story and how through patience, effort, courage, and painful honesty they had rebuilt the relationship the years had torn apart.

Now they were a happy, fulfilled family.

On the surface it looked like a fairy-tale romance but she knew how difficult it had been for both Bill and Leah.

She wondered as she told them thanks and goodbye if she had the courage and honesty to achieve what they had accomplished.

Chapter
Fifteen

The truck with the marquee and the chairs had trundled down the lane. The horses had been put into their stalls, the office building locked, and the fragrance of steaks grilling over charcoal briquettes filled the air as everyone gathered on the back porch for dinner.

Chris went around pouring punch into everyone's glass, then raised his. "For a very successful opening with my heartfelt thanks to each one of you!" The click of glasses was followed by Tallie's "Dinner's ready."

Maggie Rose, tired but relaxed, watched contentedly as people crowded the grill to pick up the succulent steaks, corn on the cob, and baked potatoes. A mixed salad graced the middle of the table along with the large peach cobbler. It all added up to a carbohydrates, cholesterol glut but she didn't think anyone, including herself, was worried about it at this moment.

"Ready for some food?" Chris asked, dropping into the chair beside her. Today was the first time she'd seen him in his fawn breeches, tan shirt, and brown riding boots. He'd always been appealing but now he was positively handsome.

"I haven't had a chance to tell you how good you look," she said, "and yes, I think I'm ready for dinner." She began to stand but he put his hand on her arm.

"I'll get our plates and thanks for the compliments. Maybe we should have Bill take a 'his and hers outfits' photo for the shop," he said teasingly.

"I couldn't do that," she protested. "I'm not a model, I'm just an office manager."

"You think?" His soft, sultry words left her with a message that made her tingle as he went over to join the group at the grill.

With everyone seated and eating, the conversation turned to the afternoon's event.

"There were a lot more people this year and it was clear they were enjoying themselves. It was like a party."

"That includes the children," Alicia added.

"How'd it go in the clothes shop, Alicia? I meant to check it out but Dan and I were pretty busy at the stables." Jerlene's hand rested on Dan's thigh.

Does she know how that looks or does she care? Maggie Rose thought as she glanced at Covey, who was eating his dinner with enthusiasm. No one else seemed to be noticing. She guessed she was too much of a prude or maybe too repressed. A smile curved her lips as the notion came that she could be just plain jealous because she couldn't lay her hand on the thigh of the man sitting beside her.

". . . and at one time we could have used four dressing rooms," Alicia was saying. "We sold all of the breeches in sizes twelve and fourteen, a handful of the leather belts, a few pairs of boots, and some children's items." She sighed happily.

"Your friend Neda came to buy," Maggie Rose told Chris. "She said she's thinking of signing up for classes."

Before she could get his reaction Bill said, "If she does I'll be first in line to take her picture, set up the mounting block, and maybe even take lessons just so I can ride with her."

"You mean ride behind her?" Dan said with a straight face.

"This isn't men's night out, guys," Chris said mildly.

"She is spectacular," Janice observed. "All the women were eyeing her and whispering. I guess she's used to that."

Janice was petite and attractive in a fairylike way. What a pity that she couldn't appreciate her own porcelain-doll beauty. For all Maggie Rose knew, Neda might wish to be Janice's size.

"Do you think Neda will carry through on riding instruction? She took an application with her."

Chris shrugged. "I've no idea." Under the cover of someone's burst of laughter, he said softly, "But if she comes to class, she'll be just another student, Maggie Rose." His meaning was unmistakable but she knew that any man, faced with a Neda McCann on a regular basis, might succumb to that voluptuous temptation. A change of subject was needed.

"Covey, you were great in your exhibition. You've

only had a few lessons but you looked like you were born to ride a horse," she said.

"That's what I told him," Jerlene said complacently.

"You saw me, Aunt Maggie Rose?" The boy blushed with pleasure as others echoed the sentiment and Bill presented him with a photograph that emphasized his correct posture and the ecstatic expression on his face. "I'm glad you finally got to see him, he's wanted you to from the beginning," Chris said.

"Is he as naturally talented as he appears to be? I know that since he's been coming out here the horses are his consuming interest."

"If he keeps on as he's going, he'll likely outstrip the other children in a few months. He has an affinity with horses. I'll teach him all I can while he's here."

"Should we be paying for his lessons, Chris?" It hadn't occurred to her before and she was certain Jerlene hadn't offered.

He looked surprised. "Of course not. He's working here; plus he's your nephew."

And your son? The smile he gave her held no hint of self-consciousness.

He picked up her empty plate and slid it under his. "Dessert now or later?"

"Later," she said because she felt full, then wondered what later Chris meant.

"Bill, did you sell many pictures?" Chris asked.

"I sold every picture of the students and quite a few people in the crowd." He pulled a pile out of his jacket pocket and passed them around. "Here are the rest." They went from hand to hand eliciting comments and some laughter.

Mr. Tallie produced a stack of small paper plates and served the peach cobbler with a dip of vanilla ice cream.

"This is worth the whole afternoon's work." Ginnie sighed. "Your cooking is superb, Mr. Tallie."

The cobbler dish was emptied and the group sat around in the reluctance to move that follows a delicious meal. Eventually Ginnie said, "I've got to go but first I want to help clean up."

Despite protests from Mr. Tallie the others good-naturedly rose and did their part. By the time that was finished and the leftovers from Leah's kitchen distributed, the heat of the day had begun to diminish and dusk was moving in. They walked to the parking lot and to their cars with final good-byes to Chris and Maggie Rose, who were leaning against her car.

When Maggie Rose started to unlock the door, Chris said, "You can't go yet."

"Why not?"

"We haven't had our dessert."

"The dish was empty, Chris. I saw it."

"You saw the empty big dish. Tallie made a small one for us. Come on."

This time they sat side by side in lounge chairs on the front porch eating their cobbler with ice cream. Chris ate in deep contentment thinking of how many nights he'd yearned for just this, Maggie Rose beside him with night coming on.

"This is restful." Maggie Rose sighed, setting down her empty bowl and leaning back to watch the last of the daylight fade from the sky. "It's cooler now."

Chris put his dish down and settled back to let the same quiet he'd sought in the predawn hours come to repose in him now. The last few days had been stressful but now the summer season was launched.

"How do you think it went?" he murmured.

"It was a huge success, Chris. Have you any reason to doubt it?"

"As far as I could see it went well, but you were around more than I was."

"Did you see anyone you knew from the association?"

"No, and I was looking. Have you any idea how many strangers were here?"

"I know at least five invited guests who brought visitors with them. You can look at the guest list tomorrow and see if there are more. The only one I recall speaking with was Mr. Kimbel, who came with Mr. Neal from the bank."

"I'll also want to see the list of new students. Dan's dropping off his résumé tomorrow. I may use him this summer after I see him ride. What do you think of my adding him as a part-time instructor?"

"Who did you use last summer?"

"A college kid who'd done some riding but I don't know anyone here who's had the same experience Dan's had."

"Did you like his work today with the kids and the horses?"

"He was fine."

"Then I guess it's all right. Chris, I noticed no one spoke about Nicky."

"I was just going to tell you he got loose. How did you know about it?"

"I saw him in the parking lot and told the man to run and tell you."

"All he told me was the pony was in the parking lot and I assumed he'd seen her. How'd you come to be there?"

"I went to my car for something and noticed a movement among the cars; then I saw it was Nicky. I was afraid to alarm her so I ran to tell the attendant to get you."

"Thank God you did. You prevented a major disaster. Cars stacked closely together are confusing to horses and had she stayed there longer it would have been difficult to get her back calmly and in time for the small kids to ride her."

"How'd she get loose?"

"We don't know. A few guests had wandered down to the stable during the afternoon and we think one of them had carelessly or unknowingly slipped the latch. Since we were lucky enough to get her back soon, we agreed not to publish the incident."

"Next year you'll need a guard posted in the stables."

"Don't worry, Tallie and I had already made that promise."

"Chris, this may not be my business but as office manager I couldn't help noting how much all of this cost. You told me to use my discretion and I took you at your word but the checks I made out for you to sign really mounted up. Are you sure that's okay?" A little frown appeared on her face as she looked at him.

Her concern added still another layer to his feeling for her. No one had really cared about him, except Tallie, since Uncle Henry had died. He had to prevent himself from gathering her up in sheer gratitude.

"I knew this would cost a lot and I saved up ahead of time so I'd have the necessary funds." He took her hand, held it to his cheek, then kissed her palm.

"Thank you for caring, honey. It means a lot to me."

The moment shimmered with possibilities. Here she was, not twelve inches away. She'd been open to him all evening, had willingly returned to the house at his request. Suddenly possessed by his hunger to hold her, he scooped Maggie Rose up and deposited her beside him on his lounger.

"Chris, what are you doing?" she gasped.

"Shhh, honey, I'm just holding you." His voice was soft and tender as he made her comfortable and stroked her back. He didn't want to scare her and so he gentled her with soothing sounds and pats as he would with any thoroughbred until he felt her body begin to relax.

It was fully dark now. Maggie Rose thought if she could pinch herself she would to see if this was a dream. Surely she wasn't actually lying in Chris's arms in the lounger on his porch looking up at the same stars she looked at from her own window when she was yearning for Chris instead of sleeping.

At first she'd been startled but there was really nothing to fear, not with Chris, her hero since the ninth grade. He would always protect her even when he was upset with her.

"This is nice," she murmured.

"It certainly is," Chris responded. "And this is nicer." He turned her face to his and brushed her lips with a whisper of a kiss, back and forth, tantalizing and slow, waiting until she let him know she wanted more.

The signal was not long in coming. She made a little sound in her throat that drove him crazy but he locked on to his control.

His lips pressed hers more firmly and he let the tip of his tongue gently probe the corners of her mouth.

This was a part of kissing that Maggie Rose had never liked. It seemed such an invasion of privacy and it wasn't at all pleasant, just messy. But this was Chris. It would be different with him so she opened her mouth a little to see what it might be like.

She felt his tremor as she let him in and he delicately explored her mouth. The knowledge that she could have that effect on him emboldened her and she let her tongue touch his, timidly at first. She was astonished at the sensation it gave her so she moved closer and put her mind to doing some delicate exploration of her own.

Chris was in paradise. Whatever else was wrong with Maggie Rose he would bet his whole farm including his horses on the fact that she was not pregnant. Not only that, he was sure she was essentially untouched. Only a consummate actress could respond as she was doing, with hesitation and heart-rending tentativeness to lovemaking. He would have to go very, very slowly because what he wanted above everything was her wholehearted trust and commitment as their relationship developed.

That was why, with a final lingering kiss, he reluctantly let her go.

"It's getting late, sweetheart. Do you want me to drive you home?"

Maggie Rose had to think about the question. She felt dazed and surreptitiously licked her lips as Chris helped her to her feet.

"I can drive but I wouldn't mind your following me," she said shyly.

She was thankful she had him behind her on the road home. She felt as if she'd drunk one too many flutes of the finest champagne and had to drive very carefully.

Chris, on his way back, remembered the other thing he'd meant to tell her but had totally forgotten once he started kissing her.

It would hold until tomorrow.

Chapter Sixteen

Chris Shealy had to laugh at himself. Here he was like the stereotypical man in the shower singing his heart out about a beautiful day. He didn't care. He'd slept like a baby straight through the night for the first time in a week with the image of Maggie Rose in his arms his final memory before he closed his eyes and his first one when he opened them this morning.

He couldn't keep his joy to himself. Had to share it with his horses as he cared for them and praised them for their performances the previous day.

"You're going to like Maggie Rose," he told silvery gray Starlight, who nudged him in reply. "I wouldn't be surprised if you turn out to be her favorite," he whispered to Windsong. "You're so much alike."

Tallie gave him a comprehensive look as they sat

down to breakfast. "What pot of gold did you find?" he asked.

"None, yet, just the rainbow in the sky." He grinned at Tallie. "As if you didn't know."

Tallie grunted. "Your pot of gold is there, son, just you keep your eye on that rainbow no matter what clouds may come." His eyes underscored his affectionate message.

"Thanks, Tallie." Chris knew he'd received Tallie's blessing.

Chris changed into his office clothes and went to meet Maggie Rose at the office. He wondered how she'd be this morning after the kisses they'd shared last night. Probably a little shy and worrying about mixing up the personal side of their relationship with the business side. He intended not to mix them up so she could be at ease. It wouldn't be hard to keep himself calm in her presence now that he was settled in his own mind about her physical condition. When he arrived in the office she was watering her plants and looking so wholesome and sweet in her simple white dress and sandals it was all he could do not to resume where he'd left off last night.

"Morning, Maggie Rose," he said cheerfully. "Hope you're rested after the great job you did yesterday."

A faint blush stained her cheek as she looked at him with a warm smile. "Good morning. I am rested. How about you?"

"Fine. In case I didn't say it yesterday, I want you to understand how much I appreciate the tremendous work you did to make the opening a success. Words, as they say, are cheap so here's a little something to go along with the words."

"You didn't have to do this," she protested as he put a folded check in her hand. When she saw it was for five hundred dollars she tried to give it back. "I was just doing the job you hired me for, Chris."

"True, but you did it in an extraordinary fashion. You thought up the logo, the use of a marquee, and resolving the last-minute problem about it. You resurrected the shop, which led to selling all of those clothes. You made sure all went well yesterday and especially by your quick action about Nicky prevented the ruining of the program. That bonus is only a small token of my gratitude and respect for your abilities."

He went on, "Come on and sit down. Before I go in to work I need to tell you something else that happened yesterday. When I ran up to my bedroom just before dinner I thought something was out of place but I was in a hurry because dinner was waiting. After I came home from following your car and went up again, I took time for a careful inspection. Someone had gone through all of my drawers and my closet."

Her eyes widened in shock. "How can you be sure, Chris? Was something stolen?"

"Nothing was stolen but I keep my drawers very orderly and it was clear they had been disturbed. Especially the papers in the desk; they'd been shuffled as if someone was in a hurry to look through them."

"The front door was locked, Chris, I know. What about the kitchen door?"

"It was probably unlocked because Tallie went to the house once or twice. It didn't occur to us that anyone would try to get into the house that way."

"Someone sneaked into the house, went up to your room, and hurriedly looked through your belongings yet didn't take anything. No money missing?"

"I never keep loose money in my room and no, nothing is missing."

"What do you think they were looking for, Chris?"

"I really have no idea, Maggie Rose. It's a mystery to me." He glanced at the clock. "I have to go but I'll see you before you leave this afternoon."

After Chris left, Maggie Rose worked on the pile of completed applications. David and Emily Walker had enrolled their twelve-year-old son, Davey. Susie Hill, eleven, Alberta Barnhill, eleven, Jess Croker, thirteen and Liyah Smalls, seven, would all have to be fit into existing classes. They wanted to start immediately. She sketched out a possible schedule for Chris to consider. To fit them all in plus three adults and other possibles Chris would have to teach six evenings plus hire Dan.

Throughout the day the matter of the person who searched Chris's room stayed in her mind but she didn't have a chance to discuss her idea with him as he called to say he had to stay late at the corporate office.

"Chris, I'm really worried about the search," she said as soon as he came into the office Tuesday morning.

"Maybe it was just one of the kids," he said.

"I don't think so. A kid would probably take something; otherwise why go into your bedroom?

I think we need to look at this from a different angle."

Chris looked intrigued. "What angle, Maggie Rose?"

"When I was spending some time with the data cards from your office it occurred to me that maybe there was a connection."

"Between the search in that office and the search in my bedroom?"

"That's what I mean, and if you add how Nicky got loose Sunday, that makes three incidents that might be orchestrated by someone who wants to disrupt your affairs."

Now that she had put it into words, Maggie Rose wasn't sure it made as much sense to Chris as it made to her. There was very little evidence but she was sure of it because no other explanation made sense.

"But why? What would someone gain by upsetting the files, letting a horse run loose, and rifling my room?" Chris wasn't convinced. "Couldn't these be random events?"

"I guess they could but the two things that happened right here in the same afternoon don't seem random to me." She leaned toward him in her earnestness. "Do you really think they have no connection at all?" Her eyes held his and she saw him begin to consider her idea.

"For the sake of argument, say there is a connection," he said. "What's the reason, the goal?"

"To answer that, I have to ask you a question. Do you have an enemy?"

"An enemy?" he echoed in surprise. "Not that I know of." He smiled. "You know me pretty well and you know this town we both grew up in. Do you think I have an enemy?"

She had to say a reluctant no because Chris Shealy was a well-liked person in town. However, he might have made an enemy if he'd been too friendly with a woman and a man in her life took it the wrong way. She debated how she could say that tactfully.

"Uh, Chris, I don't mean to be too personal but, well . . ."

"You're wondering if I overstepped some lines with a woman," he interrupted, his eyes full of amusement. "I consider married or attached ladies off limits, so I've never had a man after me. Other friendships were always mutual and pleasantly ended. Does that answer your question?" His eyes were steady and serious now.

She nodded, too embarrassed to speak.

She took a manila envelope from her desk and handed it to him. "This is your copy of the people who signed the guest register Sunday. You wanted to see the names of people you don't know. One of them might be from the association."

"Thanks, I'll look it over and also the schedule you made."

"Keep in mind, Chris, that whoever searched your room and let Nicky out should be on that list."

When the man answered the phone the woman asked, "Were you able to carry out your plan?"

"One part of it. The other part started out okay but that nosy woman from the office got in the way."

"There wasn't anything you could do about it?"

"Not a blasted thing. I'll have to plan something else."

"See that you do and try to make it work this time."

Maggie Rose had learned a valuable lesson Sunday. On Wednesday she decided to put it into practice when Covey said Mr. Tallie was going to take him to see the old orchard and maybe pick some apples.

"I didn't know there was an orchard. Did you, Aunt Maggie Rose? I'll bet there's a lot more to this farm that you and I don't know, but before I have to go back to school I'm going to try to get Mr.Tallie to show me all of it. He said Mr. Chris loves to ride over it. Boy, I wish I could. Would you like to see it all?"

"Yes, I would." It was hard to remember how quiet Covey used to be. He began talking as soon as he got into the car now and his conversation was almost exclusively about the farm.

While Mr. Tallie and Covey went to the orchard she went to the stable after ingesting half a tranquilizer. She had seen the stalls briefly when Chris first showed her the farm but she'd managed to stay only a few moments by going into a hard coughing and sneezing spell ostensibly brought on by allergies.

This time, with the excuse of making an inventory, she intended to see if she could stay calm in the horses' environment without their actual presence. If she could, it might be the beginning of her control over her panic reaction.

She stepped through the central door. There were five stalls to the right and four on the left not yet occupied, Chris had said. She began walking slowly down the aisle to the farthest stall on the right. So far so good. At the end of the aisle she began to make notes on her pad. Outside each stall was a hook for hanging halters and lead ropes. She had just noted those when she heard a noise and looked up.

Tallie stood in the door with Chica, his back to Maggie Rose. "Put the bag of apples in the kitchen, Covey. I'll be in as soon as I take care of Chica. She needs a little rubdown after carrying both of us to the orchard and back."

Maggie Rose backed as far as she could into the fifth stall. She couldn't draw a deep breath, perspiration dampened her, and the nerves in her stomach began to tighten. She slid to the floor as her legs lost their strength and dizziness overtook her.

Don't let him see me, was her last conscious thought.

Maggie Rose didn't know how long she'd been out when she opened her eyes. Why was she lying on straw? she wondered, as she tried to get her bearings. Chica and Mr. Tallie! They must have been in the first or second stall while she had hidden herself in the fifth one, thus escaping detection.

She sat up, testing her stomach, then stood up slowly. She had to get out of here.

Brushing a couple of pieces of straw from her pants, she retrieved her pad and went to the door. No one was visible as she walked back to the office, her inventory story ready if Covey or Mr. Tallie had seen her.

So much for that lesson. The atmosphere of the stables could be borne with the help of half a tranquilizer but she still had to go the whole distance when it came to being near a horse. Tomorrow she was to see Dr. Moore. Maybe he could help her. She doubted that he could but she was becoming desperate enough to try.

Chapter
Seventeen

No matter what time your appointment was, waiting was always part of the game in Dr. Moore's office. Maggie Rose supposed this was because he was a popular family physician who took his time with each patient. He was not part of an HMO and seemed to know most people in town. He'd been starting out when she was a child and was now about the age of her father. She hadn't seen him for two years but had persuaded herself to tell him the whole story. Somehow she had to make a beginning on this obstacle to her health.

When the nurse called her in for the preliminary work, Maggie Rose was surprised to find not only that she'd lost five pounds but also that her blood pressure was on the low side.

Dr. Moore greeted her with outstretched hand and a warm smile. "I heard you'd come home to stay, Maggie Rose. Got tired of all that cold weather, did you?"

"It was more that I got tired of being away from home," she answered.

"Now that you're here maybe you can help me persuade your dad to take more exercise," he said as he opened her folder. "I see your weight and your blood pressure are a little down. What have you been doing? Working too hard and not eating properly?"

"I'm afraid so," she admitted.

"And I suspect you've been under stress, too, haven't you?"

She nodded assent. His kindly tone and concern had made a lump in her throat and she realized how much emotional weight she'd been carrying that she couldn't share.

"Tell me about it, Maggie Rose," Dr. Moore said.

"I'm working as an office manager for a man who runs a riding stable. I'll have been there three weeks tomorrow. I love the job and he's very pleased with how I run the office." She paused, wondering how to go on. She had never confided in anyone the full extent of what had happened and how she felt. She was almost afraid to do so now because she didn't want to remember. Yet if she failed to tell Dr. Moore, how could she get the assistance she not only needed but wanted now with all her heart?

"Maggie Rose, I'm your doctor. You know you can tell me anything and it stays right here between you and me. What is it about your job that's so troublesome for you?"

His calm voice and specific question made it easier for her to answer.

"I go into a panic every time I'm near a horse. In the time I've been there I've had four such episodes and my employer insisted I see my doctor to find out why, as he said, I'm sick so often. I didn't tell him about how I feel when he offered me the job because I needed the job so badly and I thought I could manage to stay away from the horses since I work in the office but it hasn't turned out that way. I don't want to lose the job and I'm ashamed to tell him now because he'll know I wasn't altogether honest with him when I took the job." She could feel herself blushing and she couldn't look Dr. Moore in the eye.

"What is it about horses that causes you such anxiety?"

"When I was thirteen I was watching my girl-friend Shana, who was also thirteen, riding her horse. She was showing off a little, riding with one hand. A rattlesnake struck at the horse's leg, scared him. He reared up, twisted, and flung Shana into a tree with such force it broke her neck." She told the story briefly, rapidly.

"What an awful thing to happen! You were thirteen, now you're thirty. How many attacks have you had in these seventeen years?" Dr. Moore asked.

"I had several until I learned to avoid movies that had horses in them, and twice when I was at a parade and horses came close by. So I don't go to parades anymore. I had no more until I began this job." Now she could speak at a normal pace. Thank God she'd gotten through it.

"Maggie Rose, the first thing I want you to understand is that you can conquer this."

Dare she believe him? She wanted to with everything that was in her but look at how she'd fainted just yesterday. The attacks were getting stronger each time.

"I know it's hard for you to believe now because you've had such a rough three weeks but you can beat this, Maggie Rose, if you're willing to work hard at it."

He didn't raise his voice but the authority and firmness in it deepened. *He's so sure,* she thought, *and he's had the experience with other people, so perhaps there is hope for me.*

"What do I have to do?" she asked.

"Let me explain what takes place physically first. You see a horse. But in reality you're not seeing that horse, because horse to you means the still vivid image of Shana's horse killing her. That image represents danger so your body prepares itself for fight or flight. Chemicals pour into your bloodstream, especially adrenaline. Your pulse races, your heartbeat soars, and your lungs can't get enough air and therefore you get dizzy. Your nerves are excessively revved up so your stomach suffers. Sound familiar?" His eyes twinkled, inviting her to relax now.

"All too familiar," she gasped.

"People express these symptoms in various ways. What happens to you?"

"Heavy perspiration, can't get a deep breath, dizziness, and retching. Yesterday I fainted."

"One of the reasons the prognosis is good in your case is that you know precisely what triggered the trauma. That helps considerably as you can understand. You're not fighting an unknown."

She hadn't thought of it that way and for the first time she began to let herself hope.

"What do I have to do, Dr. Moore?"

He took out his prescription pad. "You need a little building up physically," he said as he wrote. "One is for your blood and one for your stomach. We don't want you developing ulcers." He tore them off the pad and handed them to her.

"We're going to approach this from every possible angle. I'll give you material to read about these attacks. I want you to begin yoga classes immediately and practice religiously every morning before you go to work. The stretching, flowing movements it involves teaches you how to control your body when it wants to go into the fight/flight mode. Correct breathing is vital; see if you can find a breathing coach at least for now. Then as soon as you can, begin looking at pictures of horses. After that look at them on television. Then get a video of a movie with horses. If necessary, do some yoga exercises and your deep breathing while watching it. When you feel ready to test yourself with live horses my suggestion would be not to use one where you work in case you find you're not quite ready. Find one someplace else. Come see me again in two weeks."

Maggie Rose left the doctor's office feeling lightheaded. The depression she'd battled especially since her fainting spell yesterday was gone. Dr. Moore's analysis of her condition and what she herself could do about it made sense to her intellectually. It remained to be seen if the emotional part of the equation would lend itself to a successful resolution, but she was going to give it her best effort.

She had tucked the precious moments with Chris Sunday night in the back of her mind. She could not afford to let herself dwell on them as long as she withheld from him this problem with horses. She knew with a certainty he would feel it was a betrayal of trust. That was how she would feel if he hid a vital fact from her.

Friday morning when Chris came into the office, she told him at once what she could of her visit to the doctor. "Dr. Moore said I had lost five pounds and my blood pressure was on the low side, that I should take yoga plus the prescriptions he gave me to relieve stress."

"Are you working too many hours? I know you do work for the Mailroom after you leave here." His voice was anxious. "Maybe we should cut your time here."

"Absolutely not, Chris. There's nothing essentially wrong with me that more rest and the other things he said won't fix. I think I might have been too wrapped up in getting ready for the opening, that's all."

"You're sure?" He searched her eyes.

"I'm sure."

He would not kiss her but he had to hold her just for a moment, his sense of relief was so great. They stood quietly just holding each other.

"I'll see you this afternoon," he said with a sweet smile.

I can't let him down. I will succeed, she vowed as she looked from the shop window in the distance where the horses nibbled at the grass and she thought of the day when she wouldn't have to see them from the shelter of a building.

Chapter
Eighteen

It had been hot as blazes all day and all Chris wanted to do was take off his sticky shirt, douse his head and neck in cold water, stretch out in the shade, and drink about a gallon of Tallie's excellent lemonade from an ice-filled glass.

This was not how he had envisioned spending Saturday evening. When Maggie Rose had told him yesterday morning what her doctor said, he had been filled with joy he couldn't express to her since she didn't know he'd thought she might be pregnant. All day at work that joy had bubbled up in him. When he got back to the office he asked her out to dinner. In his mind the event needed celebration.

Maggie Rose looked disappointed. "I'm sorry, Chris. I'd love to go but I'm spending several hours this evening with a yoga instructor."

He had to admire her quick action in implement-

ing the doctor's order but it didn't prevent him
from feeling let down.

"How about Saturday?"

"Ginnie and I will be in Columbia Saturday and
part of Sunday. I don't know when we're getting
back," she said ruefully.

This was only Friday afternoon, and he couldn't
see her again until Monday when she came back to
work? Why did she have to be so busy all weekend?

Didn't she know how much he needed to hold
her, how much he needed to be held by her? He
hungered for the sweet intimacy that had begun
to develop between them Sunday night.

He saw that she was looking at him uncertainly,
so his dismay must be showing in his expression.
"I can't help but be disappointed, honey," he said
as he took her hand and caressed it, "but I understand. Will you call me when you get home
Sunday?"

She promised she would and with that he had
to be satisfied, but fixed in his mind all through
his busy day Saturday was the way her hands felt
on his face, the daze in her eyes after they kissed,
the soft texture of her mouth, and the way she felt
so right in his arms.

If he could go to her now it would relieve the
tiredness he felt. He stretched again, rolling his
shoulders and thinking he'd have to stand under
the shower a long time tonight. The opening last
Sunday had been almost too successful. He now
had ten additional students with more applications
still out. It was a good thing Dan Montgomery
had turned up, but the serious consideration of
a permanent assistant might be needed. Now his
schedule was so tight he had no leisure to ramble

over his land on HS and he still hadn't taken Maggie Rose to talk to the horses. But that could wait until his workload eased a little. She seemed to know them anyway as far as she needed to in answering questions prospective students asked.

When he finally got into bed he went right to sleep. The surfeit of lemonade awakened him in the middle of the night. As he returned to bed the sound of an engine drifted through his open window. Curiously he looked out and saw a vehicle moving almost soundlessly and without lights down his lane toward the road.

He stuck feet in shoes, grabbed a flashlight, raced down the stairs and out the front door, but he was too late. The car had disappeared down the highway.

Maggie Rose had told him he had an enemy and maybe she was right. If so, where could an enemy do the most damage? To his horses, of course, especially in the dark of night when there was no one to protect them.

Filled with apprehension, Chris turned and raced to the stable with a jumbled prayer that the horses were undamaged. He pulled the big door open and turned on the light. The horses were awake, moving restlessly in their stalls, smelling the same wisps of smoke that assailed his nostrils.

Chris looked around wildly. He couldn't see the fire, he could only smell it. He looked in each of the five stalls. No fire. He started down the other four and in the next to the last one a pile of rags was smoldering on the concrete floor. The fire hadn't taken a good hold yet. He grabbed the fire extinguisher from the wall and used its contents on the rags. He started to kick them apart after the smoke disappeared, then stopped. This needed to be reported to the sheriff's office. He made a note of the time, two-twenty A.M.

One by one he calmed the horses, stroking and talking to each one until they were quiet. Next he called Tallie on the intercom and asked him to come to the stables.

Tallie hurried through the door a few minutes later, clad only in jeans and shoes. "What's the matter?" he asked in alarm.

"Someone tried to start a fire here." Chris showed Tallie the rags and recounted how hearing the car in the lane had alerted him to look at the horses.

"Who'd do a thing like that?" Tallie asked. Fire was the greatest danger to a stable and it was unthinkable in Tallie's mind to deliberately set one. "You going to report it?"

"First thing in the morning. Maggie Rose thinks I have an enemy, Tallie, and now I have to agree with her." He related the break-in at the office, the letting loose of Nicky, and the search of his bedroom.

"I didn't know about any of this except Nicky," Tallie said accusingly.

"The things that happened didn't seem worth mentioning. Tell you the truth, I wouldn't have connected them at all, and Maggie Rose did. I wasn't at all sure that she wasn't being imaginative." His jaw was set, his eyes furious. "This fire is no imagination and I'm going to find out who set it no matter what it takes."

"You can go back to bed since you have a few students tomorrow. I'll take first shift," Tallie said.

"Thanks, but there's no way I can sleep."

"Me neither." Tallie upended two buckets for seats. "Something strike you odd about this fire, Chris?" he said after they'd sat awhile.

"You mean the way it was set so far away from the horses?"

"Yeah, as if it wasn't meant to burn them but to burn this end of the stable, which would set off the fire alarm and maybe give us time to get the horses out."

"They were already restless with the first smell of smoke and if I hadn't come when I did, they would have been crazy with the smoke and the heat even if the flames hadn't actually reached them."

"You and I know that but maybe the person who did this doesn't know it."

Chris looked at Tallie in disbelief. "If he doesn't know about horses, why was he in the stables in the first place? He could've done something to the house. He knows about horses and whoever it is, he knows the horses mean more to me than the house." He was absolutely certain of this.

Sheriff Bob Snipes wasn't certain later that morning about anything except the fire. That he could see. The evidence was in front of him and as he examined the rags and sniffed the kerosene he agreed that this was not set to cause an immediate conflagration.

"I heard you had a lot of people here Sunday, Chris. How'd it go?"

They were at the kitchen table drinking coffee while Chris wrote a statement about what happened. Twenty years in office had given Bob Snipes a thorough knowledge of the families in his county.

A thin, energetic man in khakis, he assessed Henry Shealy's nephew.

"Better than I thought it would. My new office manager is very good at organization and we had almost one hundred twenty here for the opening of the summer season." He finished the statement, signed, and dated it, then handed it to the deputy who accompanied the sheriff.

"Anything happen that day to make some youngster or someone else want to get back at you?"

"Everything went smoothly. It's like I told you, Sheriff, we think someone came with the idea of creating trouble. He searched my bedroom and let the pony loose just when it was time to begin the program."

"You've no idea who might be doing these things?"

Chris knew Snipes was thinking of those years when "that wild Shealy boy" was how people knew him. He wondered if he would ever live that period down. There was no defiance in his response, only a firm resolve. "I can't figure out who has it in for me, nor why, but I do intend to find out."

"Just remember not to take the law into your own hands when you find out, Chris," Snipes warned as he took his leave.

His first Sunday student was due in an hour, which gave Chris time to shower and to call the security company he used for the apartments.

"Clayton, this is Chris. Someone set a little fire in my stable last night but I caught it before it could do any damage. I'm going to need a good man here at night from ten until six. Who can you send starting tonight?"

Arrangements were made for Art Fulton to come

on duty that night and work until further notice. With his mind at ease on that score, Chris took care of his three Sunday students.

He'd persuaded Tallie to go into town for his usual Sunday visit to see Miss Hester Mack, the lady he'd been courting for the past two years.

"I won't stay long," Tallie said.

"Take your time," Chris told him. "I'll be right here."

Tallie always said he wasn't courting Miss Hester, they just enjoyed each other's company. Now as he sat on the porch watching the horses in the front pasture, Chris wished with all his heart that he could say he was courting. Courting Magnolia Rose Sanders.

He longed for her company. Longed to tell her every single thing that had happened, to share all of his thoughts with her. Even if his earlier days of disregard for convention still tinged her opinion of him. Even if, heaven help him, she had been pregnant, he still would have wanted to share his thoughts with her. No one else made his loneliness go away. No one else engaged his trust as she did. With her he could feel at peace.

Tallie returned and sat on the porch as Chris explained about the security guard.

"You didn't have to go to that expense," Tallie said. "I could've taken the night shift."

"I know you're willing and so am I, but realistically both of us are needed to be alert and watchful during the daylight hours."

"Humph!" was Tallie's response. "You hungry?" he asked after a moment.

"I could eat a little something," Chris admitted.

Chris was back on the porch later looking at the stallion ads when the phone rang.

"Chris, I just got back," Maggie Rose said.

His heart leaped at the sound of her voice. "May I come over for a little while?"

"Please do," she said softly.

Twenty minutes later he rang her doorbell, a tight leash on his emotions to prevent him from overwhelming her with his hunger.

Maggie Rose opened the door wide and stood back. "Hi," she said, then spoke into the next room. "Covey, here's Mr. Chris now."

Chris, disappointed, picked up on her signal that they weren't alone. "Hi," he responded and said a silent prayer that Covey and Mrs. Sanders, whom he greeted, would not stay long. Not that he didn't like Maggie Rose's mother, she'd always been very nice to him and had made him feel welcome in her house during his high school years. It was Mr. Sanders who didn't hide his disapproval of Chris.

All of the conversation was about last Sunday's opening. "I've been telling Maggie Rose and Covey what a wonderful event it was and how hard you all must have worked to put it together," Mrs. Sanders said.

"It was mostly Maggie Rose." Chris smiled.

"But what you've done to the whole place! I was very impressed, Chris."

She rose to her feet. "We have to go, Covey. We just stopped by for a minute on our way home."

Chris accompanied Maggie Rose of to the door to see them off, thankful that Mrs. Sanders was not a dithering type of woman. "Nice to see you, Chris. Maggie Rose, I'll call you. Good night." She ushered Covey in front of her and walked away.

Maggie Rose walked into his arms. "Chris," she murmured.

There were no words for Chris to say. All he could do was hold on while Maggie Rose's arms tightened around him. This was what he wanted, this was the sanctuary he craved. The tension of the day began to dissipate as he drew a deep breath.

"Come sit down, Chris, and tell me what's wrong," she said, leading him to the sofa. "You've got shadows under your eyes and you're strung up tight as a bow." Her fingers stroked the flesh under his eyes as if she could wipe away the signs of weariness.

He took her hands in his. "Someone started a fire in the stables last night."

A look of horror came over her face. "The horses?"

"They're all okay."

"Thank God!" She gripped his hands as he told her the entire story.

When he'd finished she put her arms around him again. "I'm so sorry, Chris. Your precious horses. You must have suffered just thinking of what might have happened if you hadn't reached there as soon as you did." She patted and stroked, comforting him as best she could.

"You were right about an enemy," he said.

"I'm sorry to say it seems so. Did you call the police?"

"The sheriff's office. Sheriff Snipes came and I told him the whole story, but I don't know if he saw the connection you proposed, because there's no evidence like there is with the fire. But I wrote all the incidents down in my statement so it is on record."

"I don't see how he could miss it. The fire proves it as far as I'm concerned. What are you going to do about protecting the horses?"

"I've hired a security guard who'll be there every night. In fact I'll have to go soon to be there when he gets started."

"Mr. Tallie's there now, isn't he?"

"Ummm." Chris inhaled the scent of her. "You smell so good. I haven't even told you how good you look in that blue dress and I haven't asked how your weekend in Columbia went." He punctuated his words with little soft kisses on her face and neck.

She got as far as "It went . . ." when his lips came down on hers. This was what he wanted, the honeyed sweetness that was his Maggie Rose, unique to her and unlike any other female he'd ever kissed.

The tip of her tongue brushed his lips, sending a bolt of sensation through him as he opened to her. Alarm bells went off in the back of his consciousness. He knew his resistance was too low tonight to deal with that compelling influence.

He brought her to her feet for one more deep kiss before loosening his embrace.

"If I don't leave now . . ." he said.

"Yes, leave now," she murmured, still holding him, her face flushed. "Be careful, Chris," she said, walking with him to the door.

"I'll be careful." He hated to let her go.

She raised her face to him before she opened the door. "Good night, Chris."

"Good night, sweetheart." He kissed her quickly and left while he could.

Chapter Nineteen

Calmness. Relaxation. Correct breathing. Maggie Rose kept these in mind while following the instruction of the yoga video she'd purchased from Rama Singh at the end of the evening class on Friday. She'd explained that her work schedule prohibited her from joining a class but she urgently needed to learn yoga as soon as possible. Rama Singh had smiled kindly and told her yoga was a way of thinking, breathing, meditation, spirituality, and physical exercise. It was not something to be learned fast in the typical American way. Learned fast and discarded fast.

At the end of the three-hour session, Maggie Rose had a better understanding and respect for the discipline. She rose at five Saturday morning and did the best she could to follow the instructions for the beginner. She did the same on Sunday in the hotel room with Ginnie watching admiringly.

This morning she put in almost two hours and when she was finished she felt energized, her mind alert, her muscles loosened and more fluid. She had not permitted herself to think of Chris's visit last night; it would have destroyed the focus and concentration she needed for the yoga.

But now as she showered and dressed, she let the emotions she'd felt last night flow through her. She'd called to tell Chris she was back only because she'd promised to do so. His eagerness to come over had surprised her but her first glance at him as she opened her door told her something stressful had happened. Thank goodness her mother's unannounced visit had ended quickly.

When he told her about the fire she felt her heart contract. Suppose it had been the house and he hadn't been able to escape! She knew that was not his first thought. He might never recover if his precious horses had died in the fire. The horror of what that would mean to him made her want to comfort him. He had let her hold him as she prayed he would never in his life have to know that particular pain.

Yet who knew what might happen if they couldn't find out who wished him harm? What might that person do next? Perhaps attack Chris himself. That would be harder to do now that Chris and Mr. Tallie, as well as the sheriff's office had been alerted to that possibility. She hoped the security guard would also be alert at night, not sleeping on the job. She intended to talk with Chris about that.

At her closet she selected a light brown linen dress she'd bought recently, held it in front of her at the mirror, and wondered if Chris would like it. She closed her eyes remembering how he'd cov-

ered her face and neck with kisses. He'd asked her
a question about her weekend but kissed her lips
before she got the third word out, which was just
as well. She didn't know what she was saying, she
only knew what she was feeling. All those lovely
sliding sensations inside her and the little shivers
that went up and down her body whenever he
touched her.

They had made her want to touch his tongue
again and when she did she felt him almost jump.
A minute later he had said he had to go so he
could meet the new security guard, but she knew
he didn't want to let go of her any more than she
wanted to let go of him.

Maggie Rose came to herself. How long had she
been standing in front of the mirror with that
dreamy look on her face? She'd be late now if she
didn't hurry. The dress was enhanced by her earth-
tone glass beads and earrings, plus a pair of woven
leather sandals. She hurried but the echo of Chris
calling her "sweetheart" when he said good night
kept a smile on her face so that Covey remarked,
"You look happy today, Aunt Maggie Rose," when
he got into the car.

Chris would want to show her where the fire
occurred and she intended to draw on what she
had learned from yoga to see her through it. She
felt in her purse to be certain her pillbox was there.
Just in case.

Chris came in ten minutes after she arrived. In
his summer-weight navy slacks, short-sleeved white
shirt that was open at the neck, and brown loafers,
he looked relaxed and cool. He came through the
door quickly as if, she thought, he couldn't wait

to get there, making her wonder if he was as anxious to see her as she was to see him.

He came right over and knelt beside her desk chair so he was on her eye level.

"Hey, Chris," she breathed.

"There's something you need to know, Maggie Rose. Because this is an office in which we work together, and because someone might come in at any moment, I'm going to try my best not to touch you during business hours. Okay?"

"I understand."

"There's something else you need to know. It's not because I don't want to touch you. Right now I want to hold you and kiss you in the worst way . . ." His voice trailed off as Maggie Rose, mesmerized by his nearness and the beat of her blood in her ears, leaned just a little until she could lay her mouth on his. He was all male, firm, supple, and warm, his mouth a magnet she didn't know how to resist.

With a stifled groan he cupped her face gently and returned her kiss before he stood and walked over to look out the window.

Into the silence, Maggie Rose found her voice to say, "I'm sorry, Chris, I don't know what came over me." She felt flushed all over and didn't know where to look as Chris turned from the window. This time he sat in his usual chair on the other side of the desk.

"Maggie Rose, look at me," he said gently and waited until she met his eyes. "I don't want any apology because you wanted to kiss me just as I wanted to kiss you. I'm delighted, honey. But I guess we both see the problem this could be, right?"

Maggie Rose nodded. She was so embarrassed.

Couldn't she make a better response than that? Of course she could, this was Chris. She flashed a big smile at him, batted her eyelashes, and said, "I always knew you'd be a problem to me one day, Chris Shealy."

For a second he looked surprised; then he gave a shout of laughter. He looked at the wall clock behind her as he stood up. "I want to show you where the fire was."

"Okay," she said, walking out beside him. "I wanted to ask you about the security guard. Did he work out all right?"

"He said he didn't see or hear anything. He patrolled the house and stables every hour. His name is Art Fulton."

"Is he the kind of man who won't slip off to sleep, Chris? That's what worries me. The night hours are quiet, and dark. I'd imagine it's almost irresistible to let your eyes close."

"He likes night work, sleeps in the day. Brings his coffee and a radio with an earplug. Brings his cat, too, which is okay since we don't have a dog."

Stay calm, breathe deeply. Let your muscles relax. Good. You're doing very well. Keep the deep breathing going while he walks you to the stalls where the horses live. Relax. Fine. Breathe, good. Now you're leaving and you're all right.

Maggie Rose was overjoyed. She'd done it! Of course, there weren't any horses in the stables, but this was a first step.

At home that evening she put in another solid hour of yoga and another on Tuesday morning before work.

"Morning, Maggie Rose." The words were formal but the look in Chris's eyes gave another message entirely.

"Good morning. Another hot day," she replied in the same vein.

"I looked over the list you gave me of the guests on Sunday. I would like to have some time to discuss it with you at length but I'm off to work now. Could you possibly have dinner with me tonight after classes are over?"

She thought of the appointment she had with Ginnie but she didn't want to tell him no again, especially when his body language revealed tension as he awaited her answer.

"Could we make it eight o'clock?" she asked, and saw him expel a breath and relax.

"I'll pick you up then and thanks, Maggie Rose."

A few more applications had drifted in and Maggie Rose worked them into the schedule. She made a note to discuss this with Chris. Maybe tonight since this was ostensibly a "business" dinner. He was already teaching six days. He tried to give people their preferences but she wondered how long he could keep this up; it pushed him too much, even with Dan helping. She worked on the cards and thought of what to do with the shop.

But underlying all of this, she thought about Chris Shealy. What was taking place was totally new to her. Her experience with men had been limited and disconnected. She liked men but had never learned how to be easy and comfortable with them except in groups. When someone made a move toward her in a personal way, she shied off and her invisible barriers came up. Afraid to embarrass or humiliate herself in a one-to-one relationship, she pretended disinterest.

Since she saw nothing in her mirror to persuade her that a man would pursue her for herself, she could talk herself out of believing that the ones who asked for a second or third date were attracted to her, Maggie Rose, because they found her interesting.

At a dinner party in Hartford she had met Lem Norris from Baltimore, who was visiting a cousin with the idea of relocating to Hartford. He had made a dead set for Maggie Rose, disregarding the other single women who were trying to attract his attention. He had ignored her barriers and overswept her show of disinterest. Slowly she had allowed herself to enter into a regular pattern of spending most of her free time with him.

"So you finally have a relationship," Ginnie had said when they were discussing their social life over the telephone.

"Exactly what does a relationship mean?" Maggie Rose had been cautious.

"Spending most of your time together instead of going out with other people."

"We go out with the group sometimes," Maggie Rose said. "They call us a couple."

"Also," Ginnie went on, "a relationship usually implies intimacy."

After a moment, Maggie Rose asked, "How much intimacy?"

Ginnie laughed. "Come on, girl, we're both grown. You know just what I mean."

"Then this is not that kind of relationship," Maggie Rose had said unequivocally.

Lem was witty, generous, and very persistent, as the days went on, about what Maggie Rose called "the intimacy." He was a physically attractive man, clean in his personal habits as far as she could tell, and very entertaining. She had let herself relax with him but the intimacy he wanted did not draw her. His kisses were nice and they danced well together. Perhaps, she thought, she should give it a try? How would she know how nice they could be together if she never let herself find out?

One Saturday night she'd gone to his apartment for dinner. He'd made it very plain that he hoped she would spend the night with him. "I've even put satin sheets on the bed," he'd teased.

She'd almost made up her mind to accept the invitation and in her large bag had stuffed items she thought she might need. There was no answer as she rang the bell to get into the complex. She tried three times but still no answer. As she was turning to leave, Lem's cousin drove up, jumped out of his car, and ran up the steps to her.

"I'm glad I caught you," he panted. "Lem just called me."

"He called you? Where is he?"

"Come get in the car and I'll take you home," Harold said.

When they were in the car and Harold had backed out of the driveway, he answered her question. "Lem called me from Baltimore."

"Why is he in Baltimore, what happened?" Maggie Rose couldn't believe what Harold had said.

"There's no way to make this easy, Maggie Rose. His wife called last night and told him she was ready to take him back." He looked straight ahead.

"His wife?" She looked at him in disbelief.

Harold made a show of turning a corner very carefully. "He just called to tell me you were to meet him at his apartment."

"Harold, did you know he was married?"

He turned to her, distress in his expression. "Believe me, Maggie Rose, I knew he had been married but he told me they were divorced. He lied to us all."

Maggie Rose had to endure the speculation, the whispers, and the embarrassment of having been duped. She suspected that some of the group either knew or had heard rumors about Lem's marital state, yet no one had warned her. She had picked up no clues from Lem, believing him when he said he was unattached. How could she have been so naive? The one thing she was profoundly grateful about was that she'd been saved from intimacy with him.

Chris Shealy was a different matter entirely. With Chris she felt a connection. There was a bond between them almost as old as she was. It had been forged when she was nine and for some inexplicable reason had held all of these years. She couldn't explain it but it was there.

Part of its manifestation was the awareness of each other wherever they happened to be. Part of it was her surety that she was safe with him. She wasn't certain of what that might entail but she just knew he was her anchor. The most enticing, dangerous, and exhilarating manifestation was that she was physically attracted to him in ways she had only read about but had never experienced. She was slowly, in these past several weeks, learning the meaning of terms like desire, electricity between people, longing, and yearning. Like this morning, when he had just told her why he had decided not to touch her in the office. She heard his words but the longing to kiss him blotted them out and all she could do was reach over to his wonderful mouth once more. She was so hungry for him.

Her thoughts made Maggie Rose blush. Hungry indeed! She'd better watch herself, she thought with a sense of naughtiness.

Her employer might sue her for harassment!

Chapter
Twenty

"I'm scared, Mr. Chris." Alberta Barnhill, eleven and short for her age, stood near the mounting block, uncertain if she could make herself climb on to Nicky's back.

"It's okay to be a little scared the first time you try to ride," Chris said soothingly. "But I'll be right here. Step up on the block. That's right. See how Nicky is waiting for you. He's very gentle and won't hurt you. One foot over, now get yourself settled in the saddle so you're as comfortable as you'd be in a chair. You're doing fine. Remember how you're supposed to hold the reins? Good, Alberta."

Alberta held on to the reins as if her life depended upon it and hunched forward over Nicky. Chris didn't correct her but kept talking to her as he led Nicky in slow steps around the paddock several times. He knew Alberta hadn't wanted riding lessons. She was here for two reasons, because her mother wanted to boast that her child was at a riding school and because her mother wanted to flirt with him.

This combination wasn't new to him. He'd learned how to handle the ladies who came with the personal motive of getting close to him. He had learned how to be friendly in a firmly businesslike manner that made the professional guidelines clear.

It was in his interest to avoid antagonizing the mothers as best he could because he didn't want to lose the children. Teaching youngsters how to ride had turned out to be immensely satisfying. He had started the business because of Uncle Henry and because he loved horses. After a few months he found that developing methods to help children overcome hesitancy or fear, so that they could appreciate the beauty of horses and the sheer enjoyment of riding them with a certain amount of skill, had become the focus of his business. The money he earned was secondary.

Alberta, for instance, was beginning to relax and sit up straight in her saddle. He knew that by the end of her half hour, she would be ready to approach her next class with more confidence. What he would watch for was the day she came to class with eagerness. That would give him as much joy as it would her.

The satisfaction with Alberta's lessening nervousness stayed with him as he showered and dressed. It had been a good day altogether and now he was going to the best of it, he thought, as he drove in the dusk to Maggie Rose's apartment.

The way she'd kissed him this morning had been profoundly moving. He had come into the office, his heart pounding at the sight of her in her brown linen dress and glass beads. He was still filled with how she'd comforted him the night before when he told her about the fire. It had been like a healing balm to his spirit. She was his Madonna.

He had to let her know at once that it wasn't for lack of feeling that he must keep his distance while they were in the office. It was out of respect and proper decorum. She understood, she said.

What he should've done was get right up and sit in his usual chair across from her. But she smelled heavenly and her skin looked so soft as he reassured her that he wanted to kiss her. Then *she* kissed *him*. Just like that!

Despite what he had said a second ago, she leaned to him and kissed him with a penetrating sweetness that so overwhelmed him he had to walk away for a moment. This was the first indication he had that some level of need was driving Maggie Rose where he was concerned. That possibility was both exhilarating and humbling.

He had come to the conclusion that he was going to be his own worst enemy because the strong protective instinct he'd always had for Maggie Rose wouldn't permit him to let her be rushed as her emotional insights developed. He had to make sure that his own desires were kept in check as much as possible. Since he was far more experienced in this area than she, it was up to him to take control for both of them.

With this firmly in mind he restrained his impulses when Maggie Rose welcomed him in, looking delightful in the apricot dress he'd admired when they were both at Teddy's. He permitted himself one brief embrace before escorting her to the car.

In the seafood restaurant, after they gave their orders for fried shrimp, he sat back in his chair. He intended to savor every moment of this evening. "This is the first time we've gone out together," he observed. "Thank you for coming."

"I guess we can't count that time after we finished the English assignment in the library and walked outside to talk," she said demurely.

"You remember that, too?" His eyes lit up.

"How could I forget it?" she said simply.

"All these years I thought I was the only one who remembered it." It *had* meant something to her also.

"We were so young with all of life before us," she said wistfully.

"We still have most of our lives before us," Chris said softly just as the waiter brought rolls and butter to their table.

A shadow moved across her face, then was gone as she passed him the basket of bread. "The list of people who came to the opening—you said you wanted to discuss it."

"Any excuse is better than none." He smiled.

"Agreed." She smiled in return. "But what about the list?"

"There were four women and three men whose names were unfamiliar to me, so any of them could have been from the association."

"Or any of them came with the idea of searching your room."

"I guess so, but why would a complete stranger do that? It doesn't make sense to me." Chris had gone over this point until he was tired of it.

They ate their salad in silence for a few minutes, but a glance at Maggie Rose told him she was deep in thought. "What is it, Maggie Rose?"

"I was thinking that the only person I've ever heard you speak about was your uncle Henry. What about the rest of your family?"

As the waiter replaced their salad with plates of fried shrimp, baked potatoes, and a medley of fresh vegetables, Chris told her how the original Hugh Christopher Shealy had left land to Hugh Jr., to Uncle Henry, and to Chris's father, Lee Christopher.

"Uncle Henry said Hugh Jr. lost his land through incompetence, moved away, and severed contact with the family. Old Hugh left the best thirty acres to Uncle Henry, who kept it all and added another twenty. Did you know there's a brook on the property? I want to show it to you some day."

She nodded. "Covey mentioned the brook and an orchard," she said. "What about your father and his land?"

"He gambled it away. Uncle Henry said he would gamble on anything. That's why he never had money to give Mama and me a proper home. We moved a lot and Mama was sick most of the time. Then she died and Daddy died but before he did, he asked Uncle Henry to look after me."

Maggie Rose stopped eating. All of her attention was on him. The intense quality of her empathy drew from him memories he'd never spoken of to anyone.

"Daddy never lived on his land, he rented it out and collected the money. He always said he wasn't a farm boy. I was born in Charleston but when I was two, Daddy moved us to Columbia, where we lived for about a year. Then we moved to Greenville. I know now that he was always going where he thought the gambling was good and, of course, with his never paying any attention to the land, the renters cheated him. As the money got less and less, he gambled the land away."

"You didn't know what was happening at the time, did you, Chris? You were too young."

"Uncle Henry explained to me later about the gambling. My father was this man who treated me kindly when he was around but most of the time as if he just remembered that I was there and was his son. Gambling was his whole life, you see." Chris had come to terms with the fact that he hadn't been an important element to his father by balancing that fact with the knowledge that at least his father had never been mean or abusive or deliberately unkind. He accepted that he had simply been marginal in his father's life.

"It was your uncle who treated you like a son," Maggie Rose observed as if she had solved a puzzle.

"We were the only family each of us had," Chris agreed.

The stark statement pierced Maggie Rose. No wonder Chris had lingered as long as he could in her house when they were growing up. He'd been starving for the sense of family her home represented. She recalled his reason for the fireplace in his remodeled house and the yellow room upstairs. She wondered if he'd consciously known that it was destined to be a nursery. Did he remember his mother nursing him, loving him?

"What about your mother, Chris?" she asked gently.

Chris pushed his plate away. The memories he

was evoking left no space for food. He hadn't talked
about his parents since he was about fourteen,
when questions about them had surfaced in his
maturing understanding, resulting in a long conversation with his uncle. Since then he'd dealt with
what he understood, assimilated it, and buried it
as a topic for conversation.

Only now with his Maggie Rose had he felt a
desire, a need to share it.

"Mama married young, lost their first child, and
was never well after I was born two years later. She
followed Daddy wherever he wanted to go. Because
Daddy was out so much with his friends, Mama
and I spent a lot of time together. We loved each
other and I took care of her because she didn't
have much strength."

Images arose in his mind and he described them
to a rapt Maggie Rose. "I can see myself now trying
to arrange the covers and pillows to make her comfortable or bringing her a cool drink. We ate a lot
of peanut butter and jelly sandwiches I made. I
learned how to turn down the television when she
dozed off."

Maggie Rose laid her hand on his. He turned
his palm to hers and looked down at them. "Then
one winter she got pneumonia and just slipped
away," he said softly. "A few months after that
Daddy got himself killed about a gambling debt.
Uncle Henry appeared and brought me to the farm
and my life began all over again."

Maggie Rose's heart was too full for her to speak.

Chris, still looking at their entwined hands, said,
"I was five. Seven years later when I was twelve
I met a nine-year-old girl called Magnolia Rose
Sanders." *And another part of my life began!* "I am

so thankful I met her." He looked up at her to
see an expression of tender understanding as her
fingers tightened around his.

"So am I."

As the waiter cleared the table and brought coffee and a dessert menu, Chris discovered that the
residual pain of his early life had been purged by
telling it to Maggie Rose. Her comprehension and
caring had been a healing balm leaving him with
a profound sense of peace.

One day he would tell her all of this, but now
he needed to hear about her plans with the Mailroom. No more conversation about him.

"Tell me about your part in the Mailroom business," he asked as the waiter served their pecan
pie.

"The conference we went to in Columbia was
about how to successfully run a small business. Miss
Henrietta kept it going by knowing the changing
needs of her neighborhood and her customers,
and knowing how to brighten up the place every
few years with new paintings to keep it looking
fresh and with a new machine or rack of cards."

"She did and I used to notice it. It kept me
from going to the post office because I could do
everything I needed there without having to stand
in a long line. Also I could visit with people I knew."

"Exactly." Maggie Rose beamed. "That was one
of the great selling points for me when Ginnie first
approached me. I had in mind to go into business
when I left Hartford and I was going to look
around, maybe have a stationery shop or a small
restaurant. But when she mentioned her aunt's
place, I knew it was a perfect solution for me."

"Will you add something that's not there now?"

"Ginnie and I have had long conversations about my ideas on that. She's finally agreed to let me have a counter for local artists and craftsmen to sell their products. That's what I'm doing now in my spare time, identifying the people and seeing who among them will be willing to come in to the Mailroom."

Chris was surprised. "I think that's a great idea. It should do very well, especially if you have moderately priced items for sale."

After Chris brought her home, Maggie Rose was too restless to sleep no matter how she tossed and turned. She punched up her pillow several times trying to find a more comfortable place for her head, but sleep would not come.

The evening had been a surprise to her. She hadn't anticipated Chris's revelations about his early childhood. Even now the thought of how his selfish father and loving but weak mother had denied him the kind of security he should have had brought a lump to her throat. Yet he'd made himself into a strong, successful, and caring man.

Did he understand that in the way he cared for his young students, in the patience he showed them as they developed step by step under his tutelage, and in the joy he shared with them when they became confident—did he realize he was giving them what had been denied him?

Perhaps some of his father's tendencies plus the natural revolt of youth had accounted for the wildness that had characterized his early years with his uncle. But Mr. Shealy's firm hand and steadfast love had had their effects in the end. No wonder Chris wanted the stables as a memorial to his uncle!

Chris had been open and honest with Maggie Rose. She doubted that he told other people what he'd told her across the dinner table. He trusted her.

With each day that went by she did not return that trust. She could not tell him how she felt about horses. She was working for him under false pretenses. Worse than that, she was letting them grow close under that same falsity. She knew that after his confidences tonight, she'd have increasing difficulty in looking him in the eyes. Already she felt herself drawing back. She couldn't help it and she knew he would feel it. It would hurt him. But until she found a way to overcome her fear, she didn't know what else to do.

Chapter
Twenty-One

The summer season was picking up with a vengeance. Dan Montgomery was now on the payroll as a part-time instructor. By Friday Chris told Maggie Rose if the student enrollment continued to grow he might have to offer Dan a full-time job, although he didn't know if Dan could give up that much time from the car lot. He himself had pared his hours for the corporation to six and some days to four.

"They don't mind if you do that?" Maggie Rose asked.

"They only want to be sure the apartments get rented and maintained and the profits get banked, and fortunately some days I don't have to be there too long to get that done."

"Great job," she said.

"I'm fortunate to be able to tailor the job to fit

my needs," he acknowledged. "Do you want to do that here? You may if you wish."

He was sitting across from her, at ease for the first time since they'd gone out on Tuesday.

He wasn't sure what had happened but she'd been a little withdrawn, on edge. He wondered if he'd talked too much about his family. He had been certain she was not only interested but sympathetic, but maybe he was wrong. So he, also, had been rather quiet in the office. Saying only what he had to say and leaving. Yet he sensed in her a hint of the same longing he felt and caught in her eyes a time or two a wistfulness that clutched at his heart.

This morning she was more her old self. She looked wonderful all in white, glowing with health.

"You look like the yoga is going well," he said. "Would you like to adjust your hours to get more time in for it and for the Mailroom?"

"Thanks, Chris, but no. It's all working out thus far. I am enjoying the yoga a lot and it does relieve stress. You work more hours than I do, I think. Maybe you should try yoga."

"I'll tell you what," he said as he got up to go to work. He leaned across the desk and tweaked her nose. "When you learn it well enough, I'll let you teach me."

"I don't think so." She smiled.

"Why not? Don't you think I could be a good student?"

"Yes, but I don't think I could be a good teacher."

"Honey," he drawled, "you could teach me anything you set your mind to. Anything."

He closed the door softly behind him, leaving her blushing.

She hurried through her paperwork in order to be ready for the shop traffic. It was heaviest on Fridays, although there was a nice dribble of shoppers most afternoons of the week. This morning when she finished her yoga she'd decided to loosen up on herself with Chris. After all, she was doing something about the problem so she would be able to talk with him about it soon. It wasn't like she wasn't making an effort to be able to be completely honest with him.

He'd responded immediately and she felt as light as a feather in the wind. They were going to Bill Denton's annual summer barbecue tomorrow and she didn't want any barriers between them. She intended to enjoy herself fully. Her new red dress had been sinfully expensive but its subtle lines made her think of the clothes Neda McCann wore, and since she was certain Neda had been invited, Maggie Rose was determined to hold her own!

Bill's house and backyard were crowded by the time Chris and Maggie Rose arrived. Bill told people to come anytime but the grill would be lit about six and the party would get serious about eight. It had been known to last until the wee hours.

Chris had an evening student and Maggie Rose was busy with some craftspeople, so they had agreed to go late.

"Bill's party doesn't get mellow until late anyhow," Chris said, "and the food just goes on and on."

Maggie Rose was thrilled at the prospect of this,

a party with Chris and Bill. She hadn't been to such an event since returning home and she hadn't been to a real party for two years, because after Lem Norris her social life had been muted. She dressed with great care and her anticipation put a sparkle in her eyes that made Chris bundle her into his arms as soon as he saw her.

"You're going to have a good time tonight, aren't you, honey?" Her honest enthusiasm was very appealing.

"I hope so." She smiled. "How about you?"

"How could I help it? My good time started the minute you opened the door." As he ushered her into the car he thought that part of his good time would be fending off the men who would be trying to make time with her. He knew she didn't give herself credit for her attractiveness and she wouldn't understand how she gleamed and glittered tonight in her gorgeous red dress. Her inner gaiety only enhanced the total effect she had on him and any other male in her vicinity.

They entered Bill's house, Chris's arm around her waist, a deliberate statement to the prowling wolves.

"I was about to give you a call, man," Bill said. "You've already missed some of the fun."

"Magnolia Rose. Girl, look at you tonight!" He pulled her out of Chris's arm and turned her around, then gave a low growl. "Don't be trying to keep her to yourself tonight, buddy, 'cause you don't stand a chance."

Maggie Rose, blushing with delight, decided she'd try a little flirtation on Bill right away. He was safe. She'd already noticed several admiring glances from nearby men. She patted Bill's cheek lightly. In as sultry a voice as she could manage, she cooed, "All you have to do is whistle, Bill."

His eyes widened as he gave Chris a quick glance. "Take her away, Chris, before I yield to temptation."

"Chris, how're you doing? Haven't seen you for a while." A man Maggie Rose didn't know stepped into the spot Bill had vacated.

"Hey, Chuck. Good to see you. Maggie Rose Sanders, this is Chuck Green. A certified wolf looking for little lambs, so be forewarned," Chris said pleasantly.

"Now, Chris, be nice. It's a pleasure to meet you, Miss Sanders. Are you new in town?"

"This is my hometown but I've been living in Hartford for some time."

"You're home to stay, I hope."

"I am, and glad to be back."

"So are we all." He winked at her. "I hope to see you a little later." He gave a pleasant nod and moved away through the crowd.

Maggie Rose had never before had two attractive men growling over her. It must be the red dress. She knew it was made just for her the moment she looked at it. She felt Chris's hand on the small of her back as they made their way through the crowd. Bill had a large kitchen, which opened into a long, high-ceilinged living room with French windows leading out to a large deck and a lawn. It seemed to Maggie Rose there were people, conversation, laughter, and music everywhere. There must have been at least sixty people here, she thought. The atmosphere was convivial and festive.

Three long tables stretched along the back of the deck. Bill, now in chef's hat and white apron, rang some musical chimes. He put on the food tables platters of ribs, hamburgers, and grilled sausage, chops, and steaks. Salads, casseroles, breads, and beverages covered the tables. A beverage table stood by itself at the other end of the desk.

"Dinner's ready!" Bill's stentorian voice rang through the air and people began to stream to the tables.

"He doesn't do all of this himself, does he?" Maggie Rose said.

"He once told me that he does, starts days ahead and does it for the fun of it. He should have been a chef," Chris said. "Impressive, isn't it?"

As they waited to eat, Maggie Rose found that she knew a number of people and Chris seemed to know everyone. She was so caught up in conversation and laughter she forgot about eating until Chris bought her a plate of food and made a place for himself in the group around her.

It had never been Maggie Rose's way to be the center of attention or to be the leader in conversation, yet she found herself in this position now. She didn't know how it happened but she heard herself handling witty repartee and bringing up new and interesting topics that the group eagerly took hold of and discussed, usually with a mixture of seriousness and merriment.

She was not alone. Chris was a constant presence, always ready with his own humorous comments or directing a question to someone who joined the group. Never in her life had Maggie Rose felt her feminine power as now. She knew Chris stayed by her side because this was where he wanted to be. From time to time people walked by and stopped to talk to him. Several women invited him to where they were sitting. Always courteous, he refused all invitations, often with a promise to come by later. Occasionally, she saw a woman cut her eyes at her because a man had paid her too much attention. She could have told the women not to worry but deep inside she had to admit it was wonderful and flattering to feel like this.

Dan and Jerlene stopped by for a while. Ginnie and Joe Stevenson were here but they were sitting across the lawn. She'd seen Nancy Fisher, who worked with Leah in the catering business, and she wondered if Nancy had anything to do with some of the desserts now on the table. She was too excited to eat but she did get up and began to walk around with Chris.

She particularly wanted to see Neda McCann and found her holding court under a tree. She was regal in a royal purple that only Neda could wear and made it seem entirely appropriate at an out-door summer party. Maggie Rose glanced quickly to see Chris's expression. With his hand still at the small of Maggie Rose's back he greeted Neda and the other people around her. Maggie Rose felt secure in her red dress.

Neda introduced the man who was standing beside her to Chris and Maggie Rose as Donald Singletary of St. Louis. He was only a little taller than Neda with sharp features, a firm mouth, and presence.

In conversation that followed, Maggie Rose sensed that Mr. Singletary had come to take Neda back to St. Louis with him.

She said as much to Chris when they moved on. "Do you think she'll go?"

"I wouldn't be surprised. She's never seemed contented here."

Maggie Rose knew she was being naive to think that because a woman was as sensational as Neda, happiness naturally followed. But still . . . imagine looking like that! She could never look like Neda, but this night she seemed to be doing all right.

Full darkness had come but the number of small lights Bill had hung all around punctuated the night and made it seem a fairyland. The disc jockey had arrived and the deck was filled with dancers while other people sat around on the lawn to watch them. The air was warm but not humid and occasionally a mild breeze ruffled across Maggie Rose's skin.

"Let's dance," Chris said, and soon they were swirling around the deck to an old Beatles tune. They sang the lyrics and laughed at how they mixed up the words. Everyone on the deck began doing the Electric Slide. Maggie Rose and Chris were in perfect step together as they moved to the fancy footwork and turned in rhythm with the others. Maggie Rose thought she'd never been so exhilarated. When the record ended the audience on the lawn applauded the dancers, who spontaneously made a long line, held hands, and bowed as one.

Chuck Green appeared. "Is the lady allowed to dance with someone else?" His words were a challenge to Chris but his eyes were on Maggie Rose as he held out his hand.

"Of course she is," Maggie Rose said, putting her hand in his and smiling at Chris before turning to dance with Chuck.

From time to time she saw Chris on the dance floor as they both exchanged partners frequently and smiled at each other across the space. Once they ended up in the same group of four couples who were trying to outdo one another.

The disc jockey announced that the next number would be especially for sweethearts. Maggie Rose had just finished dancing again with Chuck. She didn't want to look around for Chris but she hoped he'd find her.

"This one's mine," his voice stated as he appeared from behind her and took her in his arms. The lights on the deck went out. Unlike the earlier records, this one was orchestrated with lush strings and a slow tempo of melting loveliness.

Maggie Rose floated in a space where only she and Chris existed. They moved as one, holding each other in a tender embrace, her head on his chest, his cheek on her hair. In harmony they breathed in and breathed out. When Chris whispered, "Are you my sweetheart?" she answered, "Yes," and when he said, "And I'm yours?" the statements were verbal proof of what every fiber of her being already knew and accepted.

Dancing after that seemed anticlimactic and by one accord they deserted the dance floor for a pair of lawn chairs. They were joined by Ginnie and Lee as well as Neda and her friend. They fell into a quiet conversation as the disc jockey ended his music and packed up his equipment. It was past midnight and the majority of people had left.

Bill came by and said quietly, "Don't go," so they continued to sit, their chairs touching, their hands entwined. Bill had put some quiet music on the stereo, then come to them with Nancy Fisher and three other couples. They made a large circle on the lawn and watched as two uniformed people cleared up what was left of the food.

"I'm glad to see you did have some help this time," Chris said.

"Preparing the food is a pleasure but cleaning up after is the part I can do without, so when Nancy suggested using some of Leah's crew for this, I jumped at it."

"Reminds me of when we had that party in high school and three boys started a food fight, then refused to clean it up. Said that was for the girls to do," Ginnie said.

Lee said, "Both Bill and Chris know something about that, don't you?"

"We'll never live that down," Bill protested among much merriment, as most of the people in the group had all gone to school together.

"Maggie Rose, didn't you tell the principal Chris wasn't in it?" Nancy said.

"I tried but it didn't do any good. He got suspended anyway," Maggie Rose said.

Chris kissed her hand. "My hero," he said in her ear.

"That was nothing compared to the time we played Greenville High and won," someone else said. "That was real chaos."

Memories of their high school life were dredged up even from Neda and her friend, who said high school in St. Louis had many similarities to Jamison. The talk went on to events after high school and as the conversation flowed around Maggie Rose, she felt a centeredness that was new.

She was home. This was where she belonged with the people and events that had formed her and fashioned the fabric of her life. The years in Hartford had only been a small portion of the larger fabric. No matter what happened from now on, this was where she was supposed to be.

As if he were aware of her thoughts, Chris turned to her. "Thank God you came home," he said.

Bill looked at his watch. "Let's go inside. It's time for breakfast."

"I can't believe it's one-thirty already," Neda exclaimed.

"No wonder I'm so hungry," Maggie Rose said. She recalled she'd barely touched her dinner in her excitement.

In the kitchen Bill and Nancy quickly produced omelets, biscuits, fresh berries, and hot coffee.

They all sat at one of Bill's large banquet tables and demolished the food as if they hadn't had the barbecue seven hours earlier. Maggie Rose listened to the talk but said nothing.

"You're very quiet," Chris murmured. She smiled in acquiescence.

Maybe this was her future, she mused, sharing meals and friendships with these people as they all married and began to have families. Went to each other's weddings, baby showers, and holiday events, shared car-pooling and graduations for their children.

Was it in her future that she and Chris would be one of those couples?

Sweethearts were one thing. After all, Lem Norris had called her sweetheart. But they could come and go.

Chris had made it clear that she was the focus of his attention, but he was an extremely person-able and popular man. The way attractive women had tried to get close to him all evening was evidence of that. She would be naive to envision a future because he used the term sweetheart.

It was romantic, enchanting.

But it was not the magic word.

Chapter Twenty-Two

"I've a big favor to ask of you," Chris said when he came into the office on Monday. His angular face and dark brown eyes were alight with excitement as he leaned across the desk to talk to Maggie Rose.

"Ask and it shall be given." She grinned at him, then added teasingly, "maybe."

"Will you please go to the races with me Thursday? It's an annual event on the Fourth of July."

She looked down and moved her chair a fraction. "Where are the races?"

"Carrboro, North Carolina."

"I don't think I know the area."

"It's near Chapel Hill."

"Do you go every year?"

"No, but this year I want to go and have you with me, Maggie Rose." She was hesitant and he wanted to know why. He was still buoyed up by their wonderful time together at Bill's. They'd been so close, so in harmony, all of the former shadows between them cleared away.

He was certain they were ready to take another major step in the development of their relationship. He had deliberately not pushed his advantage and had left her at her doorstep with only a deep good-night kiss. Apparently he'd been wrong to think they would both want to spend as much time together outside of the office as possible. He thought she'd be delighted at the Fourth of July idea but she was obviously hesitating.

Chris straightened up. "What's the matter, Maggie Rose? If you don't want to go with me, just say so."

"It isn't that," she said, alarmed. "I just don't know if I can. Ginnie and I had planned to spend the whole morning in the Mailroom. What time would you want to leave?"

"I don't think that would work," he stated, disappointment in his voice. "The races begin at one o'clock and Carrboro isn't next door. It'll take about five hours to get there."

"Let me see what I can work out with Ginnie, because I would like to be with you," she said wistfully.

"I know you only have two weeks to finish up for your business and if you need that time with Ginnie, I'll understand. There'll be other races." He made himself smile.

On his way to work he struggled with his frustration. It hadn't occurred to him that Maggie Rose might already have plans for the holiday. He hadn't thought about her time off, he'd only thought they'd both be free from work and could spend

the whole day and evening together. Maggie Rose
was using time away from his office to work on her
own business; he appreciated what that called for.
He admired her insight and hard work and was
sure she and Ginnie would be successful.

He was just being selfish, wanting her beside him
this Thursday, all day, without interruption. Maybe
she'd be able to work something out. He hoped
so. Everything else was going well. Art Fulton
reported no sign of problems each morning and
seemed very alert. Chris had asked Dan if he could
spare more hours and Dan said he'd see. Covey was
developing into a rider with flair; he understood
horses and might someday become a first-class
jockey. The equestrian shop was turning a profit
for the first time. He might have to hire someone
just to take care of it. Given the overall picture, he
decided he could forgo Thursday if necessary.

She couldn't put it off any longer. The day of
reckoning had to come and it might as well be
Thursday. Her breathing and yoga lessons had
made a significant difference in her ability to avoid
stress to a certain extent. She had rented a video
of a movie dealing with horse racing and had seen
it through with only an acceleration of heartbeat
but no nausea, no pouring sweat, no dizziness. She
knew other people used hypnosis and psychiatry
to help them overcome the kinds of attacks she
had but she'd decided to stick with what she was
doing.

The generating event had happened when she
was thirteen and she'd scarcely had to deal with
the traumatic effects until four weeks ago. She

didn't see why she couldn't heal herself with determination and hard work now that she'd talked with
Dr. Moore.

She wouldn't know how far her healing had progressed until she was near a horse, and she was
going to have to tell Chris about her situation.
Originally she'd planned not to. That was before.
Before the first kiss and the ones that followed,
before he had revealed his childhood to her with
utter trust, before Bill's party.

She could hardly live with herself now knowing
she had deceived him. She had to tell him the
whole truth and take the consequences before
Chris went further than "sweetheart," if that was
what he had in mind. Even if he didn't, she had
to tell him for her honor's sake.

So she rearranged her plans with Ginnie and on
Tuesday put on a smiling face as she told Chris
she could go and what time would he pick her up?
They agreed on seven o'clock.

Wednesday afternoon when Chris came home
to give student lessons she decided to test herself.
She saw Covey at his usual place at the fence watching the lesson. She put her breathing ritual in
place, then went out to stand beside him.

"Hi, Aunt Maggie Rose. Did you want me for
something?" Covey asked.

"No, I just thought I'd watch. I have a few minutes," she said.

"That's good because you've never seen Windsong in practice before. She's something to see,
isn't she?"

"She is pretty just like you said," Maggie Rose
agreed, breathing deeply and slowly as the graceful

chestnut carried the young girl, who was concentrating on Chris's instructions.

Maggie Rose didn't try to follow what Chris was saying or what the student was doing, she was only aware of herself, her physical structure, as she mentally went through some yoga movements and focused thinking while her eyes were on the horse.

She made herself stay three minutes by her watch, then went back inside. Since she was sure everyone was outside she let her joy out and danced around the office.

"I did it! I did it!"

Now she was ready for tomorrow and the good news she'd have for Chris.

Her elation propelled her into a dress shop that evening. When she opened her door to Chris on Thursday, she wore a perky white top with blue trim and matching short skirt and cap. Polished toenails peeked out of white sandals with blue trim.

Chris also had chosen white for his sports shirt and belted shorts.

He picked her up and swung her around, then kissed her soundly. "You're a blessing to my eyes and my heart, Maggie Rose," he said. "We're going to have a magnificent day!"

"I'm ready for it," she said and kissed him back in full confidence that when she returned to her apartment the worst would be over and there would be honesty between them.

The miles rolled away under Chris's effortless driving, while in the air-conditioned car they talked about Bill's party and the people she'd caught up with after being gone so long. He asked intelligent questions about her business plans and told her about his plan to buy a stallion. They stopped for an early lunch and ate it on a patio protected from the hot sun by the shade of an immense oak.

Maggie Rose found herself thinking she was enjoying her day off with Chris so much that if they never reached their destination it would be all right. They dawdled over the lunch, reluctant to leave the shady spot.

"The races will be over and we'll still be here," Chris said, leaning across the table to brush her lips with his.

"This is so pleasant, I hate to leave."

"One day we'll be back when we have nothing else to do," he promised. He didn't see her crossed fingers as she thought, *If all goes well.* She was finding that the closer they got to Carrboro the more the tension began to rise in her. She hadn't expected this.

She began to fill her mind and spirit with all she could remember from what she'd been reading and practicing for two weeks. It had worked so well when she'd watched Windsong there was no reason to think it wouldn't work well today, she told herself.

They arrived at the course and Chris parked the car and took her hand as they walked to the gates, where he purchased tickets. She could feel his rising excitement as he explained the configuration of the track to her and what they would be seeing. There were throngs of people in high spirits, gaily dressed and shouting at other people. Several shouted at Chris and one or two were close enough for him to introduce her.

He held her hand and helped her through the crowd. Suddenly he stopped. "Ben! I haven't seen you in a year. Hear you've expanded some."

Ben, a red-faced, hearty man, returned the greeting and touched his cap to Maggie Rose.

"Maggie Rose, meet Ben Sewell from Greenville. You racing one of yours today, Ben?"

"Come around to the boxes with me and I'll show you," Ben said. "His name's Silver Star and this is his first race. He's got heart but not much technique yet."

Their conversation was background noise to Maggie Rose, who was counting her breathing. They came to a long series of horse stalls and still she was able to breathe and her stomach felt good.

Ben's horse was next to the last stall, which was empty. She thought Silver Star looked a lot like Windsong but was not as elegant. She stood back while Chris and Ben walked around the horse discussing his finer points. She saw how Chris stroked the horse and it came to her that if she could keep improving, the day might come when she, too, could give horses the love that Chris felt for them.

Suddenly there was a commotion. A man came around the corner toward the empty stall leading a horse who was unwilling to be led. The gangly horse was rolling his eyes in anger, tossing his head, and dancing to the right, then to the left. The man yelled and jerked the rope. The hose whinnied and reared up on his back legs. People began to appear to help.

Maggie Rose's eyes dilated, her stomach churned, and perspiration popped out on her face. She tried to move but couldn't. She screamed, covered her face to blot out the image of flashing, killing hooves, and slid to the ground, unconscious.

"Maggie Rose!" Chris said, kneeling beside her. "Maggie Rose," he repeated as if saying her name would make her open her eyes. Someone handed him a wet cloth and he wiped her face.

"I called the racetrack doctor," Ben told him.

"Open your eyes, honey," Chris pleaded, his heart pounding as he continued to wipe her face with soft touches.

The crowd that had gathered moved momentarily to make room for the doctor, who rolled up in his vehicle, jumped out, and knelt beside Maggie Rose. He ordered people to step back to give the patient air.

A whip-thin man with kind eyes, he asked Chris what had happened as he felt at Maggie Rose's wrist for her pulse.

"A horse reared up and frightened her. I think that's what made her faint."

The doctor lifted her eyelids and listened to her heart, then felt the back of her head. "A little bruise there but her heartbeat's okay. She should be coming out of it any minute. There. Her eyes are fluttering now."

Maggie Rose opened her eyes to see two anxious faces hovering over her. One was a stranger, the other was Chris. "What happened?" she asked Chris in a thin voice.

"You fainted, honey."

Before he could say more the other man asked, "What is your name?"

"Magnolia Rose Sanders."

He held up some fingers. "How many fingers do you see?"

What a silly question, she thought as she told him, "Three."

"Good." He told Chris, "No sign of concussion;

still, she should rest awhile. I'll take you both to the first aid room."

Chris picked Maggie Rose up in his arms, then placed her in the car. He sat close, his arm around her. "Is this all right?" Her face was still pale, her mouth a little pinched.

"Yes," she said but her head leaned against him of its own accord. He looked at the doctor over her head.

"A nurse is on duty who'll monitor her," he said reassuringly.

Maggie Rose still felt a little disoriented and willingly sat in the comfortable chair with her feet up as the nurse suggested.

"We want you to rest and settle yourself but don't go to sleep."

"I'll see that she stays awake," Chris promised, seating himself beside Maggie Rose and taking her hand.

"I'll bring you both some cold water." The nurse bustled off and soon returned with two glasses of ice and a pitcher of water.

"Don't you want to go watch the race? I promise not to go to sleep," Maggie Rose said. "I'm already feeling better. I don't want to spoil your day."

"I'm not leaving you, Maggie Rose. There'll be more races."

Maggie Rose saw the worry in his eyes and felt the tenderness in his touch as he held her hand. The nurse was on the far side of the room and occasionally glanced at them. There wasn't true privacy here but they could keep their voices low if they were careful. The time had come to tell Chris how she felt about horses, but she had not expected it to be like this. Chris was worried because he thought she'd fainted because of the horse frightening her, which was partially true but was not the basic truth. She had to make him understand about her trauma and that she had deliberately withheld it from him. Her sense of honor, damaged though it was, demanded this. She didn't want Chris brushing it aside out of sympathy because she'd fainted.

She sipped the glass of water while counting her breathing until she felt an inner loosening of tension. Chris was entertaining her with stories of how he had met Ben and Ben's family.

"Chris," she said, interrupting his story.

"What is it, Maggie Rose?" He leaned toward her. "Don't you feel well?"

"Chris, there's something I must tell you."

The strain in her eyes was reflected in her voice. She saw faint alarm in his eyes as he sat straight in his chair.

"Why now?"

"Because I've put it off too long."

"Then you can put it off a little while longer, Maggie Rose. Right now you have to rest and whatever it is we can talk about it on the way home."

She opened her mouth to protest. Chris said softly, "When we're alone." He gave her another glass of water. "Let me tell you a little more about Ben and his family."

Chapter
Twenty-Three

Chris put on his left directional, passed the truck ahead of him, and moved smoothly into the fast lane after checking his rearview mirror again. He had been waiting for that break. Today he had no patience for the middle lane, and the slow lane was out of the question. He'd use the fast lane as long as he could without attracting a cop's attention. They were out in force on this holiday.

They'd left Carrboro and the Research Triangle of Chapel Hill, Durham, and Raleigh an hour ago after the nurse, examining Maggie Rose again, said she could go. Maggie Rose had spent a little time in the rest room, emerging to look very much as she had this morning. Her color was back, her clothes straight, hair and makeup attended to.

"See? As good as new," she had told him with a smile. With his arm around her they walked to the parking lot. Before he could open the car door, she turned and put her arms around him in a tight embrace.

"Thanks for taking care of me, Chris," she murmured, standing on tiptoe to kiss him.

Her touch set off the explosion of emotion Chris had been repressing since seeing Maggie Rose, pale and unconscious, on the ground. He crushed her to him, raining kisses on her mouth, her cheek, her neck, and her hair. "I thought you were hurt and I didn't know what to do," he muttered. "Don't ever scare me like that again."

"I won't," she promised. "Chris, we'd better get in the car."

He looked up to notice people glancing at them as they went by. "Sorry. Didn't mean to embarrass you." He opened the car door for her.

As he climbed in and started out of the lot Maggie Rose said, "You didn't embarrass me. After all, I kissed you first."

"You did, didn't you? I like fast women like you." He grinned, his spirits lightening up for the first time since she said there was something she must tell him.

Instinct said he would not like what she had to say. Was there any way he could delay it? They still had about four hours in the car before they reached home. If what she had to tell him was going to cause an argument or create an unpleasant atmosphere, it would be twice as bad to be in the car for so long, not able to get away from each other.

On the other hand, maybe what she had to say wasn't major. Maybe she just thought it was. No, he couldn't bring himself to that conclusion. She said she'd put it off too long and she *had* to tell him, which meant it would affect their relationship.

Two weeks ago he might have thought she was going to confirm his suspicion that her frequent sickness was caused by pregnancy. Thank God he'd made her go to the doctor and that monstrous bogey had been dispelled.

So what could it be?

Perhaps she was referring to something that had happened before she came to his office and that was why she said she'd put it off too long. So much had transpired between them that in one way it seemed she'd been working with him for months but in fact this was only her fifth week.

Following that line of thought it must have been something that took place in Hartford. An affair, perhaps, that she thought he needed to know about. If so, she couldn't be more wrong. Whatever occurred in the past was past. The same with him. What was in his past was past. He hadn't lived the life of a monk all the years she'd been away. He wasn't proud of some of his past but it was over and in the last five years he'd been intent on being the kind of man Uncle Henry would be proud of.

He now realized that he hadn't been able to have a deep love affair or come to the point of considering marriage because subconsciously he was waiting for Maggie Rose. As long as she was still single there was a chance that fate would bring them together.

Fate had done its part, he thought wryly, and now that it had, nothing on God's green earth was going to keep them apart. He guessed he'd been enchanted by her when she was nine and had crept into his lonely heart by trusting him.

Instinctively, he'd felt he could trust this solemn, wide-eyed girl. That mutual trust, secure and intact within him, blossomed from the moment she had accepted the job.

It had flourished in the way she had orchestrated the opening for him, had gone to the doctor at his request, had shown concern about the hidden enemy he must have, had comforted him after the fire, and most especially had accepted and responded wholeheartedly to his lovemaking.

Now that Uncle Henry was gone Maggie Rose was the sole repository of his absolute trust and confidence.

Therefore no matter what she told him about her past, it wasn't going to interfere with the future he envisioned them having together. He had already begun to daydream about the two of them surveying their property together on horseback. As the years would go by they'd be accompanied by one or two or even three or four small girls and boys who would all roam the woods and the pastures, wade in the brook on warm days, pick apples from the orchard, and if they wanted to, take part in the family business.

He chuckled to himself. Family business could be the riding stables, the Mailroom, or even the apartment corporation. Only his lawyer, his broker, and he himself knew he was the sole owner of the corporation.

Uncle Henry had bought the first apartment building years ago without fanfare. He drummed into Chris the necessity of owning property. Most of the profits from the farm had gone into acquiring the six apartment buildings over a twenty-year period. He had insisted that Chris take business

courses in college and Chris had complied. Daily
he was thankful he'd had the sense to do so. He
wasn't afraid of hard work and he obtained a deep
satisfaction in keeping the apartments well maintained under his personal supervision as well as
profitably managed. Soon he'd be able to buy a
seventh one.

Maggie Rose had been making a remark on the
passing scene from time to time while they listened
to the jazz tapes he usually carried. But now he
could sense that she was gathering herself to bring
up the subject he was trying to delay.

"Maggie Rose?"

She turned to look at him. Her troubled expression gripped his heart. Was he doing the right thing
in postponing her revelation? Get the uncertainty
over with and let them both deal with whatever it
was.

"I was thinking that it's been a long time since
we had that small lunch. We both need some food
so why don't we stop and eat pretty soon? After
that we can have the conversation you spoke about
in the first aid place. Is that a good idea?"

Maggie Rose felt an immense relief. Part of the
reason for the emptiness she felt was probably a
simple lack of food. Anything that would help fill
that emptiness was good.

"I hadn't thought about it, but I am hungry and
you must be also."

As they agreed to look for an attractive place to
eat she felt thankful for whatever would put off
the moment when the guillotine came down on
her neck cutting off the ties between her and Chris
Shealy. Once he knew of her lack of honesty there
would be no more trips like this, no more dances,

no more embraces. That was why she'd initiated the kiss in the parking lot. She needed it against the future without Chris. She knew she was doing the right thing but she hadn't known how painful it would be. She hadn't actually told him yet and already she was hurting so badly that she had welcomed postponement.

Meanwhile, she'd stop thinking about her position and take this last opportunity to talk about Chris's concerns.

"Shouldn't you be hearing from the association soon, Chris, or do you hear only if you're winning an award?"

"I've been expecting the announcement of the awards banquet all this week. Everyone receives that. No one knows who the winners are until the night of the affair."

"But suppose you don't go?"

"They'll see that you get the award."

"Yes, but if you knew ahead of time, then you'd be sure to attend and have all the excitement and congratulations. Why don't they tell people who are the winners?"

"From what I understand they used to but then the news spread and it cut down on the attendance. Also the wrong names got out once on a rumor and it caused a lot of confusion so now it's kept a secret until the night."

"I don't see how anyone could beat you. Everything about HS Stables is first class, the horses, the property, the instruction, and the instructors."

"If only you were one of the judges." He smiled at her and her heart turned over. How could she have done anything that would take him from her now that destiny had brought them together after all these years?

She moved on to the other idea that had been floating around in her mind.

"Chris, had it occurred to you that Dan might be the one responsible for the fire and the other things?"

"What makes you think that?" he said with a small frown. "Did Jerlene say something?"

"Jerlene and I haven't discussed Dan but I've been racking my brain thinking of who could have it in for you, and the only thing that stands out is that all of these things happened after Dan showed up."

"I did a thorough background check before I hired him because he'd be dealing with kids. He's lived in Texas since childhood, father is dead, has a mother and a married sister. No police record of any kind. Has spent most of his life doing what he's doing here, in sales and with horses. Unmarried."

"How do you feel about him?"

"He's okay. Really good with the horses and does very well with the older students. I'm thinking of seeing if the schedule can be rearranged so I have all of the younger ones and he has the older ones." He gave her an intent look. "Are you uneasy about him, Maggie Rose?"

"If I am it's probably because of Jerlene. He seems to fit the patern of the men she likes and they don't wear well as far as I can see."

"I know what you mean," he said absentmindedly. "Did you read in the paper that stupid story about me breaking up a fight?"

"I saw it, why?"

"A guy at Bill's party told me that Virgil McCoy, the one who gave me the black eye, was going around spouting off to people that he would get even with me. He says he had a legitimate beef with the other fellow because of an unpaid debt and if I hadn't stepped in, he'd have gotten his money."

"Was he at the opening?"

"I didn't see him and his name wasn't on the list, but that doesn't mean he couldn't have sneaked in."

"Did you go see him?" Maggie Rose wanted this business cleared up. She thought that since Art Fulton had been hired for night patrol, Chris and Tallie felt safe. She didn't agree but didn't know if it was intuition or just normal worry for people she cared about.

"I gave the information to the sheriff. Virgil can be hard to get ahold of as he moves around a lot. Sheriff said he's out of town but has a connection who'll let him know when Virgil shows up."

"I hope so. It bothers me that you could be in danger."

"I don't think there'll be more trouble but I appreciate your caring, Maggie Rose." His words were quiet but the last phrase was filled with meaning as he laid his hand briefly on hers.

As they approached Wilmington, Chris said, "Shall we eat here?" She nodded yes and they found a pleasant restaurant off the main street. "We could find lots of places at the beach but this is July Fourth," Chris noted.

"Crowds and noise. This is better," she agreed.

Maggie Rose ordered crab cakes and was able to eat one along with a side of coleslaw. The other one she gave Chris to eat, who obliged after finishing his softshell crab sandwich.

"I remember eating here several years ago," Chris said as they left the restaurant. "The food is still good. Did you enjoy it?"

"I did, the crab cakes were just as I like them."

Once they were back on the highway Chris took a deep breath, looked at Maggie Rose soberly, and said, "I'm ready now for what it is you want to tell me."

Maggie Rose said a silent prayer for strength to get through this. She wanted to look straight ahead but that would be too cowardly. She turned in her seat so she was facing him.

"Chris, I have been dishonest with you and I apologize. I am more sorry than I can ever say that I didn't have the courage to tell you the whole truth about myself when you asked me to be your office manager. But I wanted the job. I needed the money, as you know, and I wanted Covey to be with you for the summer so I lied to you." That was as far as she could get.

"Lied to me about what?" He glanced at her with puzzlement before looking back at the busy highway.

"Every time I'm near horses I go into panic. They terrify me. I break out in sweat, I have trouble breathing, I get nauseated. My whole system goes haywire and if I can't get away I faint."

"Are you saying that all those times you got sick, that's what it was?" There was an incredulous quality in his voice.

"Yes."

"Why didn't you just tell me the first time it

happened when I was taking you to see the horses and you said you turned your ankle?"

"I did turn my ankle, you saw how it swelled up."

"The next morning when I asked you about it you said you got dizzy, which made you start to fall, but you couldn't explain why you got dizzy. You changed on me." He looked at her, recalling the scene. "I remember thinking then that you were keeping something from me and it hurt. That's why I decided to treat you like any employee I'd hired." This time when he looked at her, his eyes were flashing. "Do you remember that?"

"Of course I do, but I never knew why you'd changed."

He scarcely heard her as he reviewed other times she'd been sick. "Two days later you brought the twins to the stable and you looked awful. I took the boys but when I looked back you were bent over in pain but you never mentioned it to me. Then you were supposed to watch Covey's first lesson but you had an excuse for not coming out. A few days later you did watch and would have fainted if I hadn't jumped the fence and caught you."

The more he recalled the angrier he became. He saw the rest-area notice ahead and pulled in. He parked as far away from other cars as he could. Then he turned to face her.

"I kept asking you what was the matter. Why didn't you ever tell me the truth, Maggie Rose?"

Beneath his agitation she heard a plea. There was no way to pretty it up or avoid the unvarnished truth but she knew this would bring on the death

knell of the beauty that had been developing
between them.

"I was ashamed. And afraid."

"What were you afraid of? What have I *ever* done
to make you afraid of me?"

"It's nothing you've done, Chris." Instinctively
she put out her hand to touch him only to have
him draw himself away. "I was hired to work around
horses but I can't stand to be near them so I was
afraid to lose my job, which I loved."

"The day I came to see you in your apartment
and we talked about Covey helping Tallie this summer you got upset when I mentioned horses. You
were speaking about yourself, weren't you?"

"Yes, I was."

"I asked you then if you trusted me and you said
it wasn't a matter of trust. That it was a matter of
Jerlene's consent."

She thought she'd never seen anything as bleak
as the eyes that looked into her soul. "But it was
a matter of trust, wasn't it?" he said.

His voice was quiet now. "*It was always a matter
of trust that you didn't have in me.* You didn't trust
me enough to say how horses affect you. We could
have worked it out."

Maggie Rose could not look away from that bleakness, even through the tears running down her
face.

The quiet voice went on. "Do you know what I
was forced to conclude about you? That you must
be pregnant. I didn't want to think it much less
believe it but the symptoms fit. That's why I insisted
you go to a doctor and I trusted you to tell me
what his diagnosis was. But even then you didn't
trust me with the truth, did you, because I assume

you told him the real cause of your symptoms,
didn't you?''

She nodded her head in assent.

Chris looked at her as if this were the final sword
thrust. He let himself out of the car and walked
away down the green grass to the far end of the
picnic area.

Maggie Rose laid her head on the dashboard.
Wrenching sobs came up through her whole being.
How could she have been so blind? She had put
her own fears above all and not understood the
depth of injustice to Chris, who had given her
his trust and demonstrated his caring from the
beginning.

She could never expect anything from him again.

Chris walked to the end of the picnic grounds
and looked blindly at the row of eighteen-wheelers
parked on the opposite end in their own restricted
spot. Their colors glistened through the tears he
would not permit to fall. Grief, anger, and raw hurt
tore at him in a way he'd never experienced before.

He yearned to be on his own land chopping
down a tree, clearing out the brush that surrounded his pastures, or even riding HS at full
speed across his fields. Anything rather than
standing here, immobile, feeling his impotence
to vent this rage that only Maggie Rose could
make him feel.

He couldn't understand why she hadn't told him.
Hadn't he always been careful with her, restraining
himself from doing anything to frighten her, and
hadn't he always shown her his trust?

He suddenly felt drained and looked around for
a vacant table. He sat down, his head in his hands.
It must be that awful reputation he'd cultivated

in his youth. He'd never done anything criminal, although some of his escapades just skirted the law. Then he'd grown out of the need to make people like Maggie Rose and her father sit up and take notice of him. Was that why she couldn't trust him? Even though she was as attracted to him as he was to her? That he would swear was true, the mutual attraction. Unless his desire for her was so strong it made him see only what he wanted to see.

But he would have bet the farm that her shy embraces and kisses were real, that she meant it when she said yes, she was his sweetheart. The ugly possibility that those professed feelings also were false propelled him to his feet and to a pounding walk around the entire rest area.

He had to get himself under control. He still had a few hours of driving to get them safely home. How was he to handle that?

Earlier today he'd told himself that what was past was past. That was when he was trying to anticipate what Maggie Rose wanted to tell him. Now he knew. And it was in the past. So be it.

Tomorrow was another day but to get there they had to finish today. So he'd return to his SUV and drive home with Maggie Rose as just another barely known passenger.

With that in mind he returned to the car and got in. He looked at Maggie Rose curiously.

Although her eyes were red and swollen and her face was drawn, it was obvious that she'd tried to pull herself together as best she could. Her hair was freshly combed, her lips had a tint of red, and her posture was erect as she met his eyes.

"I know you don't believe me, Chris, but I do apologize. And I'm sorry I don't have another way

to get home so you wouldn't have to be bothered
with me."

"Don't be ridiculous," he snapped. "I'm not
going to put you out on the side of the road. I
would suggest that you ride in the back where you
can stretch out and get some rest, as we still have
a ways to go."

She immediately climbed into the back and lay
down.

Chris pulled out onto the highway and in
wretched silence they returned to Jamison.

Chapter Twenty-Four

Maggie Rose dragged herself out of bed Friday morning after a night in which she'd finally succumbed to sleep two hours earlier. No yoga this morning. She barely had time to stand under a shower long enough to feel its revivifying effect before dressing.

She looked hollow-eyed and pinched. Cosmetics helped but nothing could make the sparkle return to her eyes, she thought. They were as dull and lifeless as she felt.

Covey was full of talk about his holiday with his mom and Mr. Dan at Folly Beach. He was tanned and had begun to fill out so that his arms and legs no longer looked so thin. "Tommy went, too, and he and I swam and played ball. I can run faster than Tommy now since I've been working on the farm," he said proudly.

"Something in here smells bad, Aunt Maggie Rose," he said, sniffing the air.

"I don't smell anything," she said.

"I do," Covey declared. "Can I look?"

"Please do."

Do sadness and sorrow have a fragrance? she mused while Covey pulled all the receipts, bills, and other junk out of the glove compartment. *Maybe that's what fills the car.* There was a song about the sound of silence. She could write one about the smell of sadness or the sting of sorrow.

Covey pulled a sandwich bag containing a portion of molding beef from under his seat. "Ugh," he said. "I left this here almost a week ago, forgot about it. Sorry." He opened the window.

"Covey! You know better than to throw it out the window. Hold on to it until we get to the farm."

The office waited, empty and silent. Maggie Rose, feeling bruised and apathetic, dreaded seeing Chris, but he did not come into the office before going to work. She worked on the never-ending file cards, brought student records up to date, ordered supplies, and prepared the three paychecks for Chris to sign when he came home.

She was thankful that parents had already arrived when he came in. She was included in his general greeting as he received the roster for Friday's students and signed the checks.

A quick glance told Maggie Rose that Chris, too, lacked sleep. There were shadows under his eyes and an edginess in his manner. This increased her sense of guilt, for as a riding instructor he needed to be alert and rested.

The burden of guilt had lain heavy on her all weekend. Nothing gave her an escape from it. Even church on Sunday had provided no surcease from her pain. She went to the Mailroom and worked mechanically with Ginnie and the two professional painters who were putting broad bands of fresh cranberry color at the top of the light gray walls. Only the Craft Corner remained to be done before she and Ginnie took possession a week from tomorrow.

She and Ginnie had decided that for the first year they would work without a salary from the Mailroom. Ginnie would continue with her job and Maggie Rose had intended to work out an afternoon shift with Chris, as that was the busiest time of his day. That would leave her free to work mornings at the Mailroom while Ginnie worked afternoons. What they would have drawn as salary would go to keeping Essie Weathers on full-time as she was now. A longtime assistant to Miss Henny, she would be invaluable in helping Ginnie and Maggie Rose learn the intricacies of the business.

"You don't look too good. I hope you're not coming down with a virus," Ginnie had observed.

"I'm okay. Just a little tired."

Ginnie continued her critical scrutiny. "Are you still doing your yoga?"

Maggie Rose turned away to pick up a paint cloth. "Didn't have time this morning. I overslept and was almost late for church." The whole truth was that she hadn't attempted yoga since the morning of the Fourth. She had lost her interest, her motivation, her energy, and her appetite.

When they had finished at the Mailroom, Maggie Rose drove home. She had slumped in a chair and looked out of the window. The same scenes played endlessly in her mind: Chris's disbelieving face, his anger, his coldness, his contempt. The way he opened the door of the car when he pulled up to her door, helped her out, said an icy "Good night," and drove away after she went inside.

She was so full of self-disgust she could barely look at her face in the mirror. No matter how deeply she probed she could not find a rationale for her refusal to tell Chris about her fear of horses. What he had said was true—that he had never given her reason to distrust him.

It was herself that she distrusted, her own weakness that made her vacillate even when he pleaded with her to tell him why she was sick. She'd been astounded and even more deeply ashamed when he said he'd been forced to conclude she must be pregnant. His thinking that had never occurred to her.

That was the crux of the matter, wasn't it? His thoughts, his concerns, his anxieties about why she kept being sick had not mattered to her. She was only focused on her own and whether she would be able to keep her job.

The job that had been so important was now like ashes in her mouth. Seeing Chris on Friday had been painful beyond belief. He had not wanted to look at her and when he signed the paychecks he was careful to move them from where she sat at her desk. He talked to the waiting parents and averted his gaze from her.

She could not bear to continue to be in his presence day after day when she was obviously anathema to him. She was thoroughly in the wrong, that was true, but even so she had her pride. She would not be where she clearly wasn't wanted.

She got up from the chair, went to the phone,

and dialed his number. He answered immediately as she involuntarily looked at the clock. It was already after ten.

"Chris, sorry to call so late. I hadn't realized the time."

"It's all right."

"I called to say I'm not coming back."

Silence. He said no words but she heard him draw a breath.

"I don't see how I can, Chris."

Silence. Then he said, "If that's your choice."

She waited for him to hang up but the connection continued. She felt compelled to say something more.

"I don't have any other choice."

"There's always another choice."

This time she heard the click and she hung up the phone. Calling Jerlene was another matter. She knew she would get a lot of flak from her sister unless Maggie Rose was uncompromising from the beginning. So when her sister said hello, Maggie Rose stated her position firmly.

"Jerlene, I know this will be an inconvenience for everyone, but from tomorrow on you'll have to arrange Covey's transportation to the farm. I won't be going back myself."

"You quit? Why? This is so sudden and I—"

Maggie Rose interrupted. "I know it's sudden, Jerlene, but you'll have to do the best you can. Tell Covey I'm sorry. I'll talk to you later," she ended and hung up the phone.

She warmed milk and, taking a cup of it with her to bed, sipped it slowly, hoping it would help her sleep. Emotional exhaustion and the milk worked together to give her a night's sleep, restoring some energy. The next morning she decided to leave the apartment and avoid the calls she was sure her family would be making soon.

She gathered her sunscreen, towel, and beach attire in case she decided to swim, and several books, then drove the thirty miles to Folly Beach. There were other early people scattered here and there, some running, a number of walkers, and a few with their dogs. She had no problem renting an umbrella and a chair. She intended to stay until she had worked through what her next step should be and regained her emotional balance.

For starters, she was definitely going to have to dip into her savings to make up the total five thousand, but more than that, she no longer had the job that was supposed to sustain her until she could get a salary from the business next year.

She and Chris hadn't discussed her staying on but she was certain that not only would it have been agreeable, but he would have grabbed at it, even on a half-time schedule. She shook her head at her self-destructive actions where Chris was concerned. She hadn't been able to find a job, he appeared out of the blue and offered her one at the salary she needed, she took the job and did good work, and then she blew it all to bits, and here she was, again without a job. And she managed to do it all in five weeks!

If it hadn't been so stupidly asinine, she would have cried. One thing about it, she'd be careful from now on about criticizing Jerlene for actions and decisions that seemed crazy and reckless.

That was one thing settled. Dipping into her savings was a necessity so she'd grin and bear it. Getting a job would have to wait since the taking

over of the business was so imminent. But she'd
begin to put out feelers.

She hoped Jerlene had taken Covey to the farm.
His being there was one of the best things that had
happened in his young life and to cut it short,
especially now that he was learning to ride, would
be cruel. She would have to check on that this
evening. Between her parents and Jerlene and Dan
helping, they should manage it if Jerlene understood the depth of her son's need to continue his
work. He was around a caring, instructive man in
Tallie and the same in Chris. They both had his
interests at heart and provided for him the casually
male environment of hard work and good fellow-
ship on equal terms that had been lacking. He had
grown in confidence and stature. The idiocy of
one adult like his aunt should not interrupt this
experience for him.

That was the second thing settled, she decided.
Whatever it took, she would see to it that he got
to the farm and back five days a week.

Her mind swung again to Chris as it had been
doing almost obsessively since the Fourth. He was
always there, the person around which all of her
concerns one way or another revolved.

It seemed strange that he had never once asked
what had caused her panic reaction to horses. She
thought it would be his first question. Yet he
evinced no interest in the cause at all. Then when
he left the car to walk in the rest area she'd
expected him to return with the question. She
meant to tell him but from the beginning he had
pursued the personal aspect of her failure to tell
him.

Pursued it in all its bitterness, as it displayed

her lack of trust in him. For Chris that was the overriding issue and it revealed to her a misjudgment on her part. She had not understood his character. She knew that in not telling him of her fear she was being dishonest. She had not followed that idea deeply enough to recognize that total honesty has its basis in trust. Trusting that the two adults involved in this case could rely on themselves and on each other to find a resolution of the issue. That they cared enough about each other and what was between them to take the risk of embarrassment or weakness or whatever they might feel because the vital issue was to preserve their mutual trust.

There was no other basis on which their relationship could develop. She saw that now. One could feel attraction in its many manifestations for various people but trust was another thing entirely. To trust was a commitment. It was built on experience, insight, and instinct. She had known Chris nearly all her life and there had been a bond between them from the very beginning. Hadn't she known deep inside that she could always depend on him, and wasn't that trust?

A barking dog following a ball that hit her chair startled her out of her reverie. A boy who seemed to be about six years old, his flushed face almost matching the red of his swim shorts, rushed up to retrieve the ball and the dog.

"Sorry," he said.

"It's all right." She smiled as she handed him the ball.

The dog wagged his tail happily as the boy threw the ball in the opposite direction for both of them to pursue.

Maggie Rose looked after them and saw a woman in the near distance, her hand shading her eyes against the sun, calling to the boy, who narrowly missed a family group lying on beach towels as he trailed the dog and the ball. A man in blue swim trunks appeared beside the woman and gave a sharp command to the dog, who bounded over to him with the ball in his mouth.

The woman swept the boy up in her arms, then set him down again. With the boy's hands securely held, the three of them ran into the water. The ecstatic dog scrambled in after them.

Maggie Rose was suddenly assaulted by so deep a sense of loss it was like a physical pain that jolted her heart. The scene played out on the beach would never be before her and Chris. She had destroyed that future.

A future with Chris had been planted in her psyche since she was nine. She saw that now. They was why she could never get seriously interested in anyone else. She was meant for him because she loved him. Had always loved him but hadn't realized it. Even Lem Norris had been a reflection of that love, now that she thought of it objectively, because he resembled Chris. That was what had attracted her, the same deep-set eyes, the tall frame, and the shape of the face. She hadn't seen that before.

The beach was getting crowded now and Maggie Rose tilted the brim of her straw hat to hide her face as the tears began to fall. Black despair gripped her. She had lost her love, her only love. He had asked if she was his sweetheart and she had said yes with all of her love reaching out to him. "And I'm yours," he'd said.

Dear Lord, how could she have thrown that away? What was she to do now with the rest of her life? There would never be another love for her. Only Chris. How would she bear to live in the same town and see him year after year knowing how close they'd been to sheer happiness with each other?

She clasped her hands so tightly together they hurt as she tried to control the tears. *Help me, dear Lord, I don't know where to go from here,* she prayed. *Let Chris forgive me for what I did.* Her stomach ached and she wrapped her arms around herself. After a while she took steady sips from her water bottle and they began to have an effect in stopping the crying.

When she was quiet she wiped her face, applied a new layer of sunblock, and laid a towel across her legs for protection from a burn. Empty and hollow inside, she stared out at the endless water. The afternoon sun sparkling on the waves held no brightness for her. There was only a void, but the gentle movement of the elemental body of water entered her senses and she gratefully slipped away into it, her closed eyes blocking out all else.

Maggie Rose gradually became aware of sound again. She heard laughter and excited screams that filled a beach at its peak. She stirred and sat up in her chair. How long had she been out of it? She was so shocked to see it was three o'clock. She held her watch to her ear to see if it was still running.

She realized she felt at peace for the first time since Thursday. While she was in the valley of despair God had heard her supplication. She was not alone and He would show her the way. Gratitude filled her heart.

She reached in her tote bag for the water bottle

and touched the apple she'd forgotten about. When her stomach growled as if in response to the possibility of being fed, she began munching on the apple.

The ocean waves danced and sparkled, beckoning her spirit to be fearless and free. She opened herself to their call and emptied her mind. On the waves came the certain knowledge that tomorrow she should return to her job with Chris. She did not question it but acquiesced.

Maggie Rose picked up her belongings and left the beach.

Tomorrow she would begin a new phase in her life.

Chapter Twenty-Five

Chris was relaxing on the lounger. Monday's schedule hadn't been as demanding as some but he was tired anyway. Had Uncle Henry been alive, he would have grumbled at his nephew to take the tonic his mother used to give him. "Builds you up and gives you pep," he always asserted.

Pep was exactly what he needed these days, but he knew full well it couldn't be restored to him from a bottle. When he was younger and uncautious there'd been a time or two when a bottle of alcohol promised to be a problem solver, but he found out the hard way how false that was.

The hardest part of the day had been trying to act as if everything were normal. When he told Tallie at breakfast that Maggie Rose had called to say she wouldn't be back, Tallie had stopped dead still. "I knew something was wrong Friday," he said. "You all had a falling-out when you went to the races?"

"You could call it that," Chris said quietly.

Breakfast continued in silence until Tallie asked about Covey.

"I don't know if he's coming or not. I hope so."

"So do I," Tallie said.

Over his final cup of coffee Tallie observed, "Maggie Rose is a fine girl. She'll come to her senses."

Jerlene, in a hurry, had dropped Covey off. Dan would take him home, she said. Covey had been subdued all morning but brightened up when he had his riding lesson. Chris let him help with the four Monday students. To questions from parents about Maggie Rose, Chris said, "She's away today."

He'd managed to get through the weekend hours by hard work. Saturday was the heaviest student day and when that was over he began clearing the brush adjacent to the orchard, a job he'd been postponing in favor of more urgent matters. By the time he went to bed he was tired enough to shower and sleep.

Sunday had been difficult. He worked as hard as he could around the stables. With Tallie he found some repairs needed on the barn and decided Tallie could do them tomorrow since it only involved making some of the strips on the back more secure with minor patches, then painting them.

"Covey'll love doing this," Tallie said. "Hammering and painting keeps him happy."

"You going to see Miss Hester today it's about time for you to get ready," Chris said.

"She's out with some church ladies at a tea or

something," Tallie said. "I'll be around if you want to go off."

"That case I'll get on with the brush clearance."

The afternoon sun was hot and the sweat poured off his face and hair, wetting the towel around his neck and the sweatband of his straw hat. He liked to keep the borders of his property neat and well defined, but here they had overgrown. He used a machetelike tool to chop with and gloved hands to pull with. The rhythm he fell into made his muscles feel well oiled, flexible, and responsive to the task.

Friday and Saturday he'd been overwhelmed with sadness. He had dreaded seeing Maggie Rose on Friday so had gone into the office only when he had to sign the paychecks. The pain associated with her was too recent, too sharp. He was glad the next day was Saturday. He couldn't dwell on her while he was teaching, so it wasn't until Sunday that the full pain hit him again. He'd never lost an arm or a leg but wondered if this was how it felt. Something that had been an integral part of your being suddenly and excruciatingly lopped off.

Maggie Rose had been a part of him since he was a kid. A quiet part but always there. His very own hidden treasure to look at and think about when his spirit called for it. Since Thursday he'd been trying to analyze why he felt that way, because if he could define it, he would know how to separate himself from it.

She was tall, slim, had wide brown eyes and shoulder-length hair. But so did many other girls. He could name four off the bat, beginning with Neda, who were better looking than Maggie Rose.

She was bright and successful in her work, proving it by rising to administrative assistant for a vice president in the legal department of a major corporation. He knew other women who were just as able in their careers.

She didn't have the blazing personality that Gwen Aiken had but she was friendly and warm in her own way.

She was loyal to a fault with her family, hardworking, yet could have fun too, as Bill's party had proved.

None of these things explained the mystery of why she was so wrapped around his heart.

He might as well admit to himself that he loved Maggie Rose. That was why her lack of trust in him devastated him. She'd betrayed that love. Just at the point where he thought they'd come so close they could tell each other anything, she hit him with this mortal blow.

Chris gave a tangled knot of weeds wrapped around a branch a vicious cut that severed the knot. He pulled the weeks away, then stood straight to wipe his face and stretch his back. He looked out across his fields. In the distance he saw two men leaning over a fence. That'd be Nat and Ed Nettles, the brothers who leased part of his acreage and could be seen most any Sunday surveying part of it. They were good neighbors and good farmers. Ed was a bachelor but Nat and Laura had five kids.

Chris wiped his face again thinking Nat's oldest must be twelve or thirteen now. Old enough to be a real help on the farm. He'd often been in their home and had hoped he'd be fortunate enough to have a happy, healthy bunch of children and a loving, loyal wife like Laura.

He could kiss that dream good-bye, he thought,

as he bent once more to his task and began chopping weeds with all his strength. Maggie Rose's call to say she wasn't coming back had been the final act. Until that moment he realized that concealed deep inside him was the hope that with her in the office eventually they'd be able to bring healing to what had happened between them.

Eventually the acute pain he now felt would dull because that was the nature of pain. His life would move along lacking brightness but he'd just have to accept it and see what time would bring.

When the man answered the telephone the voice on the other end said, "If you can't do better than you've been doing, I'll take care of it myself."

"Don't worry. This next idea'll work."

"That's what you said last time."

Chapter Twenty-Six

Maggie Rose decided she would not call Chris again. She'd just show up for work Tuesday morning and see what happened. If he ordered her away, that was his right and she'd accept it.

She spent an hour doing yoga, dressed carefully in an ankle-length soft green dress, and picked up a happy Covey, who after the first question about where she was yesterday, regaled her with how he'd helped Mr. Chris with the students.

Her heart was beating fast as she entered the office. Chris would see her car and now all she had to do was get to work and wait for him to show up.

He came in three minutes later dressed in his job outfit of chino slacks and matching sports shirt.

He stood on the opposite side of her desk. He was at ease and his face revealed nothing as he met her eyes. He said nothing at all.

She'd thought of ten different things to say but

none of them came to mind as she drank in the sight of him. She saw he wasn't going to help her, and why should he? She'd made the break, it was solely up to her to try to patch it. His eyes gave nothing away but at least he was looking at her, which he hadn't done the last time they were in this spot.

"You told me there's always another choice and I discovered that was true." She found she couldn't say another word. All she could do was look at him and hope he had some understanding of all that her statement and presence were trying to convey.

She stood quietly, holding nothing back under his continued scrutiny. There was a flicker in his eyes and she saw the muscles of his face relax.

"Good morning, Maggie Rose," he said. "You'll see the Monday registrations need some work. How're you doing with the transfer onto disc of the old records?"

"I'm about halfway through."

"Good. I'll be back in time for classes."

Maggie Rose let out her breath as he softly closed the door behind him. She had surmounted the first and biggest hurdle. She was back and he had permitted her to stay. That was all she could ask for now. With a light heart she finished the Monday registrations and resumed work on the records.

At lunchtime Tallie came in with a chicken salad sandwich and iced tea. On the tray was a small vase holding four yellow daisies.

"I figured you'd be back," he said as he set the tray down.

"Thank you, Mr. Tallie." Touched by the emotion she couldn't show Chris this morning and by Mr. Tallie's kindness, Maggie Rose hugged him and kissed his cheek. "You've always been so good to me," she said.

"What you need is to be good to yourself," he said gruffly, "and to Chris."

Her appetite was back and as she ate her food she thought of the injunction that had accompanied it. She was being good to herself in being here, since she'd never thought to occupy this desk chair again. She was going to go slowly, breathe in and breathe out, do her best work, and see what the next day would bring.

Chris couldn't believe his ears when he heard Maggie Rose drive up the lane this morning. He'd been changing to go to work and he finished in no time flat. He hadn't known what he'd say when he walked into the office; he found that all he could do was look at her.

He hadn't a clue why she was there; maybe it was to clean out her desk and prepare it for the next person he had to hire. Maybe she'd brought Covey out and was waiting to have a word with him. He didn't know. All he knew was that she was here. So he waited. Waited for her to say why she was here.

Her eyes showed signs of strain but they were no longer puffy. Her dress reminded him of the apricot one she'd worn at Teddy's. It followed all the lovely lines of her body. Her hair looked silky clean and he knew it would have her fragrance if he got close to it.

"You told me there was another choice and I discovered that was true," she said.

A ribbon of heat went through him. He searched

her eyes to see what she meant. There was no evasiveness or indecision in them, only resolution. It seemed that she meant to stay if he let her. Meanwhile, she stood calmly awaiting his verdict and letting him scrutinize her until he was satisfied about her sincerity.

The tension left his body and unloosed his tongue. He greeted her as if this were a usual off-to-work communication between them.

She was back. He had his office manager again and they would take each day as it came until her agreed six weeks was up.

When he got back for his afternoon classes he found Mr. Neal from the bank and another man talking to Maggie Rose.

"Chris, meet my friend Bob Kimbel. He came with me to your opening and has been after me to go ahead and sign up for a riding class, so I guess that's what I'll do today," Mr. Neal said.

"I keep telling him he does too much sitting at that bank," Mr. Kimbel said, shaking hands with Chris. A compact man with twinkling eyes, he smiled at Maggie Rose and at Chris. "I think he's decided to do it just to shut me up."

"Do you ride, Mr. Kimbel?" Chris asked.

"All the time. I have a few horses up in Spartanburg, where I live. You've got a nice-looking bunch here. You have a stallion, too?"

"That's my next project." Before he could say more, a couple of students arrived and he excused himself. "You're welcome to watch the class if you've the time, Mr. Neal. Maggie Rose will set up a schedule for your classes."

That gala opening that Maggie Rose had engineered was still paying dividends in new students,

Chris thought. If this kept up he would have to rethink this enterprise, maybe restructure the school to a full-time business. But then what would he do about the apartment business? He enjoyed such business issues and this would help him spend his mental faculties on something other than his preoccupation with Maggie Rose.

All the afternoons except Monday were filled now plus most of Saturday, so that even with Dan on board part-time as he was today, it was a heavy load. He even had a call or two for some Sundays but he tried to discourage them. A man needed a day off for himself.

Maggie Rose went home satisfied. The day had gone smoothly and apparently she'd found the right thing to say to Chris, for he accepted her and they were a team again. This was the beginning of the repair job she had to do and although it might be a lengthy process, at least she'd made a beginning. That accomplishment released all of the tension that had built up in her for too many days and nights. She slept so deeply when she finally got to bed after talking to a number of the craftspeople involved in the Mailroom business that she failed to hear the alarm. She overslept by an hour and had to literally scramble into pants and blouse and get Covey in order to be on time.

"Morning, Maggie Rose." Chris was waiting for her, relaxed and smiling. "Sleep well?"

She returned the friendly overture. "Too well. Didn't hear the alarm at all and had to scramble to be on time."

"Did Mr. Neal actually sign up?"

"He did and he wants to come on Saturday mornings so I squeezed him in, but take a look here at the board." She indicated where she'd had to write a name in over the top of another name. All but two of the slots were filled.

"You're going to have to get another instructor, Chris. Do you have one in mind or should I put an ad in the paper?"

"A couple of college kids have called me but they'll be going back to school in another month. Still, that might help for now. Let me see if I can get one of them, and after they leave we can put in the ad for a permanent instructor. How does that sound?"

"Sounds like a plan but the sooner we know about the college kids, the better. Shall I call them and set up interviews for tomorrow?"

"Yes. Their names are the file marked Personnel. I think that's where I put them."

"Don't worry about it. If they're in the files at all, I'll find them."

They smiled at each other in mutual acknowledgement of their smooth ability to work together as Chris started out the door.

"One more thing," he said, coming back. "The horses are in the stable for Harve Brown. He's my horse doctor and my blacksmith. He's checking the horses' shoes today. Tallie and Covey are working on the back of the barn and might not hear his truck so will you watch out for him?"

As soon as Chris was gone Maggie Rose looked in the personnel file for the names of the college students but they weren't there. Eventually she found them filed alphabetically: John Calvert, Rickey Turner, and Jane Wheeling. Telephone inquiries revealed that John Calvert already had a full-time job but the other two would come for interviews the next day. Maggie Rose hoped that Jane Wheeling would qualify and be hired. It would be nice to have another female on the farm and she might be very good for the more timid beginning students if she had the right personality.

In midmorning Maggie Rose began to feel hungry and thirsty. Recalling that she'd been too late to have even a cup of coffee, she decided to go to the kitchen and get something to eat as Mr. Tallie had often urged her to do. She made a cup of coffee and a piece of toast, just enough to hold her until lunchtime. She stood at the kitchen window eating the toast and looking out at the stables.

Suddenly she saw HS standing in the wide doorway as if he were uncertain what to do next. He looked down and moved his feet, then slowly walked over to nibble at the grass next to the fence. What was he doing loose? As she stood transfixed, Nicky appeared in the doorway. Two of Chris's horses loose.

The next thing she knew Maggie Rose was on her way to the stables, telling herself that horses startle easily so approach them quietly and slowly. She hadn't the least idea of what she should do if she got next to them, but she couldn't just let them run away. As she got closer her lungs began to clog up. The muscles in her stomach tightened and she felt the sweat on her face. She fought the dizziness and nausea that threatened to overwhelm her as she came close to Nicky.

"Nicky," Maggie Rose said softly.

The pony eyed Maggie Rose but didn't bolt. Maggie Rose said, "What are you and HS doing out?" She took hold of the pony's bridle and just held it for a moment to control her dizziness, then led the pony back into the stall. She didn't know how she got Nicky past Windsong and Starlight, who were moving restlessly in their stalls, but she did and fastened him into his box.

It was when she staggered back behind the horses to go outside in the hope of getting HS that she saw Covey lying on the ground in the other part of the stable where the empty boxes were.

You can't faint now, she kept telling herself as she slid dizzily to her knees beside the boy. "Covey," she said in his ear but he didn't answer. She put her fingers on his wrist and felt a weak pulse. Had one of the horses struck him? There was a bruise on his temple and a knot had formed but it didn't look like a hoofmark.

"Covey, answer me," she begged but he was pale and silent. Where was Mr. Tallie? Working on the barn, Chris had said. Could she get that far as weak as she was? She'd have to because Covey wasn't responding and now she was frightened. *Help me, please, Lord,* she thought and pushed herself to her feet. She felt herself weaving and gasping for breath but she made it out of the stable to see HS still at the fence as she turned to go to the barn. She had taken a few more steps when she saw Mr. Tallie running toward her.

"What happened? Why is HS loose?" Mr. Tallie's face was red, his voice sharp as he grabbed Maggie Rose's arm.

"Covey. Hurt. In the stables," she gasped.

Mr. Tallie almost lifted Maggie Rose as he helped her back to the stables, where he gently set her on the floor against the wall while he examined Covey. His face was a study in confusion. "Did HS kick Covey?" he asked.

"I don't know but I can't get him to wake up."

Mr. Tallie put two fingers on Covey's neck pulse. "Let me get HS back inside; then you can tell me what happened," he said.

Maggie Rose was scarcely aware of the big horse stepping gingerly through the doorway near her as she watched Covey, and then told Mr. Tallie what had happened.

"I was standing in the doorway. He stood there for a minute; then he went over and started eating near the fence. Nicky came out next and all I could think of was that two of Chris's horses were loose so I came and got Nicky back first. Then I turned to come out and try to get HS. That's when I saw Covey here on the ground."

Mr. Tallie felt Covey's wrist pulse.

"What's wrong here, Tallie?" A big man with a big voice had come into the stables. He instantly got down on one knee and began to examine Covey.

"Harve, this is Covey, who works with me this summer. I sent him here to get me something and I guess he saw HS loose. I don't know what happened then but Maggie Rose here saw both HS and Nicky from the kitchen window and came out to get them back. She got Nicky in and when she returned to go back out to get HS she saw Covey here on the ground."

He made brief introductions and mentioned that the boy was Maggie Rose's nephew. Maggie Rose felt Harve Brown's sharp gaze on her as he nodded, then continued his examination of Covey by gently running his fingers on the back of the boy's head.

"Contusion back here as well as on his temple."

"What does that mean?"

"Looks like something struck him on the temple

and he fell." He looked at Tallie. "Better call 911 to take the boy to the hospital so they can look him over." He switched his attention to Maggie Rose. "You don't look good either." He felt her pulse and looked in her eyes. "Feel faint?" he asked.

"Not right now." She heard Mr. Tallie talk to 911, then to Chris.

Tallie held the phone to Maggie Rose. "Chris wants to talk to you." Chris's voice was agitated. "How's Covey?"

"I don't know, Chris. He still hasn't opened his eyes and he's got a bump on the back of his head and one on his temple."

"I'll be there in another five minutes. I was on an errand and Tallie got me on the cell phone. I'm not that far away. Don't you worry. We'll get Covey to the hospital and he'll be all right."

"How long ago did the boy leave you, Tallie?" Mr. Brown asked.

"I guess it's only been about ten minutes, though it seems like much longer."

In the distance they could hear sirens and in another few minutes an ambulance came down the lane. Tallie went out to meet them. Chris arrived seconds later and came running into the stables. His face was ashen as he looked at Covey's still figure. He stepped aside for the EMS workers and went over to Maggie Rose.

He lifted her to her feet and held her. "He's going to be okay and we're going to find out who did this to him."

Maggie Rose leaned against him and felt a little strength flow back into her.

"What hospital?" one of the men asked as they lifted Covey onto the stretcher.

"Trident Medical Center is the nearest," Maggie Rose said. "Take him there."

"We'll be right behind you," Chris said. "Tallie, hold the fort till we can get back." He put Maggie Rose in the SUV and they followed the ambulance.

"Can you tell me what happened, honey?" he asked gently.

"I was hungry and went to the kitchen for coffee and toast. I was at the window eating the toast and saw HS come out of the stables. Then she crossed to the fence and started eating the grass. Right after her Nicky came out so I went down there and talked to Nicky so she let me lead her back into her box and fasten her up. I turned to go back out and see if I could get HS and that's when I saw Covey over by the empty boxes. I tried to get him to say something. Then I started to go get Mr. Tallie but he was already coming. We could feel a pulse but that's all. Mr. Brown came right after that. He found the bump on the back of his head and said call 911."

"You saw the horses before you saw Covey?"

"Yes," she said. "I need to call Jerlene, Chris, so she can meet us at the hospital."

"Use the cell phone."

To Maggie Rose's relief Jerlene took the news calmly and said she'd leave at once.

The child-care center where Jerlene worked was closer to the hospital than the farm so she was waiting at the emergency room when the ambulance, Chris, and Maggie Rose arrived.

Maggie Rose told Jerlene what had happened and was profoundly glad that Covey's mother was there to fill out the paperwork. When she was asked about insurance, Chris stepped forward.

"I'll pay whatever the costs are," he said and gave the clerk the written assurances required.

"You don't have to do that, Chris," Jerlene said, "but thanks a lot. My job doesn't pay benefits so I appreciate it."

"He was working on my property, Jerlene," Chris said gently.

Jerlene came over where Maggie Rose was standing. "I still don't understand how he got hurt."

"We're not sure but it looks like he was hit on the temple and then fell." She took her sister's hand. "I'm so sorry, Jerlene. Daddy told me I'd better not let anything happen to Covey on the farm and now here he is in the hospital." Her voice wavered and tears filled her eyes.

Jerlene squeezed her hand. "It's not your fault, Maggie Rose. Why would—" She was interrupted by a nurse, who told them Covey was awake.

Maggie Rose thought how pale and listless Covey was as he lay, eyes closed, taking up only a small portion of the hospital bed. They lined up beside him and Jerlene said, "Covey?"

He opened his eyes. "Mom?" His eyes were dull and pained.

"Yes, it's me," Jerlene said, caressing his face. "How do you feel?"

"My head hurts. What happened?"

"Your aunt Maggie Rose found you lying on the floor of the stable. You were unconscious." Jerlene was struggling now with the tears that hadn't come earlier.

Maggie Rose leaned down to Covey. "Did someone hit you, Covey?"

Covey closed his eyes. His next words were so soft that if Maggie Rose hadn't been close to him she wouldn't have heard his answer. A chill ran through her as she glanced at Jerlene and Chris to see if they had heard.

The nurse said, "We're taking him down to X ray now so please take seats in the waiting room. We'll call you when he's back." She closed the curtains around his bed and ushered them out.

They found three seats together in the far corner of the room, which already had a number of people in it. A baseball game was on the television attached to a shelf high up in one corner. There was no sound but several people were watching it. Others looked at magazines and one man was talking on the telephone near the door. A man and an elderly woman were grasping each other's hands as if that might prevent the sad outcome of whatever was causing the tears that streamed down the lady's face. A mother tried to keep her small boy from running around the room. "Come back here, Johnnie," she said from time to time.

Maggie Rose wondered how much heartache and sorrow these cream-colored walls absorbed daily and how much Jerlene would feel when she repeated what Covey had said. She put her arm around Jerlene, who leaned over onto Maggie Rose.

"Who would want to hurt Covey?" Jerlene murmured through her stifled sobs.

"That's what I asked him," Maggie Rose said, looking across Jerlene to Chris.

"Did he remember anything?" Chris's eyes locked with hers.

"He said Mr. Dan hit him."

Chapter
Twenty-Seven

"What did you say?" Jerlene sat up and looked at Maggie Rose in shock, her face tearstained and flushed.

"I asked, 'Did someone hit you, Covey?' and he said, 'It was Mr. Dan.' "

A wordless communication passed between Maggie Rose and Chris. She had suspected Dan but Chris said nothing had turned up in his investigation of Dan's references.

"But Dan wouldn't hurt Covey," Jerlene protested, trying to make sense of what her son had said. She turned to Chris. "Why would Covey think Dan had hit him?"

"Let me tell you what's been going on," Chris said. He told her about the office break-in, the search of his bedroom, Nicky's being set loose, and the fire. "As you can see, each incident was a little more serious than the one before. He must have intended to set all of the horses loose and after that maybe burn the whole stable down. He got HS and Nicky loose and then Covey came in and saw him so he knocked him out and ran."

Jerlene shook her head in confusion. "I still don't understand. What does Dan have against you that he would do those things?"

"I don't know but I intend to find out." Chris's face was set in grim lines of anger and determination. "I know Dan lives on Pine Street. What is the number, Jerlene?"

She gave it to him. "What are you going to do?"

"The sheriff has been looking for the person behind these incidents. I'm going to give him this latest information," he said as he left the room.

"I'm sorry, Jerlene," Maggie Rose said as Jerlene began to cry again. Poor Jerlene. She had such bad luck in her choices of men. She wondered who Dan Montgomery really was. There had to be some connection between him and Chris Shealy. He wouldn't have appeared out of the blue and initiated this campaign without a reason.

"Maggie Rose, if it was Dan, why would he do such a thing in broad daylight? Why would he or whoever it was take such a risk?" Jerlene was still trying to get her mind around the fact that Dan could knowingly hurt Covey.

"Because ever since the fire there's been a good security guard on duty all night."

Why was it taking so long just to do an X ray? Maggie Rose couldn't bring herself to consider that Covey was in any serious danger; that possibility was unbearable. She thought she would never forgive herself if he was truly hurt, because it had been her doing that had put him on the farm. Daddy wouldn't forgive her either.

"Jerlene, did you call Daddy and Mama?" She hadn't thought of them until now.

"No. I was only thinking of getting here. We can call them after we hear what the doctor has to say. No point in worrying them ahead of time."

Chris returned and sat beside Maggie Rose. "I gave Bob the information," he said.

"I'm going to wash my face," Jerlene said, "but I'll be right back."

Chris put his arm around Maggie Rose. "Maggie Rose, when you went to get the horses back in the stables you had a panic attack, didn't you?" His voice was soft and gentle.

"How did you know?" she asked.

"I can see it in you face. Was it bad, honey?" She nodded her head.

"But you did it anyway, my brave girl." He brought her hand to his lips and kissed it.

"I couldn't let your horses run away." With that simple statement Maggie Rose realized the totality of her commitment to Chris Shealy and whatever affected his welfare. The concept that she could work through her panic had never occurred to her, but her love for Covey and for Chris had made her transcend the physical symptoms that had heretofore crippled her. She tucked that thought away for future examination as Jerlene returned.

"I wonder how much longer it will take," Jerlene said. She looked at Chris. "What did the sheriff say?"

"He's bringing Dan in for questioning as soon as he finds him. I'm sorry, Jerlene. I know you like him but if he is the one who hurt Covey I have no pity for him."

Jerlene nodded, her face filled with misery.

A nurse came into the room. "Sanders family?" she asked, looking around the room.

The three of them stood immediately and followed the nurse back to where they'd left Covey. A young man in glasses and a white coat held a thin sheaf of papers in his hand. "Who is the parent?" he asked.

"I am," Jerlene said.

"I'm Dr. Kimball and your son is all right," he said pleasantly.

"He got the bump on the back of his head from falling backward when a man struck him with his fist. You know about that?" He looked at the three of them and they all nodded.

"It wasn't as hard a blow as it could have been but the combination of it with falling backward is what caused him to lose consciousness. The X rays show no internal damage at all. These are just contusions that will eventually go down. He needs to rest but keep him awake as long as you can and I'd suggest you take him to your doctor for a follow-up in a week or so. He can have an aspirin for headache if necessary."

With a brisk nod he was gone. The nurse brought a wheelchair for Covey, who'd been listening with interest to the doctor. His eyes were clearer and some of his energy had returned. "Why do I have to ride in a wheelchair?" he wanted to know.

"We always have to take a patient out to the car in a wheelchair. That way we know the patient left here safely," the nurse answered.

"I need to talk with Covey, so we'll follow you

home. Okay?'' Chris told Jerlene as he opened her car door for Covey.

"Okay."

"We don't know how Covey knew it was Dan,'' Maggie Rose said as they followed Jerlene.

"Right. It's hard to believe that Dan just strolled in and began letting the horses loose. He'd know Tallie and Covey would be working at the back of the barn, because we all talked about it yesterday. Still, he must have been desperate to take such a risk. It doesn't make sense.''

"Unless his time was running out,'' Maggie Rose said tentatively. "Maybe he had some kind of deadline.''

"I haven't forgotten that you told me it might be Dan,'' he said after a silence. "I just hope the sheriff is in time to get him before he runs off.''

"Is he going to let you know?''

"He said he would.''

"I think there must be a link with your family, Chris.''

"That's the only thing that sounds reasonable,'' he agreed. "It's been going through my mind.''

Inside Jerlene's apartment Covey was put on the sofa with a glass of icy lemonade. The others sat in chairs around him and Covey looked as if he didn't know quite what to expect. Maggie Rose wondered if Jerlene had already asked him about Dan.

"Covey,'' Chris said, "we all need to know just what happened this morning. Do you feel well enough to talk about it?''

"Yes, sir.''

"Do you remember everything that happened?''

Covey glanced sideways at his mother as if he'd

done something wrong, and Maggie Rose knew Jerlene and Covey had not talked about it yet. Covey felt guilty about saying it was his mother's friend who had hit him.

"I remember," Covey said, looking now at Chris.

"I was helping Mr. Tallie working on the back of the barn like you told us to. Mr. Tallie needed a special marker to measure with. He said he was getting forgetful and had to think where he used it last. It was in the stables and he sent me to get it. I saw Mr. Dan as soon as I went in. He was in Windsong's box and I wondered why he was there and why he had on a hood. He turned and saw me and hit me on the side of my head with his fist and I fell down and passed out. That's all I know."

"If the man you saw was wearing a hood, what makes you think it was Dan?" Jerlene asked.

"Mama, I see him almost every day. I know what he looks like," Covey said.

"You have to be sure, Covey," Chris said.

"You know how Mr. Dan hunched his shoulders a little," he told Chris, "and he was wearing the same black pants he wears a lot. I saw the same diamond ring he showed me one day when he was here and I smelled the stuff he puts on all the time." His voice was decisive as he ended his list, still looking at Chris to see if Chris believed him.

"He started to. He said, 'What?' and then hit me real fast." His voice wavered and tears came into his eyes. "Why did he do that?" Now he turned to Jerlene, and Maggie Rose felt her heart throb in sympathy when Covey asked his mother, "Was it something I did, Mama? I thought he was our friend."

Jerlene hugged him tight. "No, it wasn't anything

you did, Covey. We both thought he was our friend but now we know he wasn't. But it's not your fault.''

Chris was clenching and unclenching his fists. Maggie Rose sensed he was feeling the same frustration she felt and a responsibility for Covey's condition. When she put her hand on his he unclenched his fist and laced his fingers through hers.

Covey had swallowed his tears as he looked at Chris. "Do you believe me, Mr. Chris?" Even though he knew now that Mr. Chris wasn't his dad, Covey wanted Mr. Chris to believe him.

"I believe you, Covey. You did see Dan Montgomery. You've been very brave and we're all proud of you." He extended his hand and Covey, flushing, shook hands.

"We're going now but one more thing, Covey. The sheriff will be wanting to ask you about this morning."

Covey's eyes grew wide and he tried to sit straighter. "He will?"

"He'll call your mom about it."

"I'm so glad you're all right, Covey," Maggie Rose said as she hugged him.

"We'll let Mr. Tallie know because I know he's worried about you."

"I can go to work with you tomorrow, can't I?" His eyes were pleading for her to say yes.

"I'll have to wait to see what your mom says, but I hope so."

When they were seated in Chris's car he hesitated before starting it. "Do you want to go home, Maggie Rose?"

"Of course not, I want to go back to work," she said. It occurred to her that she hadn't looked in a mirror all morning and maybe she didn't look fit to be in the office.

"Do I look that bad?" she asked.

"You look fine," he reassured her. "I just thought you might be worn out."

"I want to be there when the sheriff calls you. Do you think he'll believe Covey's reasons for saying it was Dan?" Since the child hadn't see the face of the person who hit him, she was afraid his testimony wouldn't stand up to the law's scrutiny.

"I don't know, Maggie Rose. He's got some youngsters himself and he should know they see and remember what seems trivial, especially boys. It sounded conclusive to me but that's because I know Covey. Tallie often tells me how good he is about details."

"The other day he smelled something in my car that I didn't smell. It was some rotten food in the closed glove compartment. I'm certain he'd recognize Dan's cologne."

It was five o'clock and Maggie Rose was still in the office registering the last of the Wednesday students when the phone rang. "This is the sheriff's office," a voice said. "Mr. Chris Shealy there?"

Chris had just gone down to the stable so Maggie Rose transferred the call there. She waited impatiently for Chris to let her know the news. When it rang she tried not to snatch the phone in front of the parent standing at the desk. "The sheriff'll be here as soon as he can make it," Chris repeated.

It took another hour and a half before his official car rolled down the lane toward the three people waiting on the porch. Tallie had told Chris and

Maggie Rose how a deputy had come to the stables
to interview Tallie and to take photographs.

Chris was down the steps to meet the sheriff
before his car came to a final stop. After they
greeted each other Chris said, "Come up and have
a seat. Tallie's got some cold lemonade or iced tea,
whichever you prefer."

Sheriff Snipes accepted the invitation and some
lemonade, explaining to Tallie he must've already
drunk a gallon of iced tea today. Courtesy demanded that no questions be asked until the sheriff
was ready. Tallie bridged the gap by talking about
the effect the drought was having on his garden
and discussing the state of Mrs. Snipes's garden.
The sheriff's wife was known for winning awards
for her vegetables at the county fair.

His glass of lemonade finished, the sheriff said,
"I guess you'd like to know we have Mr. Montgomery in custody."

Maggie Rose let out the breath she hadn't realized she'd been holding and heard Chris do the
same. Mr. Tallie's face relaxed and they all three
sat back in their chairs as the tension left their
bodies.

"He gave us a little run," the sheriff said in his
matter-of-fact voice. "We went to his house on Pine
Street. A woman who said she was his mother said
as far as she knew he was at work at the car lot. I'd
sent a deputy there and the mother undoubtedly
called Mr. Montgomery about our visit. He came
fast out of the lot and the deputy gave chase."

"That went on for about thirty minutes. He saw
he couldn't keep on outrunning us so he jumped
out of the car and ran into some woods. It took
us a little while but we found him. Then he gave

himself up. I read him his rights but on the way back he confessed that he was in your stables and that the boy surprised him. He hit him and when the boy fell down unconscious it scared him so he took off."

He stopped talking and waited for Chris to ask him questions.

"Did he set the fire also?" Chris asked.

"He said he did, and he let your horse loose on the day of the opening."

"Did he say why?" Chris asked.

"It seems your daddy and his daddy were brothers." The sheriff waited to see how this bombshell would be received.

"He's your first cousin and his name is Daniel Montgomery Shealy."

Chapter
Twenty-Eight

Chris couldn't recall any other time in his life when he'd encountered a whirlwind of events that left him in such a tailspin. He felt as if he hadn't found solid ground for the past forty-eight hours.

One of his managers was a devout believer in astrological projections; she relied heavily on her daily horoscope. She was always trying to talk him into letting a woman she knew cast a horoscope for him. Even if she had, Chris mused as he lingered a few minutes in bed the next morning, he doubted that it would have shown what had taken place beginning Tuesday morning.

First Maggie Rose had returned to work without warning. Almost without words they had made peace of a sort that permitted them to work together in the office. Then yesterday, despite a severe panic attack, Maggie Rose had gotten Nicky back into his box and rescued an unconscious

Covey, who had been attacked and left on the stable floor. Tallie had described how Maggie Rose was weaving and gasping when she came looking for him. It was no wonder she looked so ill when he got to the scene. They met Jerlene at the hospital and Covey woke up to tell Maggie Rose it was Dan who hit him. Covey's faultless details identified Dan even though his face was hooded. Covey went home. The sheriff eventually took Dan into custody after a wild chase, then came to tell Chris that Dan confessed to trying to harm him. Dan turned out to be Dan Shealy, Chris's first cousin.

It sounded like a soap opera, he thought, especially when he relived his meeting at the jail with Dan later that evening.

His first thought, now that he knew of the relationship, had been to see if there was a physical resemblance he could identify. He saw that he and Dan had the same tall, rangy bodies, except that his shoulders were a little broader and straight where Dan's were hunched. Other than that, Dan's eyes were not as dark as Chris's but both had an angular shape to their faces. Dan's complexion was lighter than Chris's and the shape of their mouths was different.

At this moment Dan's shoulders were even more hunched as he sat across the table from Chris, unwilling to meet his eyes. A guard sat a few feet away but neither Dan nor Chris paid him any attention.

"Sheriff Snipes told me you're a Shealy," Chris said.

"Hugh Shealy Jr. was my daddy," Dan said, looking at the table.

Uncle Henry hadn't talked much about his

brother Hugh because he'd been so disappointed in the way Hugh had wasted his inheritance from their father. He'd said Hugh didn't know how to take care of the land and instead of working hard and learning, he blamed his failures on bad weather, the bad seed he was sold, how the farm machinery broke down, or anything except himself and his inept ways. Eventually he lost the land and he moved away still complaining that he'd had a raw deal. He dropped completely out of sight, Uncle Henry said.

After all the years of knowing only Uncle Henry as a relative, it seemed strange to Chris to be looking at a first cousin, someone who shared his blood name. Someone who could be a part of the family Chris had always longed for. Except that he'd tried to destroy what Chris had.

"Why, Dan? What do you have against me?"

"Daddy always said the land Grandfather gave to Henry should have come to him. He was the eldest, he was Hugh Jr., and this was the best of the land with its brook, orchard, and good fields. He talked about it a lot. As he grew older that's all he and Mama talked about and drilled into me that it was up to me to reclaim it for our family. Daddy died later and Mama moved us here to plan what to do."

"Your mother's here, too?" Chris said in surprise.

"I was getting along fine in Texas and I didn't want to come but Mama kept after me so finally I gave in. We've been here a little over a year."

"She lives with you on Pine Street?"

"Some of the time. She's the one who made me look in your office files."

"What were you looking for?"

Dan shrugged. "Just anything I could find that might be useful in getting the land back. She said you might have a mortgage on it."

Chris thought how Uncle Henry had never let his land be mortgaged and had emphasized the concept to Chris. That was one reason the purchase of the property had been conceived as a source of income. He wondered now if seeing what his older brother was doing in mismanaging his part of the family land had made Uncle Henry especially determined to do otherwise.

"Mama wanted me to come out here and ask for a job but I thought that was too direct. Then I met Jerlene in a bar and found out she had known you all her life so I hung out with her. It'd just be a matter of time before I met you. I knew luck had changed when I met Maggie Rose for the first time on the day she began working for you."

Chris made a mental leap. "Your mother came to the opening, didn't she?"

"She came with her neighbors, the Connors."

"Was it your mother who searched my bedroom?"

"She wanted to but I told her it would be easier for me so I did it to keep her from doing it. She was so sure there'd be some papers she could use to get the land back or to cause you some kind of trouble. When I didn't find anything she told me to let the horses out to ruin the show, but the only one I could manage was Nicky and that didn't work out." Dan spoke in a matter-of-fact tone, looking up at Chris occasionally.

"Then you set the fire," Chris said.

"Mama kept after me to do something else but

I would never do anything to harm the horses. I like horses and there's no way I could burn them, but I figured the smoke would set off the alarm so you could get them out before the fire got to their end of the stables."

Just what Tallie had surmised, Chris recalled. Dan, Chris thought, was too much like his father, Hugh Jr. He was a weak man, manipulated by his obsessive mother, and although he was a failure in carrying out the plans she had thrust upon him, he lacked the strength of character to reject her demands even when it endangered the life and property of people who had befriended him.

For the first time in his recital Dan looked straight at Chris. "I'm sorry about Covey. He's a nice kid and he likes horses but he startled me. He came in before I was able to get the other three horses loose. He was supposed to be with Tallie working on the barn but suddenly there he was, so I hit him and got out of there fast as I could."

The blazing anger Chris had felt when he first saw Covey had begun to subside as the day went on and now as he listened to Dan's tale of events he felt only a coldness toward this man who lacked the stamina to stand on his own feet and live an honorable life. He'd been willing to abandon any good instincts he might have had to carry out his mother's twisted greed and in so doing had gone from harmless break-ins to fire and then to assault upon a child. What would he have done next and blamed on his mother?

"Your mother is an accessory, you know," Chris stated.

"I know but they'll never catch her." A fleeting look of pride shown in his face. A pride, Chris thought, for qualities of determination, organization, and practical action, which Dan, himself, lacked. "She left the minute the law came to the door and she called me to let me know they were on their way. She always had a plan in case something like this happened."

"You don't care if she left you holding the bag?"

"It was her idea and her plan but I'm the one who carried it out," Dan said simply. For the first time Chris felt that Dan had done something right. But he had nothing left to say to his cousin and he stood up to leave.

"Before you go, Chris, how did Covey know it was me under the hood?"

"He said he knows how you stood, the pants you wore, the ring on your finger, and the cologne you wear."

Dan looked impressed. "He's a smart kid. I'd appreciate it if you'd tell him I'm sorry I had to hit him and for whatever good it does, I apologize to you, too, Chris."

All Chris could do was look at Dan. "I'll tell him," he said and walked out.

He certainly would tell Covey what Dan said because no child needed to carry that burden of betrayal of an innocent friendship. God knows it was hard enough for an adult, he thought, as he climbed out of bed and dressed to begin his morning chores.

When Maggie Rose arrived in the office he was waiting. She looked like a cool breeze in a soft pink dress and pink sandals. Her face looked rested as she greeted him with a "Good morning, Chris" and the radiant smile that always made his heart turn over.

He couldn't resist going to her and holding her close for a long moment.

"Good morning to you," he said tenderly before he released her. "We have a lot of catching up to do, honey. Can you have dinner with me?"

She looked at the Thursday schedule. "Your last student leaves at six and Ginnie and I are beginning inventory tonight at eight. I can stay for an hour or so. Is that all right?"

"Wonderful. Tallie can run Covey home but I intend to see Jerlene and Covey later tonight about Dan. I have to hurry but I'll be back at noon. Also, reschedule the interviews for tomorrow."

Maggie Rose was eager to know what had transpired between Chris and Dan. She assumed that something from that exchange was what Chris had to tell Covey. Whatever else the catching up was to bring between her and Chris was a matter of destiny.

Yesterday's drama had left her so exhausted that she had dropped into bed and slept dreamlessly for nine hours. She hadn't reflected on what she'd done with the horses or what that meant for the future. Each hour as it came would bring its own decisions and she was comfortable with that. Just as at some point yesterday the decision had made itself known to her that whatever relationship had or had not occurred between Jerlene and Chris, Covey was someone else's son. Not Chris Shealy's.

* * *

The last student had rattled down the lane in his pickup truck. Chris came to the office door where Maggie Rose was working on the file cards.

"Give me five minutes for a fast shower, then meet me in the kitchen."

Maggie Rose closed up the office, retrieved her bag, and went to the kitchen where Mr. Tallie had left their dinner ready. She took the salad from the refrigerator, dropped the corn on the cob into boiling water, and heated the baked chicken in the microwave. She put a pitcher of iced tea on, filled the glasses with ice cubes, and set the salad dressing on the table.

Chris flew down the stairs just as she lifted the corn out of the water.

"You really are fast," she admitted. "That was six and a half minutes."

"Bet I can beat you," he said, kissing her cheek.

"Watch it, Chris," she said, laughing, as she set the plate of hot corn on the table. "You can't beat me," she said in response to his bragging.

"One day we'll see," he said and was delighted at her hot blush.

"Tell me about you and Dan," she said as soon as they began their meal.

Chris told his story slowly, taking time to eat, and particularly to savor Maggie Rose's rapt attention. To feel the weight of her comments and sympathetic comprehension, an emotion he thought had been lost to him forever.

They were eating the sliced watermelon Tallie had set out when she asked, "How do you feel about Dan, Chris?"

"I don't feel vengeful," he began thoughtfully. "I'm not angry as I was at first. I think it's a waste and a shame that the only other Shealy is a man who's lost his way as Dan has. I guess he has two points in his favor. He was sorry about Covey and I felt that was as sincere as a man like that can be, and he would not hurt the horses."

His analysis was well reasoned and demonstrated again to Maggie Rose the generosity of spirit she knew to be an integral characteristic of the man. But she saw the shadow of bleakness in his eyes and knew he had experienced again a sense of betrayal, this time by a kinsman. Without hesitating she got up and went to him.

She made room for herself on his lap and putting her arms around him, sheltered him in her arms. "I'm so sorry you found your cousin only to lose him, Chris," she said softly.

Chris hadn't realized the sharpness of that particular sword until now, when Maggie Rose asked him how he felt about Dan. All his life he'd yearned for family, and fate had sent him a first cousin who turned out to be an enemy. He'd met him without knowing he was kin, then found he was and consigned him to incarceration. He held Maggie Rose tightly and let the tears flow.

When he was quiet again Maggie Rose took his face in her hands and kissed both cheeks tenderly. Then she made as if to rise but Chris held on to her. "Don't go, please." She settled back on his lap.

"I want to ask you about yesterday, honey. Help me to understand how you were able to deal with the horses."

"When I saw them my only thought was that they were loose and shouldn't be because they could run away. When I got near them I had the same symptoms I've always had but somehow the need to make them secure took over and I just kept working at it through the nausea and dizziness. When I got down to look at Covey I was afraid I'd faint on top of him. Then I managed to get to my feet and stagger out to get Mr. Tallie. I guess he thought I was drunk, because I could feel myself weaving and I kept trying to draw long breaths but I couldn't. So he had me sit down and propped me up until you came."

"When you had time to think about it, were you surprised, Maggie Rose?"

Maggie Rose's gaze had been directed toward the window from which she'd seen the horses but now she looked at Chris with the same expression that had ensnared him when he had asked her what her name was twenty-one years ago.

"I had no idea I could do that, Chris. Nothing I read suggested it. I guess a strength you didn't know you had takes over when a crisis of real importance occurs. If you had asked me if I could do that I would have said no. Yet when it happened I didn't think at all. I just went into action to save your horses." Her eyes asked him to share the wonder of it all.

His awareness of her was so keen it cut his breath. He could see the tiniest feature in her face, could feel the blood coursing through her veins, could smell all of the fragrances emanating from her, could sense the depth of every breath she drew. He was swamped with emotions he didn't know how to handle. He wanted to make her his in every way possible, to put his imprint on her and hers on him. He wanted to bind them together for the rest of eternity.

All he could do was hang on tight to her, his face buried in her hair, murmuring her name as if it were an incantation, until the tide of emotions began to subside. How could he ever have imagined that any other woman could fill him with such heartache, sorrow, joy, and happiness!

"Thank you, my dearest Maggie Rose," he said.

"I'm so glad I was able to do it." Maggie Rose had felt the tumultuous flood of feeling that had overtaken Chris. She had held herself very still, uncertain of how to respond, because it seemed to her they would both be tossed around if they weren't careful and she had no idea what the result would be.

But now Chris was calmer, so she brought up the item that was on her part of this catching up.

"Chris, I'm going to have to leave soon but I thought we might talk about what's going to happen after Saturday. That's the end of my six weeks."

"I need you to stay, Maggie Rose, on any schedule you can arrange, although I understand it'll be on a part-time basis. Have you and Ginnie discussed it?"

"Ginnie can see her clients better in the morning and evening, which works out fine for me. I'd be most useful here in the afternoons when the students and parents come."

"That's perfect. Is the Mailroom open on Saturday?"

"Yes and that's going to be my big Craft Counter day because people like to shop on Saturday so I have to be there."

"I understand and that's okay."

She stood up reluctantly. "I really must go," she

said but turned in his arms and held up her face
for a kiss.

He brushed her lips. "Are you my sweetheart,
Maggie Rose?" he whispered.

"Yes," she breathed.

"And I'm yours," he answered and crushed her
to him in a reckless kiss.

Chapter Twenty-Nine

"How are you this morning, Covey?" Maggie Rose asked as the boy hopped into the car Friday morning.

"The bump on the back of my head has almost disappeared. See?" He turned his head so she could feel where the bump had been.

"I see. The one on your temple is flatter, too."

"Mr. Chris came over last night to tell me and my mom about Mr. Dan. They're cousins," he said as if he found it hard to believe.

Covey, like Chris, had no cousins to grow up with and had always wanted some. Tommy was the only friend he'd had all his young life. Maggie Rose could understand how Covey thought having cousins was always a good thing. He was coming up against some of the hard realities of life this summer, she thought.

"Mr. Dan told him to tell me he was sorry to hurt

me. He didn't mean to. He knew I was supposed to be with Mr. Tallie and when I came in it surprised him so he hit me and ran away."

"People do stupid things that they're often sorry about later," Maggie Rose said.

"That's what Mr. Chris said."

They rode in silence for a few minutes. "Can I tell you a secret, Aunt Maggie Rose?"

"Of course."

"When I came to the farm I wanted to find out if Mr. Chris was my dad like I heard one of the boys at school say."

Maggie Rose was so startled she almost jerked the wheel. That boy must have heard the old gossip from a careless parent. Poor Covey. Would he have to go through his whole life wondering and looking for his father?

"Did you find out, Covey?"

"Yes. He's not my dad but I like him a lot anyway," he said calmly.

"How did you find out, Covey?" She wondered if it was the same way she found the answer to that same question and thought it was ironic that both nephew and aunt had embarked on the same mission.

"I knew how I'd feel," he said with an utter conviction that Maggie Rose couldn't question, but she saw him look at her to see if she would believe him.

"I understand, Covey," she said with the same conviction. And she did. She hoped there would be some understanding about what had happened to Covey when she and Jerlene and Covey met at her parents' home after work. They had been agitated when Jerlene called them after she'd brought Covey home, and had taken her to task. Knowing their father, she'd told Jerlene this morning she'd be there to help calm him down when they went to dinner.

Chris was in the office when she arrived to say he was going to work but would be back at ten for the interviews.

"But first . . ." he said, taking her hand and pressing it to his cheek, then kissing her palm before releasing it. "I know what I told you about being in the office, et cetera," he said with a wry smile, "but it seems I must at least touch you."

"I know," she murmured, her eyes locked with his.

Ricky Turner, dressed in jeans and a white sports shirt, was five minutes early for his interview. He was a well-spoken young black man who'd grown up in Arizona riding horses, he said. Chris took him out to the stables. Forty-five minutes later Chris came back to take Jane Wheeling through the same routine. While waiting for Chris, Jane had told Maggie Rose that although her parents were Swedish, she herself had been born in Virginia and raised on a horse farm. Maggie Rose wondered which of the two Chris would choose. Both seemed to be well qualified for the job.

Chris agreed when he discussed them later. "But I'm choosing Jane because she can give me more time. Ricky's major is engineering and he'll be carrying a heavy load when he goes back to school. Jane is liberal arts. She said she's going to college to please her parents but all she wants to do is work with horses. She'll arrange her classes so she can give me every afternoon and maybe more!"

"When is she starting?"

"Monday."

On the way home Covey said, "I met the two people Mr. Chris was talking to about coming to work here."

"What do you think about them?"

"They're both nice but I hope Mr. Chris hires the lady, because she was telling him how she's been in horse shows since she was my age. I want to learn all of that and maybe she can help Mr. Chris teach me."

"That's the one he hired." She watched Covey's face light up and was thankful that something had happened to give him joy.

Maggie Rose gave Jerlene full marks for strategy when she saw Jerlene had brought Tommy with her. They met in the driveway.

After greetings were over and Covey had been examined by both grandparents, Ada Sanders said, "Dinner isn't ready yet so you boys can go outside. I'll call you when it's time to eat."

Maggie Rose exchanged a look with Jerlene. They were in for a full-blown lecture but at least Covey was out of the way.

They were invited to sit in the living room and as soon as they were all there, Maggie Rose watched her father sit ramrod straight in his well-worn leather chair, his hands clasped.

"Your son," he began as he looked at Jerlene, "is our only grandchild. Your mother and I have helped raise the boy. He is very precious to us. We don't understand how you and your sister could have put him in such a dangerous position that he was assaulted!"

Now he turned his fierce gaze on Maggie Rose.

"Do you realize he might have been killed? Supposing that madman had a gun or a knife?"

His gaze swiveled back to Jerlene. "That madman that you brought into your home. When are you going to learn some sense about the men you choose, Jerlene?"

"Calm down, Frank," Mama said. "Watch your pressure. The man did not have a gun or a knife and Covey is all right. That's what we have to remember and be thankful for." She looked at her husband anxiously, lovingly.

How many times when they were all growing up had this scene taken place? But it still had power because of Daddy's personality and the underlying fact that he loved his family. There was always more truth than not in what he had to say in these parlor lectures. Maggie Rose thought that he was the one person who could make Jerlene cry as she was doing now, because they were too much alike.

"Did you find out why Dan did what he did?" her mother asked.

Maggie Rose had steeled herself for this meeting and began to answer all the questions and explain all that Chris had learned. Jerlene had stopped crying but since she didn't seem to want to enter the discussion, Maggie Rose embarked upon a defense for the two of them.

"So you see, this campaign against Chris had been planned long ago. When we all met Dan Montgomery he seemed to be a nice person. None of us had a reason to suspect him and he'd been very helpful with the riding school. That's why he was offered the job as part-time instructor. Even the students like him. I don't think it's fair, Daddy, to put this blame on Jerlene and me or even Chris.

Do you think for one moment that either of us would have let him stay if we had a suspicion he'd come to harm? You and Mama aren't the only ones who love Covey!"

Maggie Rose felt moisture come to her eyes but she refused to let it fall and held her father's gaze until she saw it soften and his face relax.

"I might have been a little hasty in what I said," he acknowledged, "but all I could think of was what might have happened to the boy." He blew his nose in a snowy white handkerchief. Turning to Jerlene he said, his voice gentle, "Jerlene, daughter, take your time and try to find yourself a good, decent man."

"I will, Daddy," Jerlene promised in a tremulous voice.

Maggie Rose answered the phone Saturday evening knowing it would be Chris.

"I've missed you today, sweetheart. May I come over?"

"Ginnie and I will be working at the Mailroom but you're welcome to come there if you wish."

"I wish and I'll see you there soon. I've something to show you."

Ginnie and Lee Stephenson were wiping off the front of the counter section. She told Maggie Rose that he'd come by and she pressed him into service. Chris said he'd be here later also, Maggie Rose told Ginnie, who said that the more hands they had, the more they'd get done tonight and wouldn't have to do tomorrow.

Ginnie opened the door to Chris when he

knocked. She said, "Hi" and directed him to go help Maggie Rose in the storage room.

"Bossy, isn't she?" he told Lee with a smile as he was on his way.

"Not always," Lee quipped and winked at Ginnie, who made a face at him.

Maggie Rose was opening a box. She looked up when Chris appeared in the doorway. For a moment they were motionless; then Chris was holding her and she was holding him.

"The day isn't right when you're not there," he said between kisses.

"I know. All day I've been thinking of you." She pressed against him and kissed him fiercely.

Control, Chris told himself. *Remember where you are. Control,* he said while the hunger for Maggie Rose danced through him. He began to pull himself away from her. "We'll never get your work done this way." His voice was shaky as he leaned his forehead against hers.

Maggie Rose reluctantly let him go and went back to her box. "You said you had something to show me."

He handed her a stiff white envelope. She opened it and saw it was an invitation for Mr. Christopher Shealy and guest to attend the awards dinner dance given by the South Carolina Riding Association at the Carlton Hotel in Beaufort on Saturday, July 20, at seven in the evening.

"Very impressive," she said. "I'm glad it finally arrived. . . ."

"You will be my guest, won't you, Maggie Rose?"

"Of course," she said, then added with a giggle, "If I can find something suitable to wear. I'll get Alicia right on it."

"That's just a week from tonight. They don't usually wait this late to send the invitations."

He looked at the stack of boxes. "What are we doing here?"

"First we have to fill the card racks with the new cards."

"What about the craft items?"

"That's tomorrow's job. The people will be bringing them in then because we didn't want the risk of having them any longer than necessary because of insurance."

The four of them ended the evening sitting on the floor and eating a large pizza Lee ordered.

Chris followed Maggie Rose home, the need to prolong his time with her eating at him, but all he did was hold her and kiss her gently before saying good night. But on the way to the farm he wondered just how long he could hold out.

Sunday at the Mailroom was a longer proposition but Chris was content as long as he could be near Maggie Rose. He saw how talented she was in dealing with the craft artists and in helping them arrange their wares to the best advantage. He admired the number and variety of candles and holders, jewelry of all kinds, bowls, dishes, and vases that graced the shelves and glassed-in counters. Each one had a price tag and he saw most of them were no more than twenty-five dollars.

When they left the Mailroom at five o'clock Chris suggested they stop for dinner so all she'd have to do when she got home was rest and get ready for tomorrow's opening.

"How about Shoney's? I know you like a large salad bar," he said.

"I can deal with that," Maggie Rose said. Some

of the smaller, more distinctive restaurants were closed on Sunday in Jamison but she could make a satisfying meal from the variety of salad items and fruit at Shoney's.

They sat in a corner booth and took their time, winding down from the work they'd done. "If we could, Ginnie and I would give you free service for the hours you've put in last night and today. But we can't give away stamps. You and Lee were a great help, Chris."

"It was a pleasure for me and I mean that. You don't seem to understand that all I want is to be near you, sweetheart." His voice was soft, his eyes burning into hers.

"When you look at me like that I feel funny inside, Chris," she whispered. "I can't think and I sure can't eat. Dr. Moore wants me to gain back that five pounds I lost, you know."

Chris looked away and tried to turn down the fire that flared up so easily in Maggie Rose's presence. He rummaged around in his mind for a safe topic and remembered he'd meant to discuss her new salary.

"We haven't talked about your salary for your new hours."

"Too much else has been happening," she said. "Of course it'll be less than the generous salary you've given me during these six weeks."

Chris managed to give her a look of surprise. "Are you going to work less hard than you've been doing?"

"Of course not." She was puzzled by the question.

"In that case your salary won't be any less." He looked smug as he finished that maneuver.

"But I'm working fewer hours, Chris," she protested.

"Doesn't matter." He was unmoved.

"But it does matter, Chris. I can't accept that salary."

"What did you earn in Hartford?"

"Thirty-two thousand."

"Then your salary will be twenty-two thousand. Case closed."

She sat and looked at him as he gave her an innocent smile. She decided to ask him the same question she'd asked him when she was spending freely to make the opening a success.

"How can you keep on spending so much money, Chris, if you don't mind my asking?"

"I don't mind at all. I'll tell you what only my lawyer and my broker know. The apartment corporation I work for belongs to Uncle Henry. It's a part of his estate. He set it up as a trust fund for me."

He loved the way her eyes opened when she was surprised. She absorbed the information; then comprehension dawned. "That's why you do the work yourself. You save on salary but more importantly you can be assured you're managing your uncle's investment in the way he would want you to."

"Exactly. You can see it isn't going to strain my finances to pay your salary. I'm confident your work is worth it."

Although Maggie Rose continued to raise questions, in the end she had to let it go and accept his decision in good grace.

Chapter
Thirty

An early thunderstorm rolled through Jamison, waking Maggie Rose at five on Monday morning. She welcomed the cooler air it left behind, washing away the humidity. Thank goodness it had come now instead of later. *Don't rain on my parade,* she thought.

Rain didn't keep people from mailing a letter if they had to get it off but sunny weather made it more likely they'd stop in to buy stamps or a card or to see who was there and visit. Aunt Henny had never let the Mailroom become a lounging hangout for folk with nothing to do but she hadn't discouraged short visits between friends. Ginnie and Maggie Rose wanted to keep the same environment. People who weren't in a hurry would be the ones to look at the Craft Corner.

She thought how as a child when her sisters were playing house with their dolls she was always the

one who played at having a store or a bank or a
dress shop. But somehow the reality of being in
business had been sidetracked not only by the lack
of money but also by the lack of confidence that
she could succeed. Yet the desire had been there
ready to come to the forefront when Ginnie had
proposed this partnership.

Now she was excited and thrilled at the fulfillment of this dream. Today was the beginning but
who knew where it might end in the years to come?
As she slipped out of bed to begin her yoga, she
gave thanks for the blessings that had brought her
to this day.

Later in the morning Maggie Rose looked at
the busy Craft Corner and counted as one of her
blessings the choice of Mrs. Helen Reid to take
care of it. Helen Reid was a widow living on Social
Security and when Mama had suggested her name,
Maggie Rose knew it would work. A former department store clerk, "Miss Helen" now spent her time
knitting and doing cross-stitch. "I can do that at
your place as well as at home, and the extra income
will be welcome," she said in her dignified manner.

A lovely display of flowers had arrived as soon
as the Mailroom opened. The basket now sat on
the end of the counter and most people com-
mented on its beauty and read the card: *Congratulations to Ginnie and Maggie Rose from HS Stables.*

Maggie Rose was feeling proud of performing a
complicated sale on the computerized register
when a familiar voice said, "A book of stamps,
please." Daddy with Mama beside him were on the
other side of the counter, smiling proudly at her.
"Guess I'll have to switch my business from the
post office to here," her daddy said.

"Guess you will," Maggie Rose replied.

A few minutes later she saw Chris come in. He smiled at her and wandered over to the Craft Corner where her parents were examining everything on display. She saw her mother engage Chris in conversation, and then her father talked to him and shook his hand. Her parents left and Chris waited until the line at the counter had been served. For the moment there was no one behind him.

"Had an interesting conversation over there at the Craft Corner. I'll tell you about it this afternoon."

When Maggie Rose completed her first morning at the Mailroom counter she was pleasantly stimulated at how well she had done. Essie Weathers had had to come to her rescue only once. As she drove to the farm she made a vow that by the end of the week Essie would not have to rescue her.

She smiled at the notion that from now on she'd think about her morning job and her afternoon job. She was a lucky woman because she liked both jobs. As she entered the office and settled at her desk she felt as if she were coming home. The demands on her at the Mailroom were new, here all was known and comfortable. She wondered how Jane Wheeling felt on her first day here.

She soon found out when Jane came in to meet the first Monday parents and to take the children to the stables. "I love it here," she told Maggie Rose as they waited. "Everything is in first-class order and the horses are lovely. Do you ride?"

"Not yet," Maggie Rose said.

"You're going to love it, I promise you." Her smile was infectious, her blue eyes sparkling, and her blond hair bouncing. Maggie Rose wanted to believe her and thought how good Jane was going to be with the students as she imbued her enthusiasm for riding into them.

Chris came into the office late in the afternoon. "You certainly had a successful opening," he observed. "Didn't you think so?"

Chris was sitting in his customary chair, his fingers busy plaiting three strands of leather into a belt. He'd been showing Covey how to do this and found it a useful ploy to distract his need to touch Maggie Rose when he was in the office with her.

"Yes, I do, and I'm anxious to talk with Ginnie this evening to see how the afternoon went."

"Your Craft Corner is going to be a moneymaker. I heard Miss Helen make several good sales. Getting her was a great idea."

"Mama suggested her. I saw you talking with Mama and Daddy."

"I guess it's true that every cloud has a silver lining. Your mom was gracious as she always is to me but Mr. Sanders really surprised me. He thanked me for taking care of Covey and paying the medical bill. Then he shook my hand for the first time that I can remember. I must be making a little progress in his opinion." The touch of cynicism in his words was belied by the pleased smile he gave Maggie Rose.

"He also said that between him and Jerlene, Covey would get to the farm every day. I've been meaning to ask you, how's she getting along?" he asked with concern.

"She's pretty quiet right now. Home every evening with Covey and they do things together. I think she took to heart what Daddy said." She

related to Chris the gist of their confrontation with
their father.

Chris listened with a sober face. "She's had a
rough time. I wish her luck."

The rest of the week flew by for Maggie Rose
with her two jobs as well as conferring in the evening with Ginnie or shopping with Alicia, who was
hard to please.

"I don't see why I can't wear this one," Maggie
Rose said, showing Alicia a lovely silk peach-colored
dress.

"Nice, sis, but not for this occasion. I want you
and Chris to be the most distinguished-looking
couple there."

"What a hope! I just want to be decently dressed,
not embarrass Chris."

"You have never given yourself credit for your
figure and how to dress it, Maggie Rose. You've
long legs, a flat tummy, and a reasonable bustline.
I don't know what else you want. What we're looking for is something in black that's extremely well
cut to look smart and sensual at the same time.
Trust me," she said as she dragged Maggie Rose
from store to store.

By Thursday they were both becoming discouraged. Then Alicia remembered a small dress shop
a colleague had recommended.

She told the middle-aged, smart-looking woman
who asked if she could help precisely what they
wanted. The woman looked at Maggie Rose
appraisingly, then disappeared. She returned with
what Alicia instantly knew was the perfect gown for
Maggie Rose.

"Persistence pays off," Alicia said as she looked at Maggie Rose in the dress. "Wait till Chris sees you in this!" She laughed as Maggie Rose blushed.

One of the indulgences Chris had permitted himself was to have an experienced tailor in Charleston make his evening wear. Off the rack was acceptable for most events but he loved the ease and comfort of after-six clothing that was perfectly fitted to him. He gave one last glance at the black jacket and pants trimmed in satin, the white, pleated shirt accented by its black studs and gold-trimmed black cuff links, and his black satin bow tie. He wore thin black silk socks and black oxfords. He straightened his black silk cummerbund. He passed the brush over his close-cropped hair once more and went to pick up Maggie Rose.

Alicia opened the door to him. "Hi, Chris. Have a seat. Cinderella's almost ready," she said and disappeared down the hall.

Chris was too keyed up to sit. He stood looking out the window, hoping the evening would turn out as he planned. He absentmindedly watched three small children throwing a ball to each other with none of them catching it but having a good time running after it.

"Hello, Chris," he heard behind him. He turned around and there she stood.

She took his breath away. Chris could only stare as if he'd never before seen this gorgeous woman in the elegant black strapless gown who stood before him, her eyes warm, her smile tender and shy.

Her hair was arranged in soft curls on the top of her head, accenting her graceful neck and shoulders. She wore a silver necklace with an onyx stone around her neck and onyx studs in her ears. Her long, long legs looked marvelous in sheer black hose, and black patent sling-back heels adorned her narrow feet. She carried on her arm a shocking-pink silk throw.

But her dress! Again and again Chris's eyes returned to the dress and the way it highlighted every lovely line of her body. Thank God there was to be dancing tonight so he could hold her in his arms.

"You are absolutely stunning, Maggie Rose," he said finally. "You take my breath away." He took her hand and bowed over it in homage.

Her eyes sparkled with delight. "Alicia will be so pleased you like the result of her work, and I am too. You're looking wonderful yourself."

Alicia, satisfied with her efforts, followed them to the door. "Have a blast," she ordered.

Beaufort was only sixty miles south and the time flew by for Chris as he and Maggie Rose talked and laughed with each other. Promise spun in the air around them, reminding him of the high school prom night they'd attended when they each had come with someone else but had gravitated toward each other all evening. He touched her hand.

"Remember prom night?"

"You took Nicole and I was with Marvin but we spent a lot of time with each other. After one of the dances you took me outside and kissed me." She sighed. "I was so thrilled."

"So was I," Chris said. "I'd been wanting to kiss you all evening but I had to work up the nerve to do it."

"I've always wondered why you didn't ask me to go to the prom."

"I wanted to but I was so sure your dad wouldn't let you go out with me."

"I'm sorry to say you're right."

"Every time you came home I wanted to take you out. Did you know that?"

"I'd no idea." *Ginnie was right,* she thought.

"My reputation was so bad I was afraid to ask."

"You, afraid?" She didn't understand that at all.

"I was afraid you'd say no and I didn't want to hear you say it." He looked sheepish as she impulsively leaned to kiss his cheek.

The knowledge that Chris had been interested in her all those years was a wonder to Maggie Rose. Ginnie had surmised it but now it had been affirmed by Chris himself. It lit a spark within her and by the time they arrived at the Carlton Hotel and were ushered into the ballroom she was glowing.

Fifteen tables seating ten each filled one section of the huge room. At the door two hostesses greeted people and gave them cards with their table number. "You and your guest are at table three," the lady told Chris, eyeing him appreciatively.

"These places are so cold." Maggie Rose gave a little shiver. Chris took the silk wrap and draped it across her back. His fingers lingered on her velvety skin, adjusting the cloth. She stood perfectly still with all of her senses aware of him.

"Better?" he asked softly.

"Yes, thanks."

On the way to their table several of Chris's acquaintances intercepted them. One was Ben Sewell, who introduced his wife, Gloria, professed his happiness at Maggie Rose's recovery, and told Chris his horse had made an excellent showing in the race.

A red-faced man with a shock of white hair held out his hand to Chris. "I'm Jim McDougall from Lancaster. I hear you have a nice little riding school near Charleston."

"Nice to meet you, Jim. I'm Chris Shealy and this is Maggie Rose Sanders."

"This your first time to one of these?" he asked Maggie Rose. He didn't try to hide the admiration in his glance.

"Yes, it is," she said.

"I hope you enjoy yourself." To Chris he said, "Hold on to her tight."

"You can count on that!" Chris said as McDougall gave him a wink and moved away.

Of the four other couples at their table, Maggie Rose found that two of them were from Wilmington, one from Orangeburg, and one from Florence. Their friendly conversation centered on horses. Since she neither bred horses nor raced them, there wasn't much that she could contribute, but occasionally as they ate their beef or chicken, green peas, and herbed rice with apple tart for dessert, someone would ask her a polite question that had nothing to do with horses. She appreciated their courtesy and hoped she wasn't disappointing Chris.

As dessert was finished and coffee cups refilled, a portly man appeared on the stage. "I hope you folks enjoyed your dinner"— a small applause — "and I want to move on to the program so the dancing can begin. My wife has made me promise to dance every dance with her so naturally I am anxious to begin. Especially since I haven't danced since this occasion last year.''

A hearty laugh from the audience met this humor.

"First I want to introduce the other members of the board. Please stand wherever you are.''

As the names were read, Maggie Rose with everyone else looked around to see the men. As he came to the last two names she felt Chris grow tense.

". . . Jim McDougall and Bob Kimbel!''

Chris didn't turn to look at her but his hand grasped hers tightly and held on as the first two sets of awards were announced and the recipients walked up to receive their framed certificates.

"The third-place award in category three goes to the Blueberry Hill Riding School in Florence.'' The man and woman who sat across from Maggie Rose hugged each other joyously. "We've finally made it,'' they said and went to the stage, their faces beaming.

"The second-place award goes to Vargo Stable in Lexington.''

Chris was as tense as a drawn bow, and Maggie Rose rubbed his arm.

"The first-place award goes to HS Stables in Jamison.''

She felt Chris jerk and the people at their table began to applaud. Chris stood. "It's your award, too,'' he told Maggie Rose and held out his hand.

I've done it, was all Chris could think as he took what seemed a long walk to the stage, the applause ringing in his ears. He knew his was the first black-owned school to win a top award but he hadn't done it for that reason. He had done it to honor the man who was his father in all but blood.

He received the award, then turned and handed it to Maggie Rose. The crowd roared its approval as she blushed and held it to her heart.

The rest of the evening passed like a dream for Chris. People surrounded them with congratulations. The newspaper took pictures of all the winners and did brief interviews.

When that was over he and Maggie Rose, with one accord, moved onto the dance floor eager to have an excuse to hold each other. It was like coming home. No conversation was needed as their hearts and bodies communicated with each other.

When the music turned bluesy and funky the crowd of dancers loosened up. The other six black people Maggie Rose had met earlier danced in a group with her and Chris. Afterward they exchanged addresses with promises to get together in the future. Bob Kimbel came up, introduced his wife, Shirley, and asked Maggie Rose for a dance while Chris partnered with Mrs. Kimbel.

"Now I understand why you came to see us twice," Maggie Rose said.

"I needed to see if the great impression I received at the opening would hold up on an ordinary day and I found it did. Chris Shealy can go far if he keeps up his fine work."

"He sees the stables as a memorial to his Uncle Henry, who raised him from the time he was five," Maggie Rose confided.

"I'm doubly glad he earned the award," Mr. Kimbel said.

Two dances later the same exchange was made with Jim McDougall and his wife, Marlene, and later still with the board chairman whose name Maggie Rose learned was Murray Pope, and his wife, Crystal, who said flirtatiously, "Despite what my husband said, we do dance with other people and now we get to dance with the best-looking couple here."

When Maggie Rose and Chris compared notes later, Maggie Rose said, "She was right, you know. There's no other man here as handsome as you. But she didn't have to flirt with you like she did, batting her eyelids and being coquettish."

"Jealous?" Chris smiled at her but inside he was gleeful. Maggie Rose was feeling possessive about him!

"Should I be?" Now it was Maggie Rose who was batting her eyelashes.

"Not unless I'm permitted to be jealous of all the men who can't take their eyes off of you."

"I guess we're even," Maggie Rose said but added with mischief in her eyes, "but you better watch it, buster."

After the next dance Chris said, "Let's go to the beach, take off our shoes, and walk in the sand."

"What a wonderful idea!" Maggie Rose said.

Ten minutes later they'd left the hotel, parked the car near the beach with their shoes and hose in it, and were walking on the beach with a blanket over Chris's arm.

They could see a few other people who were also enjoying the night breeze, the starry skies, and the gentle sound of lapping waves.

In this peaceful space the cumulative emotions of the evening began to demand an outlet. They had been walking hand in hand lost in their individual thoughts.

Suddenly Chris stopped and spread the blanket, then seated Maggie Rose on it and himself beside her. He took her in his arms and turned her face to his.

"May I take you hair down?" His fingers were busy before she could say yes. He ran his hands through, arranging her hair so it fell around her back and face. "This is the way I like it."

With his hands in her hair he kissed her, his lips soft on hers at first, then harder as he pulled her closer. She put her arms around him and responded with all her heart.

When they were both breathless, he pulled away until he could see her face. There were stars in her eyes and his heart felt as though it would come out of his chest. "I love you so much, sweetheart, I've been loving you all of these years, Maggie Rose, I love you, love you, love you." He rained kisses on her as he repeated the litany, on her hair, her eyes, her lips, and her cheeks as he paid his homage.

Maggie Rose felt a great stillness inside as his declaration of love reverberated through her system, recognizing the fulfillment of its destiny. Hosannas and hallelujahs followed. Chimes filled the air around her as she said, "My beloved. You have all my heart, Chris. I love you."

The enormity of their pronouncement stilled them as they looked into each other's eyes.

"Will you marry me and be my wife, my help-meet, and the mother of my children, Maggie Rose Sanders?"

"I will." Her voice, though soft, was firm and committed. He pulled a box from his pocket and took from it a delicate gold band set with nine small diamonds. Placing it on her finger, he kissed it and asked with a small smile, "Do you know what the diamonds stand for?"

"I can't see them for my tears," she said in a shaky voice.

"The nine is to always remind you I've been yours since you were nine and I looked into those same sweet brown eyes that I'm looking at now."

Maggie Rose threw her arms around him and wet his shirtfront with what she assured him were tears of joy that she couldn't hold inside. He petted her and called her sweet names and soon she was able to dry her eyes.

"I'm sure I look frightful," she apologized.

"You look beautiful," he said fervently. "The next thing is, how soon can we be married, sweetheart? I know it can't be as soon as I want it, which is tomorrow, but in two or three weeks?"

Maggie Rose held his hands and looked at him pleadingly. "Chris, I can't marry you until I can ride a horse without fear."

He started to protest and she gently placed a hand on his mouth. "Please, please listen to me. When I was thirteen I watched my best friend get thrown from a horse that was frightened by a snake. She died instantly of a broken neck and I had nightmares for months of the horse's flashing hooves when it reared up. The doctor told me that each horse I see now is that horse and that's why I get panic attacks. I'm working on it and I've made some progress. You can see that yourself. But, Chris, it's because I love you so much and we've both suffered because of my reaction to horses that I cannot come to you to be your wife and the mother of your children with this disability."

She fell silent and waited, looking at him anxiously. Would he understand? She knew it was asking a lot of him but it would be worth it for their future happiness.

Chris was horror-struck by her story. Little Alberta Barnhill had been only a year and a half from thirteen. He imagined such a thing happening to her, the emotional devastation it would cause especially if not treated immediately with sensitive mental and psychological help. He felt ashamed now that he had been so overwhelmed by his own pain at what he saw as a betrayal of trust that he had not even thought to ask Maggie Rose why she felt as she did about horses.

He folded her in his arms now and tried to let her know his sorrow at what she had gone through and his shame at not seeking to understand. "I'm so sorry, sweetheart, and please forgive me if you can for not trying to find out at once why you feel this way about horses."

They held on to each other for mutual forgiveness and comfort. "When do you think you might be ready?" he asked, caressing her face.

"I don't think it'll be too long but I can't set a date. Believe me, I'm as anxious as you are, Chris," she said as she linked her arms around his neck and kissed him.

Chris returned the kiss and, knowing the force of the hunger burning him, smiled at Maggie Rose as he helped her to her feet, shook the blanket, folded it, and with his arm around his fiancée, made his way to the car.

Chapter
Thirty-One

Streams of light poured through the stained-glass windows above the heads of the choir as they filled Salem Baptist Church with their opening song of praise and gratitude. A respectable number of worshippers filled most of the auditorium but as Maggie Rose slipped hurriedly in she saw that Mama and Daddy had managed to save a place for her beside them in their usual pew.

She took her place beside Mama and joined in the singing. When the hymn was concluded she whispered hello and sat back, her eyes closed, as Deacon Ward offered a prayer. "We thank Thee, O Lord, for leading us out of the wilderness of darkness and error and into the light," the mellifluous voice intoned.

Maggie Rose felt that Deacon Ward was reading her heart. Involuntarily she caressed the ring Chris had put on her finger, a symbol that the two of them had found the light of certainty, of truth and commitment. Her being was filled with gratitude and joy.

As the prayer ended she felt Mama's hand on hers. Mama looked at the ring, then looked at her with surprise. "Chris?" she whispered. Maggie Rose nodded. Mama smiled and directed Daddy's attention to the ring. Maggie Rose held her breath as Mama told him "Chris." He studied her for a long moment, then as if coming to a decision, blessed her decision with an approving nod and smile. She felt Mama's arm around her shoulders and nestled against her like a child. This kind of nurturing was what Chris had been denied, having lost his mother when he was five. She made a vow that she would be the best mother she could be to their children and the best wife to Chris, willing to learn and to grow. She loved him but love alone was not enough. Patience and persistence would be needed as well as knowing there would be instances of the same error the deacon prayed about, but the light could always be reached with will and effort.

Maggie Rose settled back to listen to the sermon. Reverend Dawson preached about summer being the season of fruition and what that meant spiritually while she made plans for attaining her readiness to marry Chris.

When the service was over Maggie Rose followed Mama and Daddy to the parking lot, where they waited for Alicia, who after divesting herself of her organist robe, appeared with Jerlene and Covey in tow.

"I didn't see you two in church," Mama told Jerlene and Covey.

"We sat upstairs, Gramma. I like it better 'cause I can see everybody," Covey said.

"Sit wherever you like, just come," Daddy said, using his gentle voice and looking at them with a pleased smile.

"Look what Maggie Rose has!" Mama held Maggie Rose's hand out.

Alicia gave a little squeal and threw her arms around Maggie Rose. "I had a feeling this would happen." In excited tones she described to the family how she had dressed Maggie Rose for the awards dinner and how wonderful she and Chris had looked together.

"I'm happy for you," Jerlene said as she and Covey examined the ring.

"Why are there nine little things around the ring?" Covey asked.

"Chris said he put in the nine diamonds because that's how old I was when he met me."

"You were younger than I am!" Covey said, wonderingly trying to understand.

"Did he win the award he wanted?" Jerlene asked.

"Yes. HS Stables was named number one in their category. You should have seen Chris. He's worked hard for this in memory of his uncle and he was so pleased," she told Daddy.

"Seems the boy has finally grown up," Daddy acknowledged.

"When's the date, Maggie Rose?" Mama said eagerly.

Maggie Rose know she had to be firm with Mama about this or she'd plunge ahead for the sheer joy of finally getting her daughter married. "Mama, Chris and I haven't set a date yet so please don't do anything now. You'll be the first to know when we do. Okay?'' She held her mother's eye until she saw her reluctant acceptance.

"But couldn't I just—" Mama began.

Daddy said, "Ada, they'll let us know. We won't do anything at all until then."

Maggie Rose had to deal with the same impatience later that evening when she told Ginnie her news. After the first excitement had tapered off, Ginnie's next question was, "When's the big day? We have to start planning now."

"We haven't set a date yet."

Ginnie's voice was disbelieving. "You haven't set, why ever not?" She interrupted herself, and then went on full tilt before Maggie Rose could answer.

"What do you and Chris have to wait for? It's not like either of you had been married before and had that to contend with, or kids. Goodness know you're old enough, you've known each other forever. What are you waiting for?" She paused only because she'd run out of breath.

"Ginnie! Stop talking and listen to me. We. Have. Not. Set. A. Date. But as soon as we do, you'll be the next one to know after my family. Okay?"

"I hear you, Maggie Rose. Sorry I got carried away. But I'm so thrilled for you both. Now tell me how the awards dinner dance went."

At breakfast Sunday morning, before he picked up his fork, Chris said, "Tallie, I found the pot at the end of the rainbow last night."

Tallie's eyes gleamed. "You popped the question and she said yes?"

"That's what happened." He felt Tallie would understand the triumph in his statement.

Tallie's hand shot out to give Chris's a firm shake. "You got a fine girl," he said, "and she's got a fine man."

"Thanks, Tallie," Chris said. Then he laid the engraved award at Tallie's plate. "You helped us win this. I'm sorry you never want to attend because you should have been there last night."

"Henry would have been proud," Tallie said.

As they resumed their meal, Tallie said, "Decided on when yet?"

"No, not yet."

When Tallie took more waffles from the warming oven he said, "I'll be ready to move out whenever you say. Married folks don't need a third person around."

"Tallie, this is your home like it's mine and like it will be Maggie Rose's. I'm not moving and you aren't either. End of discussion," Chris said firmly.

Tallie served the waffles, sniffed a little, and no more was said.

On Monday afternoon when she went to the office, Maggie Rose examined the contents of the Riding Establishments file. Of the seven there she selected three and called each one asking about the instruction. The person who answered the phone at Emerald Lane identified herself as the owner of the riding school. Her warm, mature voice and her answers to the questions Maggie Rose asked sounded like what she was hoping to find. An appointment was made for later that evening.

The school was at the end of a winding lane with

a neat, modest house in the front, the stable and fields in the back. The woman waiting for Maggie Rose had a weather-beaten face, eyes that had looked at life and liked most of what they'd seen, and a welcoming smile.

"I'm Emerald Lane," she said. "Come in and tell me what was behind the questions you asked."

They sat in the small office while Maggie Rose told her what she needed. "I don't know if you'll accept me, because I'm deathly afraid of horses, a fear I'm determined to accomplish so I can get married."

"I've heard a number of stories over the years but yours is a new one. Don't leave out anything," Emerald said. She sat relaxed and attentive as Maggie Rose told her everything after saying it was a confidential matter.

When she came to the end, Emerald said, "I've been working with horses and people since I was twelve years old. I'm about to retire and I take only a few students. What I like most is to bring horses and people together in mutual respect and understanding. I'm not a psychologist but I'd be comfortable working with you if you think you can trust me."

"I'm ready to begin." Maggie Rose was certain Emerald Lane was the answer to her problem. The same assurance she'd felt at the beach was with her now.

The next evening she began a routine that started with exercises increasing her knowledge of and familiarity with horses in general, followed by a visit to become acquainted with one of Emerald's four horses. It took her six successive days before she could put her hand on Roxie, the horse she liked best, without nausea symptoms.

Emerald was with her every step talking her through her symptoms, encouraging her to breathe, assuring her Roxie was perfectly safe and that in her mind, Maggie Rose really knew she was. This was not the horse of her nightmares. By the end of the third week Maggie Rose was able to mount the horse while Emerald spoke to her soothingly and walked Roxie around just as Maggie Rose had seen Chris do. Maggie Rose was ecstatic!

The weeks for Chris had been a seesaw of excitement and anticipation on one hand and calm composure on the other when he tried to rein in the fever of his emotions.

Five days a week he saw Maggie Rose in the office. They played a dangerous but necessary game of indifference to each other. She wore her engagement ring on a long chain around her neck to prevent questions from the parents with their unavoidable comments and allusions. When they saw each other outside of the office, their hunger for each other frequently reached a boiling point.

On one such occasion they were sitting on Maggie Rose's couch having coffee after seeing a movie. Awareness of each other was so keen it was painful. Their verbal conversation had petered out as communication on another level had taken over.

Chris put his cup down, took her cup from her hands, and set it beside his. He tugged her into his lap. She came willingly, put her arms around his neck as his went around her. They stared at each other, their faces edged with overwhelming need.

With an incoherent sound Maggie Rose pulled his face down to receive her kiss. He responded with gentleness, which soon turned into something passionate and fervid. She answered and it seemed to her they were suddenly caught up in a blazing fire. She couldn't get enough of him. She couldn't get close enough, her hands wanted to feel the texture of his skin, the scent of his maleness filled her nostrils, the rasp of his breathing sounded in her ears, and the taste of his mouth intoxicated her.

Chris knew he loved Maggie Rose, had probably been in love with her for years, but he was awestruck as the depths of that love revealed itself to him. Nothing he'd ever experienced had been like this. The landscape before him was totally new.

His emotions were a battleground for the confluence of physical desire and a primitive possessiveness with a protective devotion and tenderness. He knew that if he permitted the fire that was barely in check to flare out of control it would damage something infinitely precious, something vastly beyond the present moment for Maggie Rose and for him.

He raised his mouth from hers, settled her against his chest, and with slow, calming hands caressed her back until they both were restored to a relative ease.

Into the silence Maggie Rose observed, "There's so much I never knew before. Every time we're together I learn more and I'm filled with wonder. How could I have lived to be thirty years old and been so unaware?" There was a smile in her voice.

"Maybe I was like Sleeping Beauty waiting for the right prince to awaken me with his kiss."

"Thank God you waited," Chris said fervently.

Following that eye-opening evening, Maggie Rose asked Emerald Lane if she could have an additional thirty minutes in the evening and if they could work out extended time on the weekends. She hadn't realized the toll this postponement would take on the two of them. Chris especially was becoming more fine-drawn; the relaxed ease had gone from his body, and although he never pressured her about what she was doing about overcoming her fear of horses, she could feel the tension in him as the days turned into weeks and the first month had passed.

On the Saturday ending the fifth week Maggie Rose called Chris when she knew his last class was over.

"It's such a lovely evening I thought I'd bring some ice cream and sit on the porch and eat it," she said.

"I'm waiting," Chris said.

A rain shower had come through long enough to blunt the heat of the afternoon, and the air on the porch cooled their faces as they ate their ice cream and talked about the week.

"Jane's working out well with the kids?"

"So well that she wants to work full-time and take night classes. She and I are beginning to work out an events program so the students can participate in shows on a regular basis. I haven't been able to do that before."

"Have you thought of putting all of your energy

and time into this, Chris, and getting someone else to do the corporation work?'' Maggie Rose was sure this was a direction that would give Chris the greatest fulfillment.

"It has been in the back of my mind," he acknowledged. "It's something we can talk about later, maybe even expand the school physically." He looked out over the fields. "There's lots of land here."

"I've only seen this part here," Maggie Rose said. She turned to look into his eyes. "Maybe we could take a ride and see it all."

Everything in Chris came to a standstill. Her eyes were steady and filled with love as she met his gaze unflinchingly.

"Now?" he managed to say, his voice husky.

"Yes, please," she said. "Now."

He rose and drew her to her feet, his eyes never leaving hers.

"Are you sure, Maggie Rose? I don't want to rush you."

"I'm sure," she said and led the way down the porch and onto the path to the stables. She meant to demonstrate her lack of fear and her ability to rely on the instruction she'd received from Emerald.

In the stable she went to Windsong, talking to her as she approached the horse's left side. When she had Windsong's acceptance, Maggie Rose began to put on the bridle, taking her time so she could remember what Emerald had taught her. She took as much time putting on Windsong's saddle. She was so intent on getting it all correct she forgot about being afraid. Emerald said that would probably be the case the first time she rode with Chris.

Chris stood watching her, filled with love and pride. Once again she'd demonstrated the intelligence and competence he'd seen at work in her management of his opening, in the reorganization of his office, and in the Mailroom.

Once she'd prepared Windsong and given the horse time to become accustomed to her, Maggie Rose led her to the mounting block and mounted her correctly. Seated, her back erect, she looked at Chris for approval.

He came beside her on HS, leaned over, and kissed her on the mouth. "You are wonderful," he said with utter sincerity.

This time he led the way, describing to Maggie Rose what she was seeing including the orchard, the fields lying fallow, the acreage leased out to the Nettles brothers, and finally the brook.

Riding on the back of a horse made the land look different, Maggie Rose discovered. She couldn't ride fast yet but she could imagine the exhilaration Chris felt riding swiftly over the land knowing how it had come down to him from his grandfather and that he was its custodian. Maybe they would have children who would have the same understanding.

They dismounted at the brook.

"Having you here at the brook with me is a fantasy come true," Chris said, taking her by the hand and seating her. He tied the horses to a nearby tree, then lounged down beside her. "This was my favorite place when I was growing up."

"I can see why," she said, lying back and looking at the dusk through the leaves of the overhanging branches. "It's peaceful and the water makes a little music of its own."

He resisted the temptation to lie down beside her and instead he asked her to tell him what she'd been doing to get to this point with Windsong.

"Do you know Emerald Lane?" she asked.

"The Irish lady who's forgotten more about horses than I ever knew," he said.

"That's the one. She's been working with me these past five weeks."

Maggie Rose had a sudden image of her prone position and scrambled up as she told Chris the details of her recovery program.

"I'll be eternally grateful to Emerald," he said, "and we'll invite her to our wedding."

"Chris, you've been so patient," Maggie Rose said, leaning against him.

He put her head on his shoulder and supported her back as he listened to her proposition about the wedding.

"We can do this several ways. We can go any day and be married in a private ceremony, then have a reception later. We can be married at my parents' home, which will only take a week to arrange, and have a reception later or we can have a church wedding but that will take longer to arrange. I'm willing to do whatever you wish."

Chris pondered his choices. Now that she had filled her own prerequisite, as far as he was concerned she was his wife and he would like to consummate the marriage right here and now in the cool of the evening beside his brook. It seemed a natural conclusion to him. Fitting, appropriate, and highly desirable. He turned her face to him and kissed her, then searched her eyes asking the question. Her answering kiss was a gentle acquiescence as she softly caressed his cheek.

Her quiet submission to his desire aroused in him his protective instinct, rendering the present situation untenable and dictating what his choice must be.

"This is the only wedding you or I will ever have, sweetheart, so let's do it right. We've waited this long, I guess we can survive another four weeks. Is that all right with you?"

The radiance in her face as she turned to him clutched at his heart. What a joy it was going to be to try to keep that emotion in her.

"One condition. You're going to have to give me at least an entire week for our honeymoon," he said.

"Gladly! Where are we going?"

"Wherever you like. Bermuda, Hawaii, London, Paris—your choice."

"I've always wanted to see the white beaches and the clear blue water of Bermuda," she said hopefully.

His eyes lit up. "That's my preference, too!"

HS and Windsong looked up to see the man human swinging the woman human around as they laughed out loud. They watched the strange sight for a moment, shrugged at each other, and went to nibbling the succulent grass.

Epilogue

Summer's heat still lingered but its weight and humidity had been diffused by approaching autumn so that this first October Saturday, although sparkling and fresh, was shirtsleeve warm. It had brought out a constant stream of people to the fairgrounds for the annual big event. The fair had been going on for three days and would end on Sunday but today always brought in as many paying customers as the first two days combined.

Covey was hopping with excitement as he and Jerlene pushed through the masses of people.

"Can we go on the rides first, Mom?"

They went from ride to ride for the next hour. Covey jounced around in company with other kids, enjoying himself despite the absence of Tommy, who was in Columbia with his grandparents.

Jerlene sat when she could find a bench near the rides, musing at the difference in her son since they'd been here last year. Then he'd been a quiet, reserved boy, sometimes difficult to understand

and to reach. Since his summer at the farm and his introduction to horses, he'd become more outgoing and confident. The latent intelligence she'd seen in him was now apparent.

There was a change in her as well. The episode with Dan had forced her to take an honest look at herself. Her father's sorrowful words of advice about taking her time to find a decent man had found a home in her heart. Dating one man after another no longer held an appeal. She valued herself and her time in a better way now and spent time with her family and especially with Covey, who had proven to be more interesting than some of the men she'd known.

Then there was Maggie Rose. Like Covey's, her summer at the farm had resulted in a life change. Her marriage to Chris two weeks ago had been so lovely that even now in the midst of the noisy crowd around her, Jerlene had only to close her eyes to see Maggie Rose in her long bridal gown coming down the aisle on Daddy's arm, her eyes only on Chris, tall and handsome, waiting as if paradise were coming toward him. Jerlene, as bridesmaid along with Alicia and Ginnie, could see his rapt expression clearly and she prayed with all her heart that one day she would be blessed with finding such a man.

"Mom, is it time for the rodeo yet?" Covey was beside her looking at her watch while he read a crumpled program he'd stuffed in his pocket at the gate. "I don't want to miss any of it."

"Why don't we get something to eat and take it with us? It's a little early but the sooner we get in that line, the better seats we'll have."

They found that several other people had the

same idea but even so they ended up in the third row where they could easily see and identify the horsemen in the ring. The program began with an announcement that this rodeo had experienced professionals from all over the world riding some of the best horses in the rodeo field. The standing-room-only crowd was going to get its money's worth, the announcer said, so sit back and enjoy yourselves.

What followed was a breathtaking spectacle of magnificent horses trying to unseat magnificent riders. Each rider's name was announced but couldn't always be understood because of the noisiness of the crowd. Jerlene and Covey were enthralled, their eyes watching every rider and every movement.

The riders who managed to stay on their horses came close to the fence to look at the audience and acknowledge the applause. Sometimes one would make a cocky bow, or raise his arm in triumph, or wave his hat. Others just looked and smiled.

The last rider was a tall black man who rode with grace and ease, controlling his fractious mount with competence. When he came to the fence to take his bow, Jerlene and Covey stood with some other people to applaud him. As the applause built he circled around and came again to the fence looking intently at the crowd, then made a sweeping bow before he rode off.

"Mom, can we go see him?" Covey asked.

"We can try but I'm not sure if they'll let us in," she said.

The stables were a little distance from the stands and were protected from the public by a barred fence but the open space in front of the fence held a chattering crowd of autograph and souvenir hunters around the rodeo riders.

"There he is, Mom," Covey said, heading toward the tall man with at least twenty people around him.

"Covey, wait." Jerlene restrained Covey. "If we stay over here until he's through, we'll have more time with him."

"Mom, I don't want to miss him," Covey wailed.

"I promise you, Covey, we won't miss him." Her words were so positive, Covey subsided. He watched the man and saw him raise his head from signing someone's hat. He looked around and saw them. He looked straight at them, then gave a little nod and went back to signing autograghs. Covey knew Mom had been right.

When he was finished the man walked over to them.

"I saw you in the stands and I was coming to look for you," he told Jerlene. "I knew I'd recognize you." He took her left hand and looked at it, then held his out for her to see there was no wedding band.

"Who is this?" he asked Jerlene while looking at Covey.

"This is my son, Covey Reed Sanders."

Jerlene watched shock, surprise, and then joy pass across his face. He turned to Covey.

"You don't know how happy I am to meet you, Covey. My name is Matthew Covey Reed." He crouched down until he was on eye level with Covey.

Covey searched the brown eyes, looking for the truth his heart was telling him. He saw there what he hadn't seen in Mr. Chris.

"You're my dad?" he breathed, almost afraid to say the words for fear their sound would make the reality vanish.

"I'm your dad and you're my son." The man's arms went around the child, whose shorter arms went around the man's neck, both holding on for dear life.

Jerlene, witnessing what she thought would never happen, wept quietly, happily.

"We need to go where we can talk," Matthew said. "Wait here for me."

"How much time do you have?" Jerlene asked when he returned.

"Long enough," he said, holding her hand, his arms across Covey's shoulder. "Is it possible to go to your place?"

"Of course," she said.

When they were in the car Matthew turned to Covey in the backseat. "Son, I need to talk to your mother alone for a while. Is there something you can do while we talk?"

"I'll play outside until you call me." Covey was so happy he could sit outside for the longest time just thinking about finding his dad.

"Jerlene," Mathew said when they were alone, "are you angry with me?" His square face was sober, his long brown eyes intently searching hers.

"Not anymore. I went to the rodeo every year hoping to see you; then I gave it up. I have never told anyone, including Covey, who his father is. Where have you been, Matthew?" She didn't want to cry in front of him but now all the loneliness and yearning she'd tried to compensate for with the presence of other men in her life burst out.

Instantly he took her in his arms and his own

eyes grew moist. "I've been all over the world, Jerlene, and this is my first time back here but I've never forgotten you. Never forgotten our lovemaking those two nights in my truck. You were so sweet, so loving. You told me you were eighteen but in thinking about it later I wondered if you were." She made a little negative movement without raising her head from his chest. "You were seventeen?" A nod. "Is that why you didn't write me?"

"I was ashamed and then I lost your address."

"I'm so sorry you had to go through all of that alone, but I'm going to try to make it up to you and to Covey if you'll let me."

She sat up and wiped her eyes. "I don't understand."

"When you met me I was twenty-one; now I'm nearly thirty-two and I'm leaving the rodeo. I want a stable home life and I'm getting a second chance in finding you and our son to make that happen. If you let me, I want to court you and Covey and let your family get to know me and then I'm going to ask you to marry me. Of course, I'll have to get a job but I don't think that'll be a problem."

Jerlene wondered if Daddy would find Matthew to be a decent man. She was fairly sure he would. In any case, she was going to give Matthew the chance to prove it. Matthew was waiting for her answer, not bothering to hide his vulnerability.

"Covey and I will let you follow your plan, Matthew," she said.

On the Sunday after Thanksgiving, Matthew Covey Reed married Jerlene Sanders and Covey Reed Sanders.

Dear Readers,

Since I last wrote to you we have all suffered through the horrific events of September 11, 2001. In my personal life, I have lost my husband of many years, who was not only my friend but also my staunchest supporter.

It is easy to let fear dominate us when tragedy occurs but we must fight it. For fear anesthetizes us. It keeps us from moving forward to find whatever life still has to offer us.

Maggie Rose discovered through trial and pain that she had to find the will to conquer her fear, and in doing so, opened herself to a fuller life and to her love for Chris.

Thank you for your many letters about *Destined*. I look forward to your reaction to this new story from Jamison, South Carolina. Your comments are greatly appreciated and very encouraging.

Adrienne Ellis Reeves
PMB #122
975 Bacons Bridge Road
Suite 148
Summerville, SC 29485-4189

ABOUT THE AUTHOR

Born and reared in Illinois in a family of seven children, Adrienne Ellis Reeves has lived in Arizona, Bermuda, California, Connecticut, New York, North Carolina, and, presently, in South Carolina.

She and her late husband, William Reeves, met in Greensboro, North Carolina, then settled in California, where they raised their daughter and their two sons. Six grandchildren and one great-grand now grace the family.

Adrienne travels extensively in the interest of the Baha'i Faith. In addition to her novels she has published articles and a children's book, *Willie and the Number Three Door.*

Her interests include the theater, reading, music, cooking and quilting, and anything else that comes up that might add something unique to her life.